DAYLIGHT AWAKENS

A Novel

Kathryn Horsley

Vendera Publishing

Chapter 1

Once upon a time, the earth was flat, toads caused warts, and the sun protected the humans from my kind. But time changes truths, beliefs adapt, and facts are revised. There is only one certainty that has transcended across the sands of time flawlessly. The crippling and unchanging reality that suffering will forever be an inescapable constant.

There are beliefs that I held a century ago that have become lost to me now. The sun that once burned into me, today only flits across my skin in an unnaturally, delicate way. The enemy I once hated now sleeps next to me, letting her devotion hold me tenderly. The blood and cries that used to lull me to sleep are no longer my most comforting escape.

Not that I do not still enjoy taking a life. Because I do. I take lives. I take them often. And I do enjoy each one very much.

I would wager that most creatures, especially humans, take pleasure in the suffering of others. Vampires simply do so with flair. Humans will tell you they don't, but they are terrible at lying.

Humans say that it is not the turmoil but the rise above it that makes the trauma of another so appealing. But that is propaganda. I suppose they must tell themselves that.

They don't want to believe themselves capable of enjoying the downfall of another so wholly. If they were to accept that they simply enjoy watching others squirm, it would be difficult for them to remain so pious. And we can't have that, now can we?

Humans lie to themselves and say that that they have risen above the barbaric ways of their predecessors. But they haven't.

I know this because I have met their predecessors. I was one. I remember their past because I lived it. And I have watched as each century presents new faces and new clothing in attempt to hide the same apathetic hearts.

The basic lust for pain is overwhelming; it is consuming, and it is not contingent on being a vampire. Even peaceful yoga instructors rubberneck as they drive past an accident in a desperate attempt to see a glimpse of a crimson-stained body draped with a thin blanket.

Like moths to a flame, humans cannot help but be swallowed by the temptation to watch someone in torment. They are nothing but beasts hiding behind fleeting benevolence.

Only vampires have the courage to embrace their nature. We do not simply witness pain; but we cause it. Other species waste their energy pretending not to be horrifically intrigued by death while vampires bathe in their cravings. Our indulgence comforts us and cools our ever-burning desire to rip into another victim.

I suppose it is because, unlike other species, vampires cannot refuse our reflex to kill. Participating in physical torment is not something we are capable of excusing ourselves from. No vampire can sustain their life without taking another's. It is not a choice; it's an obligation. One that we might as well enjoy.

The sun was meant to naturally limit our carnal compulsions. And it has done that for centuries. It prevented numerous killing sprees by my fangs, but something changed inside of me. Something that was never meant to.

Without Krista, I would have no reason to stop myself from walking into the daylight and taking what I want, when I want it. But with Krista, I have a new reason to limit myself, to not be the killer I could easily become.

She is my new sun. The center of my universe and the only light in my dark world. She unknowingly keeps my appetite at bay as much as the sun ever could. She sees a light in me that I thought had been consumed long ago. A light that I will attempt to preserve for her.

When Krista looks into me, she sees the man who loves her and the vampire who paid a price to leave with her. I lost everything that night; but to me, it was that night that I gained my whole world. She sees a man who would do it all again.

She sees *me*. Not a monster. And I need to keep it that way.

So, I wait. I pace myself. I conceal as much of that side of me as I can from her. Obviously, Krista is aware of what I am, and what I do. But knowing I am a vampire is not the same as being confronted with it day after day. It is not the same as seeing me switch off my emotions and let my hunger take over me. And it certainly is not the same as watching me delight in it.

Ten years have passed since I first touched the sun. Ten years without that simple restriction to slow my appetite. Ten years of restraining as much of my vampire-self as possible by limiting hunting, and only feeding on Julia in areas that can be easily concealed by clothing to name a few ways.

However, there are still obligations to be satisfied and needs to be met. So, tonight, while Krista was running in the light of the full moon, I found myself chasing after something much more tempting than a night sky. After all, vampires will be vampires. And humans will always be prey.

Despite being able to walk in the sun, I still prefer night for hunting. The daylight still skims across my skin in a foreign way. My eyes prefer the dark, and screams are easier to conceal in the night. Without question, the darkness is where monsters can truly live.

Before the sun comes up, the dredges of humanity emerge. That should have been the first clue for the girl who sat next to me. No decent human would be drifting through the streets in the wee hours of the morning like I was. Especially not in places that entertain ladies like her. So, when I asked the blonde to join me in the car, she should have said no.

But she didn't.

Now as the water runs over my skin and the last remaining hint of her vivacity disappears in the drain, I close my eyes savoring the smell of her last moments once more…

*   *   *

"Where are we going?" she asked curiously.

Looking over, I smiled at her to put her at ease. "Not much farther. I like my privacy with this."

Not more than twenty, she smirked at me as her long hair tumbled over her shoulder and she slid her hand on my thigh. "I can be private in a car," she said with a wink.

I pushed her hand from my leg purposefully as I told her flatly, "Not this car."

My words made her squirm in her seat but not for the reasons she should have. Her anxiety was not based on fear as it should have been. It was merely caused by her impatience to be paid and move on to her next job.

The sun still needed another hour to make its debut. The dense forest protected me for a while longer by snuffing out the beams before they reached the soft, mossy floor. Still, I had intended to be home before the sun was at its brightest.

"We're here," I told her as I slowed the car to a stop.

She looked around at the trees as I parked the car in the middle of the path as though I expected no other soul to stumble upon us.

"I need you to get out of the car," I told her directly.

When she only blinked her concern at me, I informed her calmly, "You see, this is my friend's car and even though, she does know what I aim to do, I did promise not to stain the seats. So"—I waved her away with my hand—"shoo, shoo."

However, she did not move so I continued my explanation. A more thorough explanation. One that always prompts a human to run.

I smiled lightly as shook my head. "I couldn't use my own car. My girlfriend would know you were here. She would smell your trashy perfume."

I looked over at the girl as her eyebrows came together irked by my words, but I continued speaking before she could think to comment. "Even if I managed not to get your blood on the seats, she would know I murdered you," I said matter-of-factly.

Her pupils dilated as my words left my lips and I could not help but to chuckle lightly as I said, "I mean, you got in my car. Of course, she's going to assume that I killed you. It's what I do."

Her breathing sped up, fast and heavy, pulling more and more oxygen into her body as her fight-or-flight responses began to take over. I could smell the spike in her glucose levels as her body dumped it into her bloodstream, ready to utilize the quick energy it provided. But it would not be enough to save her.

Dropping my smile, I leaned close to her and let my inner darkness dance over my next words, "Now you're going to run, and you are going to die. Because *that's* what you do."

Keeping my face near hers, I could feel her hot breath on me as her hands began to tremble and her lip quivered. I reached past her and pulled the lever to release her door. The door swung open as I added coldly, "Now run. It's more fun that way."

Frozen in fear, she sat shuddering in the passenger seat. However, I wanted her run. I needed her to.

I let my eyes turn black slower than necessary simply to add to their eeriness as the sweet stench of fear rolled off of her. Her eyes grew wide as mine grew darker. The monster in me begged to be set free.

I let a sinister smile spread across my face. That did it. That pushed her to scream. A piercing, screechy scream that was fueled by terror, and terror alone. She bolted from the car and into the trees with the knowledge that something, not someone, was coming for her.

I sat in my car allowing her a head start, despite it being completely futile for her. The weak hope a head start offered would only add to the delicate smells of dread and panic when I did inevitably catch her.

My skin tingled with anticipation of such an exciting meal. The chase really did make it so much more satisfying. The taste of her blood was worth the wait. The way her body pumped her bloodstream full of delicious hormones.

I have tasted them thousands of times. Cortisol, epinephrine, adrenaline. They all add to the sensations of feeding in their own way. Like any drug, the added hormones that drove her body beyond its limits, would give mine a gratifying surge of power. Lingering in my own muscles far longer than feeding on any sheep, the natural additives in a helpless, fearful victim's blood was more nourishing and so much more rewarding.

With my monster raging, I exited the car and ran in the direction she had disappeared. Alone and afraid, her body naturally constricted the blood vessels to the skin so it could flood the vital organs with oxygen and nutrients. It was a natural response meant to fuel her escape. However, it only made it easier to track her.

Her scent hung in the air like the humidity of a Southern night, clinging to my skin as I pushed through its sticky, sweet allure. Being faster than her, I caught up to her quickly.

I grabbed her by the hair, jerking her to a stop and threw her to the ground. Her feet scrambled to push her backward, away from me, as I stood over her.

"P-Please," she stammered.

I knelt down, placing my hands near her on the soft moss that lined the forest floor as she continued to whimper pointlessly, "Please don't hurt me."

"They always say that," I said stoically.

Leaning over her, I inhaled her panic like the sweetest perfume. My monster lavished in the delay of my kill, savoring each moment of her tears rolling over her supple flesh. I placed my hand on her throat, feeling her heart pound against me. Allowing her to watch my fangs extend, I kept my face near hers simply so she could see her impending death as it approached.

Her body shook with her sobbing as she feebly voiced, "Please. I'm just a kid."

But I did not care. She was not innocent.

Still, I loosened my grip on her neck and leaned back slightly. "How old are you?"

"Seventeen," she said between broken breaths.

My eyebrows furrowed with her words. So young. Such a shame. I let my eyes change back to green and my fangs recede as I stood up. Staring at her, I rubbed my hand across my lips, thinking as she sobbed on the ground.

"Go," I told her quietly.

"You're letting me go?" she asked but she did not need me to answer. She clambered to her feet and looked at me briefly. "Thank you," she said timidly.

She started to run but her feet did not take more than two steps before I grabbed her hair and slammed her back against a tree. The tree shook with the force of her body, but I doubted her fear allowed her to feel the full impact of it.

I chuckled cruelly as I wrapped my hand around her throat once more. The sweat from running full speed had begun to cool on the back of her neck, allowing chills to form under my fingers. I let her watch my eyes glaze to black once more with a twisted smile on my face as I leaned close to her ear. "Humans are so quick to believe what they want to hear."

As my fangs pressed against my gums, I inhaled the sweetness of her fear once more, and whispered tauntingly, "Silly little human."

Then without any further delay, I sank my fangs deep inside the delicate skin of her neck. She screamed until the blood in her throat drowned out the sounds. She pushed against me until her hands became raw, and she cried until the salt from her tears left white streaks on her skin. But it was not enough. It never is. I laid her limp, lifeless body down on the dirty ground with my greed and my monster satisfied for one more night…

*　　*　　*

The shower carries those delicious smells away. However, it cannot take the vitality her life supplied to my own body. That is why we kill, isn't it? A life for a life, so to speak.

My thoughts are cut short by the bathroom door opening and the sound of Phoenix's voice, soft and playful, "When I said you could use my place to clean up once in a while, I didn't realize you would be interrupting my sleep quite so often."

Through the steam on the glass of the shower door, I see her red hair shining and I smile at her blurry shape as she passes me.

"Well, I don't want to take this smell home, now do I?" I ask rhetorically.

She answers anyway, "Well, you could." I see her milky figure slide onto the sink counter as she finishes her thought, "If you weren't so hell bent on dating a werewolf."

My lopsided smile spreads across my face. Even though, Krista has never asked me to keep my dietary habits discreet, I have been reasonably successful doing that.

Krista knows I hunt but that doesn't mean I should flaunt it. So, I try to not bring home the stench of death or blood on my clothes, and obviously avoid talking about feeding on a human nonchalantly. I also go out of my way to be sure not to feed on my sheep in front of Krista, and so far, it has been working rather nicely.

"I mean, seriously," Phoenix continues, "you're so neurotic, you'd think you were dating a bloodhound." Her tone turns playful. "You even leave a toothbrush here. Which I did not authorize, by the way."

I chuckle lightly to myself as the water drips from my hair, making a tapping sound on the tile of the shower floor.

I figured that toothbrush would be a bane to her when I placed it there. Phoenix will never be comfortable letting a man get close enough to leave a toothbrush.

Despite knowing her for centuries, our relationship has always been mostly business. Rarely more pleasure than quips and catty banter has to offer. But then again, the fact that we have never been more than friends is likely why we still are.

Sliding the shower door open slightly, I peek my head out just enough to make eye contact with her. "About that. Would you mind asking Jesper to pick up a new toothbrush for me next time he's out? Mine is getting old."

Her eyebrows rise but she is not actually angry as I flash an exaggerated smile at her and lean back out of view to continue washing.

"Honestly, Nicolas, what is a guy supposed to think when I bring him over and your toothbrush is by my sink?"

I do not often speak so candidly of private matters with women, but this time, I cannot help but to laugh lightly. "Oh, Phoenix, I doubt anybody you bring home would be fool enough to believe you plan to keep any man long enough him to warrant bringing a toothbrush."

At the sound of her sharp inhale, I can nearly see her jaw drop, but she is neither shocked nor appalled by my bluntness. I laugh to myself and remind her, "Besides, you don't bring men here."

Which is mostly true. She does bring human men here. Humans are easy to let in. They are weak and vulnerable. Easy to manipulate and defend yourself against. Besides, the human men she brings here are not concerned by a toothbrush when a woman who looks like Phoenix invites them into their bed.

Vampires, however, we are a different story. Phoenix is not the trusting type and will not invite vampires in for such a frivolous thing like intimacy. Even after I pulled her from a burning house, it still took nearly a century for her to trust me enough to let me know her address.

That is not to say that she does not go to their houses. Because she does plenty of that. She is a vampire after all. And vampires are well known for succumbing to the greed that fuels all their most ravenous desires.

"Just because I never brought *you* home doesn't mean I never bring anybody. I happen to prefer men who are a little more choosy about their partners," Phoenix says teasingly.

Rinsing the shampoo from my hair, I joke, "Are you saying I'm easy?"

The suds run over my fingers and trail down my back but there is no sound coming from Phoenix. Leaning back into her view, I see her with raised eyebrows, looking at me incredulously. It is as though she had been waiting for me to peek at her simply because there are no words that could say what the look on her face does.

I laugh and return to rinsing. "Yeah, yeah, but only when I'm single." I begin my second wash and rinse cycle on my skin to be sure that no traces of the girl from the car comes home with me. "I am rather good at monogamy, don't you think?"

"Surprisingly so. But then again, Krista is a dog who could quite literally bite your head off, so I suppose there is some added motivation to consider." She giggles at her own response before continuing.

After a moment of silence, Phoenix asks me, "How are things going with you guys, anyway?"

"Good," I tell her simply. But being with Krista is better than good. She is everything I have ever dreamed of for myself.

Dating Krista has had its fair share of obstacles, but it has been so worth it. Sure, she is a werewolf and, sure, her family hates me and wishes I were dead. But none of that seems to matter when I'm watching her emotions scroll across her face as she reads a novel, or when she subconsciously hums bits of songs as she tinkers in the garage.

The way Krista twirls her hair with her finger when she is deep in thought; it is as though she is willfully wrapping me up as well. Calling her mine has been the best ten years of my existence as a vampire.

I shut off the water. "Why do you ask?"

She sucks in a heavy breath and exhales it forcefully. "Just curious. Can't a girl be nosy?"

I pull down the towel that I had draped over the rail of the shower door and wrap it around myself.

Phoenix is never simply curious. She is an impeccable tracker. If she wants to know how my relationship is going, she will uncover it for herself without my help.

"I know you better than that," I remind her as I open the door and step out, keeping myself covered.

She sits on the counter next to the sink, in skimpy night-shorts that are not much bigger than panties, and a tank top that is clearly too large but somehow still holds her just right. Her red hair is tossed about but appears to have been at one point a sloppy ponytail. The strands of red frame her face as she looks at me with a noticeably forced smile.

Since I am using my towel for coverage, I grab a second towel from the cabinet. "Out with it."

I hear her skin stick to the granite as she shifts and crosses her legs on the cold countertop. "Krista is a wolf."

"I've noticed."

"She smells horrible,"—I chuckle lightly at that exaggeration—"and she hung that gaudy cross on your wall—"

With a wide smile, I interrupt her, "That cross belonged to her grandmother and you know it."

The large cross in our living room was definitely not my idea of pleasing wall art. However, like most committed men, I found myself outvoted when it came to our home décor.

Phoenix teases playfully, "None of your friends can go in your house with that thing hanging there, glaring at us. Not even me."

"Well, you're the only vampire friend I have left, and you don't like visiting, so—" I say shrugging, although that is not entirely true. I still have Luther. And he is a vampire friend. Well, he's a vampire anyway.

Yielding, she rolls her eyes. She holds a ring box toward me. "I found this."

My eyes rest on the cherry ring box. A little box that lights when it's opened, casting its brilliance on a ring that was never meant for Phoenix to see. A ring that Phoenix would never understand.

It was plain and meek before. Not like Krista at all. But now it is updated and beautiful. Something new and different brought into my life that changed the way my world is seen—just like Krista.

The old silver band, polished and shining, boasts a new blue-green stone, striated with white mottling, in the shape of a droplet. And though any non-vampire would assume it is a teardrop, the shape is that of a drop of blood, the very thing that gives me life, and keeps driving me forward. Krista is that for me. My entire purpose.

I try to keep my voice light as I tell her, "Rifling through my clothes now?"

"When they're in my house," she retorts flatly.

I stare quietly at Phoenix. She knows that is no ordinary box. She knows what waits inside. My future pending on a piece of soft metal.

"That's my mother's ring. I just thought it could use a box. Try not to read too much into it, deary," I say attempting a futile lie.

Phoenix knows that I often carry my mother's ring with me. I have nearly lost it more than once simply by not being able to return to where it was hidden. It is the only thing of my human life and therefore, I must bring with me if I intend to keep it forever. Which I do.

Phoenix scoffs at my avoidance. She is no fool and my inept lie only insults her intelligence. But how would I even begin to explain the standards of dating a werewolf to Phoenix? Should I tell her the many times I have asked Krista's father for his blessing? Every six months for the past six years. Would Phoenix even care?

Phoenix doesn't even like Krista that much. She merely tolerates her for my sake. Hearing that I have spent so much time devoted to making her my wife would only disgust Phoenix.

For every normal vampire, courting a werewolf is such a pathetic way to spend one's time. But I am not normal, and I do want to marry Krista. And I can live with being a pathetic vampire, just so long as I am not a pathetic husband.

Phoenix raises her eyebrows with a small sigh. Laying the ring box in my hand, she asks teasingly, "Oh, Nicky, must you always lie to me?"

I smirk to myself. "Well, don't consider yourself special. I lie to everyone."

She laughs lightly at the truth in my jest. "And yourself if you think this would ever work."

Leaning back against the white backsplash, she crosses her wrists over her knees delicately. As she looks up at the ceiling, I let my towel drop. It plops against the cold tile floor, but I too am lost in my own mind to hear it.

I set the ring box near the sink and stare at it quietly. It must work. It has to.

When I think of my future, Krista is the only thing I see. The only thing of importance. Everything else is replaceable. Everything except her.

Phoenix's voice stops my wandering thoughts, "I worry about you, Nicolas."

I look over at her but say nothing as I slide my pants on, and she does not wait for my response. "Werewolves are not like us, Nicky. They are one being with one mind, and they only have room for one love."

Knowing where she is going, I drop my eyes sullenly. I have heard this warning from her before. Heard that a werewolf is one and the same as its human form. Not separate beings like the way I view them. Their feelings and thoughts intermingle wholly and inseparably.

The human in a werewolf may feel one thing. However, if a wolf decides it knows better than its human host, their wolf may override their human feelings. And suddenly, the human will feel the same as the wolf. They are simply more wolf than human.

Bonding, that's what they call it. The wolf finding its soulmate; that one partner who will help further their species and complete them in a way that no other can.

Tara has tried to explain it to me before. Bonding is like colors on a wheel, she said. Some elements complement, while other contrast in beautifully. The colors speak to your soul in a language only you can hear. Together, they paint order in the chaos. Suddenly, the life you had before your mate looks dull and gray and there is nothing you would not do to keep this all-new spectrum of your own.

It does not happen frequently. However, I know of at least one wolf it did happen to: Finn, a member of Tara's pack. His wife loved him dearly until one day, she stopped.

Her wolf may decide to protect itself by choosing a mate with greater power and position. In that instance, she could no longer feel the love she once held for Finn. Her new love for Saul felt just as real, because it is real, and now it always will be. Once a wolf has chosen, it will never change its mind or its heart again.

Phoenix continues softly, "Vampires love because our hearts tell us to. Wolves love for very different reasons. Wolves love for power or offspring, sometimes both. What can you offer in those regards?"

Nothing. I can offer neither for Krista.

"You cannot genuinely tell me that her wolf would choose to love. You cannot continue her species and you hold no position within a pack. But some werewolf out there can and does. And when her wolf meets its mate, her feelings for you will be over. Turned off like a switch. Ring or no ring."

And she will love him unequivocally. I will be nothing to her, because when push comes to shove, Krista is simply more wolf than human.

"I am aware of the risk," I tell her emphatically. Regardless, any amount of time with Krista is time I will relish forever. Loving her is worth the risk of losing everything.

"Your relationship is a time-bomb. There is an expiration date. Even if you don't know when, there is a fallout coming."

Phoenix leans toward me, laying her fingers on my arms more gently than she normally is. "Do you remember that wolf you had me track down in Alaska? Roderick Brooks?"

Tara's son, Roddy, had gone rogue and disappeared from his pack. Yes, I remember. I remember having Phoenix track him down for me at the request of his mother. I remember finding him and then lying to Tara about his whereabouts. Yes, I remember Alaska.

"What about him?"

"Do you know he's getting married?"

Married? That's absurd. I am practically his uncle, and nobody mentioned this to me.

I meet her eyes questioningly and ask her, "And how, pray tell, would you know this before I do?"

She shifts herself slightly, shrugging nonchalantly. "I figured if he was important enough for you to leave him alive, he must be important enough for me to keep tabs on." Then smirking oddly, she adds, "In fact, his upcoming marriage is to a woman."

I snort lightly. "Preposterous. Roddy is gay." It is the whole reason I lied to Tara about finding him in Alaska all those years ago. Phoenix knows this, she found him there with a man. How proud of herself she was at discovering his dirty little secret.

Phoenix sighs heavily as though I have missed her point completely. "*Roderick* is gay. His wolf is not."

She smiles widely, pleased with herself for knowing while I clearly did not. "The obligations to the pack far outweigh their own obligations. Roderick is a werewolf and his wolf decided it was time to begin contributing to the continuation of their species. And it found itself a partner that fit the bill."

She crosses her arms over her chest proudly. "I suspect that he is just as much in love with her as he has ever been with anybody. And he will never stop loving her because—"

"Wolves love for life," I finish for her grimly. At least, bonded wolves do.

Hearing the sorrow in my voice, her smirk fades. Biting her bottom lip, she watches me regretfully, sorry to have gloated so much. Phoenix lays her hand on my arm gently.

If Roddy's wolf can change his heart, there is no reason to believe that Krista's wolf cannot do the same.

Quietly, Phoenix explains, "I'm afraid a wolf is not free to love a vampire forever."

And my fear is that she may be right. Krista loves me—that I do know. How her wolf feels, now that is mystery. There is no rational reason for Krista's wolf to choose me. But still, I cannot accept the logic of this as truth.

"You know there is a chance her wolf will never choose its own mate," I dare to suggest such a glint of hope. After all, bonding is less common than not.

Phoenix chuckles as though she finds my resistance to her logic exhausting. She sighs as she slides off the counter. Patting my shoulder, she starts past me, teasing lightly, "I'll toss some coins in a wishing well for you, yeah?"

But she knows I will need more than a wish and handful of coins to keep Krista, even if I refuse to admit it.

Her footsteps are quiet as she heads toward the door. And just as I slide my shirt on, I hear her feet spin around on the tile.

"Oh, I almost forgot. There is another matter I wanted to discuss: word on the street is that the Genesis are recruiting a gun for hire. The hit is an acquaintance of yours but it's especially hush-hush. I know you have waited a long time for him to get placed on the chopping block *but* apparently, the Genesis is paying mad money to keep you out of the loop on this one."

There is only one person she would bother mentioning to me. Only one person I want dead. But still, I look at her gravely. "Who's the mark?"

"Salem."

My creator. But not my savior. Much like a scientist who causes a plague but leaves someone else to create the vaccine. Salem only destroys. He does not create. He does not heal. He does not help. He is a black stain that cannot be purged. The only cure for him is to be burned from existence. Burned and forgotten.

Salem changed me into this monster all those years ago. He was the one who let me watch as he killed Ann, my human love, in an alley and left me writhing in the dirt. There is something about knowing that he is still alive and breathing out there somewhere while my mother, Marcella, is not, that feels wrong. It feels unjust somehow.

Reaching in the cabinet, I pretend to grab another towel from the shelf but instead only rest my hand on the soft fibers as I ask, "Why would the Genesis want him dead?"

I cannot imagine anyone who wouldn't want him dead. He has been practically invincible, cowering under the shield of the Genesis for so long. That eccentric cult of crazies is the only reason he has been left untouched.

"Rumor has it that he killed Amelia."

Amelia, really? I wonder why. Well, it doesn't matter anyway. Murdering the leader of such a demented cult does certainly warrant his assassination.

"And this next part is extremely classified. It's so off the record that the man who told me is no longer alive, if you get my point. Apparently, the hit isn't for her murder; Salem is a target because he took a journal with him."

A journal? Why kill Amelia for a journal? And why is the Genesis more worried about that journal than Amelia?

"What's in the journal?"

Phoenix shrugs. "Rumors only say it's valuable, but my guess is it's something they already know but do not want you to discover. Why else work so hard to keep you from finding out?"

I think about her words for a moment. Killing Amelia is out of character for Salem. He is a coward. I can think of no reason for him to give up the safety the Genesis provides. And for a journal of all things? It doesn't make sense.

Salem is finally exposed. He is all alone and vulnerable. I could kill him. The Genesis is looking hard for him. It's only a matter of time. Someone *is* going to kill him. Might as well be me. I mean, killing your maker never helps as much as it should. But it would feel good. Better than good.

Although she does not propose it as an invitation, Phoenix leans her shoulder against the doorway in a sultry manner. She does not wish to seduce me, and I am not even slightly inclined to bed her. She merely stands perched against the door-frame in her most frequent stance, one of persuasion and enticement. It is the way she naturally stands when she wants a man to bend to her will.

"You know you want Salem dead." That is a vast understatement. "And we both know you want to be the one do it. If another takes his life, you'll forever feel dissatisfied because his death rightfully belongs to you."

She did not need to say that last part. I know what she's hinting at. And she's right. He is mine to kill. And the Genesis knows my feelings for Salem. They are fully aware that they did not need to hire a hitman when I would kill him for free.

There must be a reason they want to keep me out and that is all the more reason for me to dive in.

"If the Genesis doesn't want me knowing, why tell you?"

Phoenix scoffs at me. "You underestimate me. I don't *need* them to tell me anything. I have my own ways."

"Well, if you're so good, what's in the journal?" I ask with a smirk.

She lets out a strained chuckle. "The only way to know that for sure is to go get it and read it for yourself."

Tempting. I do owe it to myself to see what they are hiding from me. And it may be my only real chance to find any answers at all about what they want from me.

It could be dangerous though. For me, Krista, and Phoenix. It is hard to say what exactly the Genesis would be willing to do to keep me from the truth.

Looking at her, I try to keep my tone flat and prevent the swirling thoughts flooding my mind from showing, "But why kill Amelia for a journal? Why not just steal it? Doesn't add up."

Shaking her head, she adds with a lighter tone, "I don't know, Nick. Why does a dog bite its owner?"

Sighing, I ask in a playfully tone, "Do you think he has rabies?"

Phoenix's mouth twists, holding back a grin. Raising her eyebrow, she crosses her arms over her chest and tells me sarcastically, "Yes, Nicolas. Salem has rabies. That's it. You've figured it out. Congratulations."

I smile at her until she rolls her eyes at me and presses her back against the door. Smiling, she asks, "So what do you think?"

I'm thinking it would be thoroughly enjoyable to slay Salem and that I will be thoroughly disappointed if I received news that someone else did it. But that is not what she is asking.

"Are you in?" she asks with a glint in her eyes.

This isn't about Salem; it can't be. My concern must only be for the journal. Going after Salem could put everyone in danger, and he is no way worth that risk. But the journal? It just might be.

I stare at her for a moment watching the hunger grow in her eyes as she anticipates my response. Finally, I exhale forcefully. Keeping my tone low which only emphasizes my British accent, I reply, "You find that tosser and I will pull that journal from his ashes before they've even settled on the floor."

A wide smile spills onto her face as she rubs her palms together excitedly as she bites her bottom lip.

"I haven't had a good mystery in so long and I know just where to start," she says happily.

She spins around to leave, grinning wildly. But my words stop her in the doorway once more.

"By the way, Phoenix"—I let my face grow serious before continuing in a sobering tone—"I screwed up last night."

Her eyebrows begin to furrow with confusion and concern. I walk over to her and take her hand delicately. But I cannot hold back the impish grin that spreads across my face.

Faking a wince, I continue, "I know you told me not to but I may have picked up another prostitute and Jesper *may* be cleaning out your car as we speak."

She sighs exasperatedly, letting her arms drop dramatically to her side. It is not the first time I have asked her sheep to clean the car after my exploits. And she reacts much as I expected her to.

Exaggeratedly groaning, she shoves me back playfully. "Nicolas Vincent Rider! Stop putting trollops in my car," she screams despite her smile.

Smiling sheepishly, I walk toward the door to leave the bathroom. "What can I say? They love me." Shrugging, I add, "Besides, I didn't get any blood in it this time."

Phoenix follows me toward door, not letting me escape her inflated wrath. "I'd rather smell the blood. That cheap perfume clings to the seats."

"Next time, buy leather," I joke.

"My car smells like a gypsy, Nick." She tries to force a scowl, but her grin gives her away. She shakes her head at me. "Why do I put up with you?" she asks without anticipating any answer.

My lopsided smile flashes across my face. "Because you're a masochist."

Phoenix huffs and fights back an irritated smile. "Well, no more. No more borrowing my car. No more free showers—"

I interrupt her by kissing her on the cheek. Staying close to her face, I look into her eyes and say softly, "Thank you for the shower, Phoenix. I don't know what I'd do without you."

She smirks. "You'd use your own car and your own shower. And Krista would know exactly how many people you kill when she goes out."

I nod seriously. "Yes. And I'd probably be single because of it. So again, thank you for the shower, Phoenix."

She smiles softly at me, no longer pretending she is annoyed, and leans her back against the wall.

Letting my lopsided smile charm her, I ask sweetly, "See you for the next full moon?"

Rolling her eyes, she crosses her arms over her chest. "Yeah, yeah. Keys will be in the glove box."

Chapter 2

The smell of blueberry muffins fills our little home as I type away at the computer. Not my typical vampire home, this house has windows that have not been painted or sealed to keep the light from pouring in. There is no basement. There is no stench of blood. And judging by the rather large wooden cross glaring down at me from above my desk, there is no indication that a vampire would live here at all.

The house is small enough that it does not have a separate space for my writing. Therefore, it must be in the living room and it must be in this exact place. The place Krista deemed it fit best with the style of the room and décor. The same place that just happens to be under the cross I strongly urged her not to hang. But just like my desk placement, I lost that argument.

As I write another article, the wooden cross quietly watches me. At one time, I would not have been able to even sit under it. I would have been forced to look away by some unseen force. An immense weight would have pressed against me, compelling me to escape. I would not have been able to touch it, or move it, and I certainly would not have been able to share this space with it. The towering pressure of such a symbol would have either drove me out or drove me mad.

While the cross no longer bears down on me the way it once did, the weight of it hovering over me still forces me to look up occasionally and stare at it as it judges me heavily. The stopping and starting is very counter-productive to my writing. Yet, so far, it has not been a convincing or compelling reason for Krista to re-home it.

I can feel its watchful glare urging me to look up at the dark wood. The cross does not move. The wood does not creak. It does not shake and fall from the wall like in the movies when some evil force is near. It does not change in any way at all. It simply stares at me, letting me feel its weight. Or perhaps it is simply the burden of my own guilt that it calls to the surface that looms over me.

"What?" I ask the cross flatly. "What do you want me to do? Kill a more contributing member of society?"

But there is no response; it only stares back at me.

"I didn't think so."

Sighing, I shift in my chair in attempt to refocus my attention to the task at hand. However, instead of my eyes finding their way to the computer screen, they stop on a picture of Krista on my desk. My lopsided smile spills across my face as I remember the day I snapped that photo.

A hurricane in the South had brought a storm up the coast causing us an unexpected layover in New York. Tired of watching people in the airport, we decided to make the most of our six hours before any flights would be leaving.

The clouds rolled in as we ducked into a record shop to escape the rain. A little hole-in-the-wall kind of place, the shop smelled strongly like the cardboard sleeves that contained the vinyl records. I watched her as she thumbed through the rows of various artists, smiling each time she found one that brought some fragment of nostalgia.

Just as I raised my camera to take a soft, sweet photo of her thumbing through the albums intently, Krista snapped her head up, grinning excitedly. *'This one is coming home with us,'* she said as she rocked an Otis Redding album between her hands. And *click*. I snapped the picture of my soaking wet, exceedingly happy, and captivating better half.

Little did I know that the same Otis Redding record would again feature in a prominent memory later that same week. One that was starkly contrasting the happiness captured by this photo. Because exactly five days later, I found myself affronted with my own deceptions and the anger those lies produced.

Leaning my head back, I rest my eyes and I can still hear the harsh words of our most severe argument to date...

*   *   *

I realize that Krista is capable of understanding the necessity of my hunting, but I am not fool enough to pretend that she should have to accept it. So, I hid yet another murder to protect her, big deal. Every vampire does. She is literally blowing this out of proportion.

Exhaling forcefully, I attempt to calm the anger stirring in myself. However, it does little to dissipate much of my frustration with the entire situation.

I mean, honestly, what does she expect?

"We're supposed to be partners, Nicolas. Or did that slip your mind too?" Her words are sharp, cutting through the tension that crowds the space between us.

"Oh, I'm sorry," I say exaggeratedly. "I didn't realize vampires are supposed to snuff out all our dietary instincts. I guess I will just have to starve then."

With a low chuckle, she shakes her head in frustration. "You're not hearing me," she mutters irritably.

She's right. I'm not listening; I'm only reacting.

I snap with a crispness to my British accent, "Well, in case, you didn't notice, I happen to be a vampire. And vampires just so happen to murder people. All of us, in fact, flit about in the wee hours massacring people. For fun."

Fury bursts out of her as she snaps back at me, "I don't care what all the other vampires are doing, Nicolas. I'm not dating an entire fucking species! I'm dating you and I happen to care about what you're doing, especially when it is different than what you *say* you're doing."

The heat of my anger has been creeping through me, slow and rhythmic like a bass line. It gently escalates, seeking out intensity and suspense with each passing second, until it suddenly pulses to a peak.

"When I drag some poor soul into an alley and I say, '*Hello, my name is Nicolas and I'm a vampire,*'"—I say in a mocking tone—"they don't think I'm about to invite them for crumpets and tea." I can hear the childish tone in my words but I cannot stop them. My anger pushes them out of me like a crowd vacating a subway, shoving against one another to be the first. "No, they know exactly what that means. A vampire means teeth, and blood, and pain. And I'm sorry if you missed that memo somewhere but that's me. That's what I do."

Her hands tremble with her words but it is not fear that shakes them. "Stop talking! Stop. Just listen. For once in your life, will you *please* stop talking?"

Rolling my eyes, I chuckle to myself. Truth is, it doesn't matter what she has to say. I cannot change the hunger inside me. And to be frank, I don't think I would even want to.

With a deep breath, she attempts to keep her tone flat as she says slowly, accentuating the importance of each word as though I'm a toddler, "It's the lying."

She takes a breath. "It's the secrets. It's the scheming. It's looking me in the eyes and lying to my face. That's what breaks me, not the murder. I wish it was the murder that has me so furious. I wish it was that simple. But it's not. The murdering, I'm okay with," she says crassly. "Do you realize how insane that makes me feel? I feel like a monster just saying those words aloud."

Well, heaven forbid she feels like a monster for dating a serial murderer, I sneer to myself.

"What exactly do you want me to say here?"

"The truth," she says firmly. "Always the truth."

I scoff at her words. "You seriously think that knowing would make you feel better?" I ask scornfully.

Shaking my head, I step closer to her. The heat in my words grows flat but still contemptuous as I tell her, "You want truth? You want to know how I enjoy the way their tears roll over my fingers when I sink my teeth into their neck?"

Tears well up in her eyes. However, I'm sure it is not because of my words. Instead, it is the sheer volume of overwhelming emotions crashing on one another like waves during a violent storm that draws them out. So, I continue.

She wants truth, so she should know what she is asking to hear. "How their blood is more decadent when they're afraid? That I can literally taste their fear? That I prefer it? Or what about the fact that I do not value a human's life any more than you value a bologna sandwich?"

"No," she says quietly.

"No?" I repeat sarcastically. Of course, she doesn't. Who in their right mind would want to know such things?

Her tongue rolls over the front of her teeth under her lips as she pulls her tears back, refusing to let them fall.

"What I want, is to live in the gray." With a deep breath, she attempts to regain her composure before continuing, "That area that is absent of lies but is also simultaneously lacking details. I want to be able to ask you where you were and know that you are being truthful. Like normal couples."

I snort under my breath. "Normal."

My reaction reignites a heat in her that had just begun to subdue. "Yes, normal," she says dismissively. "Most couples are happy with knowing that their spouse was at the store. They don't need to know how many cans of beans were on display, how many clerks were working, or even what color the shelves were. Most people are happy with honesty and without details," she snaps.

"Most couples do *not* want to know if their spouse was out slaughtering humans. Most people would rather pretend their spouse was at a store because most humans want the lie so they can remain oblivious to such things altogether. There's a phrase for it: *'Ignorance is bliss.'* Why can't you let this be?"

She steps closer to me, clenching her teeth as she rubs her temples. She closes her eyes briefly before beginning again, "Truth is about trust. If you can't trust me enough to be truthful, then maybe we shouldn't be together at all."

Not be together? Her words take me aback and I stand silent as she continues.

"I'm not asking for much," she continues. "I don't need details. My compliance in all this is burden enough for me to bear. I just want to know that when you're speaking to me, I am not a fool to believe it."

She isn't asking for anything I should not be able to offer. She should not carry my conscious on hers. But I cannot comply. I know cannot. Lying about my meals is practically a reflex at this point.

I want to shield her from knowing the darker parts of me. I cannot bear for her to see me as a monster, and I fear that the truth will drive her away quicker than the lies ever could.

I should tell her that. I should make her understand why it is so difficult for me to be honest about this. But instead, defensiveness still rings in my tone as I tell her coarsely, "Well, I hate to be a burden."

With an exasperated sigh, Krista glances off to the side to avoid rolling her eyes at me just as the door swings open. Neither of us look at Julia as she carries a bag of groceries in each arm, but we aren't looking at each other either.

"It's getting dark out there," Julia chirps as she walks past us to set the bags on the table.

"Is it?" Krista asks in attempt to dissuade Julia from noticing the tension suffocating us, much like a parent would hide an argument from their child.

However, it does little good. As Julia turns around to fetch the other bags from the car, she notices the tight lines of Krista's brow.

Julia walks over to us. "Are you okay, Miss Krista?"

"I'm fine," Krista replies.

She places her hand on Krista's arm delicately. "You don't look fine."

"I am. You don't need worry about me," Krista tries.

I can hear it in her dismissive tone. She wants Julia to leave. We both do. There are still so many things left unsaid. So much frustration pushing at us both, spilling out of every fiber and flooding the space between us.

Julia shakes her head. "Yes, I do. Nicolas said that your happiness takes precedence…"

I sigh exasperatedly. Just leave, Julia. *'Krista's happiness takes precedence.'* Are you kidding me? You're going to give her those words, my words, to use against me, right now, at this very moment?

But Julia cannot hear my inner dialogue and cannot discern situations as a normal human would, so she remains oblivious to my seething and as she continues, "…even over his own orders. You are my first priority."

Just leave. That's what I mean to say, but before I can throttle my anger back, I abruptly snap, "Bugger off, Julia!"

I hear the cracking sound of Krista's hand only seconds before I feel the sharp sting it leaves on my cheek. Julia's mouth drops open as she stands awestruck, unsure of what to do next.

My fingers touch my tingling face instinctively, but I do not immediately look at Krista.

Normally, a strike like that only proves to create a swirling storm of fury, a driving force toward the cusp of madness. But not this slap. No, this slap is much different. This slap drains me, emptying me of all my anger in an instant.

In that first moment, I feel surprise. Shocked that Krista would strike me at all. I crossed a line. Sure. An invisible line that I knew was there. I spoke too harshly to Julia, who, in all fairness, has the mind of child. And in doing so, I managed to evoke a rage in Krista I have not seen before.

As I stand there silently, a team of emotions fill every crevice left inside of me that have otherwise been vacated by my receding anger.

Not be together? Those words ring in my ears once more. Those are the words she used. Krista has never used words like those before. Never even close to them.

My words and my actions were unnecessary, but I will not apologize for the murders. I needed those, and I enjoyed them thoroughly. But there were lies that did not need told. So very many lies. And I have no one to blame but myself. I put myself here. Pitted against the only person who has ever truly been for me.

I was so worried that the truth could push Krista away that I didn't consider that lying to her could do the same. My impulsive, rash behavior toward Julia could cost so much more than I am willing to pay. What if she begins to see that our worlds are just too different? What if my behavior and lies have caused a big enough rift between us to cause our future to crack and fall?

What if I cannot fix this?

I stand, overwhelmed by the panic-inducing thoughts swarming my mind as Krista says to Julia with a tightness in her voice that is reserved for me, "I'm not fine but I will be. For now, just please leave us."

Julia nods and walks toward her room. Krista waits for Julia's door to shut behind her before she looks at me crossly.

She stares, choosing her words and tempering her anger before she adds sternly, "Don't come to bed."

Without another word, Krista walks toward the bedroom. She does not slam the door because, despite being younger than me, Krista does have much better control over her emotions than I do. I let out a shaky exhale and collapse onto the chair closest to me.

Not be together? That is what she said. Like a ghost, the words waft through my every fiber. As though I'm barely even present, they leave me chilled to the core feeling suddenly fragile and dangerously alone.

For hours, I sit as quietly as I am able. Vampires do not require sleep the same way other creatures do, which is helpful because tonight, sleep would have evaded me regardless. For hours, I am alone with my thoughts, replaying the evening in my mind. Each time, my words and my actions seem to become more crass and coarse. Each time, I find myself more and more to blame. This is my fault and if I lose her, that will be my fault too. Krista did nothing wrong. She asks for very little from me, yet I offer her even less. She is right to be angry with me.

Several rooms away, Krista attempts to fall asleep and forget this night ever happened. I listen to her quiet sobs, acutely aware of just how culpable I am.

At some point, I bring the rest of the groceries inside. Careful not to disturb anyone else in the house, I put them away quietly, unaware of the time. Time is not important right now. My forever is on the line. The only thing of any importance in this moment is figuring out how I'm going to buy myself another chance. A chance to do this right; to be the man she deserves. A chance to be Vincent, instead of simply Nicolas.

I hear the door open. It is only Julia, but still, I stand as she enters the room. Julia's hair is tussled about. Her sleep was not disrupted by my outburst. She will never process it the way a normal human will, but regardless, an apology is due.

"Julia," I start.

She looks at me happily and says with a yawn, "Good morning, Nicolas."

"I hope you slept well."

Julia nods with a smile.

"Good." I hesitate to gather my words before I continue, "Listen, about last night… I shouldn't speak to you like that."

She shrugs dismissingly. "You can speak to me any way you like."

Julia is right. A sheep does not take my tone to heart. Their entire existence is to please their master. And for Julia, that's me. If it pleases me to be rude, then she is happy to endure it.

"Yes, I know that. But that doesn't mean I should." Julia looks at me curiously as I continue, "Going forward, will you do me a favor? Can you correct me when my words are harsh toward you?"

Julia asks uncertainly, "And that would make you happy? My correcting you?"

"Very."

She shrugs again. "Okay, then. I'll correct you."

"Thank you," I tell her quietly. Then, gesturing toward the stove, I ask her, "Would you like some tea?"

Julia smiles wide. "Yes. That would be delightful."

She follows me to the counter and watches as I pour her tea into a mug.

"Nicolas?" Julia starts. "Are you allowed to speak to Krista any way you like?"

I chuckle to myself. "Oh heavens, no."

As I hand her the mug, she nods and adds, "Then I think that some humility might be in order this morning."

Humility. How very astute for a sheep. "I think you're right. You know, Julia, you just might be more insightful than I give you credit for."

"It's not insight. It's my duty. You told me that her happiness is your happiness. And I think an apology would make her happy."

Looking over, I see Krista standing in the hallway watching us with a small, forced smile. So much of last night still weighs down the corners of her mouth.

"Then I shall give her a genuine one," I pretend to whisper to Julia.
Julia grins at me the way a child would, full of hope.

"Will you excuse us, Julia?" I ask her softly.

Nodding, Julia walks back to her room, blowing the steam from her mug of tea. As Julia passes her, Krista walks toward me. Her eyes should be puffy from a night of crying but instead, they are delicate in their sadness; a benefit of being a werewolf, I suppose.

"Tea?" I ask Krista, procrastinating the conversation we both know is coming.

"Do I smell coffee?"

I nod. "I made that too. I wasn't sure what you would be in the mood for."

Krista stops by the counter next to me and reaches for the coffee pot. Without looking at me directly, she pours the coffee into the other mug waiting on the counter.

Despite thinking of this moment for the past few hours, I'm not sure exactly what words will justify my apology. I simply start softly by saying, "Krista, I'm not good at this."

Lifting the mug to her mouth, she looks at me over the rim with the copper flecks in her eyes catching the light. "Humility? Oh, trust me, I'm aware." She smirks.

Hopeful that her smirk is a good sign, I smile lightly back at her. "At being honest."

She takes a sip of her coffee then shifts uncomfortably, unsure of where this is going. "Nicolas, I don't want to fight anymore. I've thought about this all night, and I already have the solution."

What does that mean? She knows the solution? She can't know what that is. I haven't even begun to clarify, or attempt to justify my behavior, or even ask for a chance to rectify any of it.

She certainly did not decide that deception would be acceptable. Nor can I imagine that she has decided to end our relationship. Not because I believe it would be an irrational response, but because I simply refuse to embrace that possibly.

Unsure of exactly what conclusion she has come to, I ask her leerily, "May I explain myself first?"

With a long exhale, she sets the mug on the counter and looks at me waiting hesitantly.

"I am good at talking. I am very good at saying what people want to hear. But as far as being genuinely open with another person…" I grimace as I shrug. "Not controlling the narrative is not something I have ever had much use for."

Her eyes grow softer, but I need to finish my thought before she interjects, so I continue, "I have spent centuries perfecting how to lie. It comes more naturally to me now than the truth ever has."

Krista opens her mouth to say something, but again I cut her off. "It will take time. I can't promise that it will always be smooth, I will find the gray area that you want to live in. It won't be the same shade every day, some days it will be darker than others. But I promise you, if you bear with me, I *will* find a middle ground where I can be both truthful and discreet."

With a heavy sigh, Krista looks around the room. I can see the thoughts racing through her mind as she twists her lips.

"Nicolas," she says gently. "Sometimes you are so much like a wolf that I forget you're not."

"You forget that I'm not a werewolf?" I ask, raising my eyebrows skeptically.

Warmly, she smiles at me. She sets her cup of coffee down on an end table as she walks into the adjoining living room. "Sometimes you are so very arrogant and stubborn"—she grins at me—"but you can also be selfless and loyal. Like a wolf."

She flips through the sleeves of records slowly, searching.

"Like with Tara, and Marcella. And me. You always protect, always forgive. Like we're your own little pack. You have killed for each one of us simply because you believe you can bear it easier than we can. And you live with those sins so we don't have to."

I can bear it easier. That is true. Murder is easy, and once you have done it enough, it is possible to even find some type of comfort in death.

"But you don't have to bear it all alone." Krista puts a record on and moves the needle to the center. As the song begins, she reaches her hand out toward me.

As I walk toward her, she adds softly, "A pack means, nobody ever has to be alone. No one person carries the entire burden."

As Otis Redding's "Pain in my Heart" plays, I take her hand in mine.

"You are my pack and I will carry your burdens, if you let me," she whispers gently. She wraps herself around me. Her warmth has never felt more comforting. The heat of her skin through her shirt soothes my angst that still clings from last night. My body sinks into hers, like exhaling after a long day.

"Sometimes I forget that we have not always lived by the same rules and expectations," she continues tenderly. As we sway to the music, she looks up at me. "Words are easy for you. Letting me into your world, however, is understandably much harder."

That is true. What I worry about the most is that without the lies, her smile will not be as radiant. It will be clouded with the realization of what my life costs so many others and tainted with the culpability of knowing the truth and doing nothing to stop me.

But that is a fear I will simply have to face. Because if I do not try, I will most assuredly lose her to my lies.

Krista rests her forehead against mine and nuzzles her nose next to mine as she adds, "All night I thought about us, who we are, where we are. And I realized that as much as I want you to learn to be open with me, I also need to learn to be patient with you."

I close my eyes allowing the warmth of her hand against my chest to bring me comfort as my mind begins to settle into my own little reality. The reality in which she belongs in my arms. There are no werewolves, no vampires. Just us. Two beings meant to be one.

I do not know why fate would pair a vampire with a werewolf so completely. All I do know is that for centuries, I believed Ann was the only person I would ever truly love. And I wholly believed I deserved to lose such a gift.

No woman has ever replaced Ann in my dreams nor my heart. None. Not Claire, not Hannah, not even Kate. Not until her. Not until Krista walked into my view. That moment. That brief moment, changed everything.

When Krista is near, I do not miss Ann. I do not feel like a vampire. And I do not long to drink her blood. All I want is to hear her voice calling my name when she smiles. I want her warm hand to reach for mine in the dead of night. I want her to continue dancing with me. Forever.

No person, in nearly six hundred years, has ever made me ache for them so completely. She is undoubtedly the only thing I want for myself. Without her, I have no future. Without her, I cease to exist...

*   *   *

The rush of air and the movement of the thin sheers that cascade over the windows as the door opens distracts me from my wandering mind.

As Krista steps inside our little home, the light pours in from behind her, framing her delicately, and I cannot help but smile at the sight of her. She smiles and nothing else seems to matter.

Her eyes seem to light up when she looks at me. "Hey, handsome," she says fondly.

"Hey. How was your night?" I ask her as she walks toward me, but I already know the answer. The rosiness of her cheeks tells me of the invigorating run she had. It tells me of the freedom of letting the moon trickle against her fur, and of the renewed sense of vitality spending an entire night in her most true form awards her.

She leans toward me and kisses me on the cheek, wafting me with the heavy scent of wolf and moss, and something else—maybe rabbit? But the smell does not distract me from the softness of her lips on my skin.

"It was fun," she says simply as she slides onto my lap, straddling me and draping her arms over my shoulders.

"I bet it was," I tell her with a smile.

"And how did you spend your full moon?" she asks playfully.

The full moon. The only night I can guarantee that she will be running in the woods in her wolf form all night. The only night I can be sure that I will have enough time to hunt, shower, and return home before her.

My hands naturally rest on her hips as I say smoothly, "The same way I always do; missing you."

Despite my omission of murder, that part is true.

She smiles warmly and kisses me gently on the lips. Keeping her face close to mine, she whispers, "Good answer." And kisses me once again.

With her face inches from mine, I ask her with an obliviously fallacious, seductive tone, "Krista? Do you dream about it?" My lips brush hers with my words. "Chasing down little rabbits and slaughtering them? With their soft little fur and their fluffy little tails?"

Giggling softly, she smirks and answers with a sarcastic jest, "Oh, please. The way they look at you with those beady little eyes,"—she clings her tongue dismissively—"they have it coming."

Her fingers twist at my collar as I smile my lopsided grin back at her as I agree, "Perhaps."

Her hand glides over my neck along my shirt collar. "You're very warm," she states almost as a question.

Krista may not understand my world completely, but she is no fool. A warm vampire is a freshly fed vampire. "Mm hm," I mumble, trying to avoid this line of conversation.

She looks toward the closed bedroom door that used to belong to Julia. "No sheep though?"

"No." I shake my head as I admit, "Not yet."

Creating a new sheep is not a simple task. At least, it shouldn't be. There should be months of research. The subject should be minimally missed or, better yet, not missed at all. It takes time to pick a specimen whose life is worth wasting.

I look toward the door, but it has not been Julia's door in quite some time. Not since she passed away in her sleep peacefully. After all, a sheep only lasts so long. No human body can withstand so much feeding without withering away.

"I miss her, too," Krista says quietly, misinterpreting why I looked at Julia's door at all.

It has been months since Julia passed and finding a replacement sheep is necessary. That much is true. But unlike Krista's misconceptions, I do not miss Julia the same way she does. I miss the convenience of having a walking, talking bag of flesh readily available any time I begin to feel a bit peckish.

"I just need more time. To find the right one," I tell her reassuringly.

However, that is not the only reason I am postponing the inevitable. It is not for lack of research. Research is easy. Sometimes lengthy, but easy just the same. No, my delay is to avoid seeing that sadness in Krista's eyes. The sadness of Krista realizing exactly what a new sheep will take from her.

She is happy here. In this suburb, with her mechanic job, with the local werewolves to mingle with on full moons. She's settled in. She's comfortable. I simply cannot hunt for a new sheep without ultimately uprooting us. Again.

I cannot possibly expect to pick a local and keep her at our home inconspicuously. And how would I explain to my neighbors that we replaced Julia with a younger version?

I was so convincing with my backstory for Julia that introducing another human would be suspicious. After all, there is nothing suspicious about me taking care of my mother who was plagued with mild dementia. Because that's who they believed Julia was.

She starts to open her mouth to say something, but I interrupt softly, "Sheep are not like other victims. They still have a heartbeat, and they stare at you every day. A constant reminder that their life been stolen."

Bodies can be hidden, but a sheep is in our home. A victim that Krista cannot escape.

A sheep means taking a human from a perfectly normal life, with perfectly normal friends, and loving family, simply to create another drone. A sheep means robbing a human of their life and depriving their families of the answers concerning their disappearance.

Gently, I glide my hand along her arm toward her neck. "It has to be the right one. I promise, that when they're staring back at you, it will matter."

Yes, it will matter but only to Krista. I can manage to separate my feelings about the life my sheep could have had versus the one I provide them. Krista, on the other hand, has had no real practice at being so removed.

Cradling her cheek with my hand, I let out a long exhale. I brush my thumb across her skin, feeling the heat of her flesh under my finger as I tell her, "We should go somewhere. Just us. Grab the passports and go."

I pull her toward me so that her forehead rests on mine as I let my hands glide over her warm neck as I continue, "I'm thinking Fiji. Huts over the water. Sex on the beach."

I move my lips close to her ear, letting my breath leave a trail of goosebumps along her skin as I add, "Sand in uncomfortable places."

She giggles lightly. "And just when are you wanting to go on this trip?"

My hand slides along her back, curving her body against me as I whisper back, "Sooner the better."

Moving my lips along her jawline, I feel her chest press into me with her breath as I continue, "We could leave today."

I press my lips to hers and feel the warming of her skin against me. My hand loses itself in her hair as I kiss a path along her neck.

Her heart pounds loudly as it picks up its pace in response to the way my hand glides along her ribs. Her scent wraps around me, caressing me in a way that no werewolf musk should ever tempt a vampire as her fingers trail over my skin.

Pulling her toward me, I start to press my lips to hers once more, but she leans back just enough to see my face.

Smirking, she asks softly, "And did you forget that we're going to my dad's next week?"

A mischievous smile, the type that a child has when they actually do get caught with their hands in the cookie jar, scrolls across my face. "I haven't forgotten." I only hoped that she would have.

Her fingers untie themselves from my hair as she slides her hand along my neck and rest them on my chest. Looking at me from the tops of her eyes, she asks despite already knowing the answer, "And am I right to assume you're planning on using this trip to Fiji as an excuse not to come with me?"

There is no part of me that wants to stay with her pack in Lock-wood Estates. Not for any amount of time. Not for any reason. Not even for one night.

She is already aware of my feelings toward her home and her pack but instead of telling her any of that, again, I simply try an undeniable truth, "Fiji is so much better than the Lock."

With a displeased sigh, she leans back, raising her eyebrows incredulously. Her tone has more despair than I expect. "Yes, it is. But my family isn't in Fiji, Nick. You said you would come with me this time. I knew you were going to do this."

I run my hands through my hair as I let out a forced exhale. I know my excuses will not appease her but hopefully they at least work well enough to get me out of going back to Montana.

"I can't go next week. I have to work. I have deadlines that simply cannot be moved," I try.

She looks over at me skeptically. "But you can move your deadlines for Fiji? You write, Nicolas. And you can write in Montana. Believe it or not, we do have computers there."

We have. She does not notice the way she subconsciously lumps herself together with Montana. But I notice. It's where her heart is. Where her pack is. Montana is where she belongs. However, it is somewhere that I do not.

I tell her softly, "There's more to writing than simply having a computer." I take her hands gently, hoping my touch might ease her. "You need the right atmosphere, mood." With a smirk, I add, "A muse helps."

She stares at me for a moment, considering her next words, then lets out a forced exhale to remove her mild discontentment with me. "Nick, you promised. You've bailed on me the last seven times. I'm running out of excuses to tell them."

"You don't have to tell them anything." I rub my hand along her arm as I say gently, "They don't want me there any more than I want to be there."

Her eyebrows rise as she asks wryly, "And whose fault is that?"

I scoff. Seriously? "Mitchell's."

Mitchell's fault. Hands down. He's the entire reason I do not have my own family to go visit. The fact that he is her brother is the only reason I haven't killed him yet. Oh, and I do mean, yet.

But I do not say all my thoughts aloud. Instead, I rub my hand across the back of my neck, trying to remove the disdain I feel for him from my voice before she expects me to respond further.

"Mitchell killed my mother, so I'm sorry if I don't feel much like singing 'kumbaya' with him," I say curtly.

She lets out a rueful sigh and tells me gently, "No. I know. And I don't expect you to."

I can hear the heaviness in her voice. Her unsuccessful attempt to hide the burden of caring for us both soothes my rash irritation, leaving only empathy in its place.

She rubs over her forehead as she considers how to continue. "It's just…" She looks up at me suddenly very sure of what she wants to say. "Nick, I love you both. But neither of you make this easy for me."

She holds my shirt collar in her hands and forces a small smirk. "I mean, seriously. The last time you two saw each other, you threw his car in the river." She raises her eyebrows to add emphasis.

A slow smile spreads on my face as I remember how angry Mitchell had been when he found his car, nose-deep in the cold water of the Bitterroot. It warms me to think of it still.

I look up at her softly and shrug. "He wasn't in it."

But I had wish he had been.

She lets out an exhausted chuckle. Her shoulders begin to relax as her fingers roll over the buttons on my shirt.

"Nicolas, I need you," she starts quietly. "I need you there. With me. Just this once."

There it is. The words that seal my fate: *I need you.* I don't need her to explain further but she continues anyway, "When you're not there, I get asked all sorts of things. 'Why aren't you with a wolf?' 'Don't you want children?' So on and so on. They don't ask when you're there." Because they are cowards.

Looking up at me, she lets out a heavy sigh. "And Simone will be there. And she's pregnant, Nick. Like *big* pregnant. And I just… I just can't. Not alone. Not this time."

She swallows hard, trying to pull back the sadness that fills her eyes. But that does little good. Even if she could hide it, I would still know her grief is there. The grief of knowing the pregnancy that she lost as a teen will be her *only* pregnancy. That is the price she pays for loving me. And as happy as she is with me, she will always mourn for the family she has dreamt of. The family that has both a husband *and* children.

"Okay," I tell her gently.

"Okay?" she asks, raising her eyebrow. "Just like that?"

Resting my hand lightly on her cheek, I glide my thumb along her jawline. "Just like that."

A warm smile lights up her face delicately so I add, "And since it doesn't look like my prayers of Mitchell getting hit by a bus are going to be answered anytime soon, I suppose I can try to play nice just this once."

She rolls her eyes, but her smile is warm as she shakes her head. As her hands run over the buttons on my shirt, her eyes wander briefly. And I cannot help but to wonder what her mind is skimming across.

When her eyes meet mine once more, I can see the sincerity in them and with a tender voice she tells me, "Thank you."

But she does not need to thank me. We're a team. If she needs me, I have to be there. That's how this works. I don't have to like it; I just have to show up.

I lean my forehead against hers, gently resting my nose next to hers. "But afterward, we go to Fiji."

Reaching up, she holds my wrist near her chin loosely. "Deal."

Her fingers trail over my forearm lightly, leaving a tingling warmth behind them. I close my eyes as I focus on the way her skin traces over mine. In this moment, there is no world around us. No Mitchell, no pack, no Genesis, and no sheep. I am not a vampire, and she is not a werewolf.

There is only the two of us and the delicate smell of moss and dew that permeates the air around us. The simple scents hold me in a calm embrace, much the same way she caresses me. Warm and inviting, it is no wonder that she can lose herself in the forest so easily. As she sits on me, flooding me with the sweetness of the trees and the warmth of her body, I find it difficult to think of much else.

Her hand glides over my chest as my breaths grow heavy and her fingers tangle themselves in my hair. Aware that she can hear my heartbeat picking up its pace and feel my skin warming under her fingers, I lean my lips toward hers slowly and allow the deliberate pace to add to her own suspense.

Under my thumb the rush of blood floods her flesh and I feel her body relax against me. Her voice is quiet as she asks, "What are you doing?"

"Thinking about Fiji," I whisper suggestively.

Kissing her softly, I part her mouth with mine and drag my tongue along her lip. I can hear her heartbeat quicken matching my own.

Despite the way her body warms under my touch, she pushes my hands away with a weak giggle. "Oh, no, no, mister. I have to go to work."

But my only retort is with my lips as I press them to the warm space behind her ear and let my hot breath graze over her skin.

I can hear the smile in her voice as she emphasizes each word, "Nicolas, I am filthy."

Keeping my lips against her skin, I reply, letting the gravelly hunger show in my voice, "Maybe I like you dirty."

She laughs but there is desire behind it. Her fingers twist into my hair and she pulls my head back slightly. Keeping her face close to mine, she says teasingly, "Fiji will have to wait until after work."

With a tender kiss on my cheek, she slides off of me and she starts down the hallway smiling back at me over her shoulder.

As I watch her disappear along with any hope of her entertaining my ideas of a prequel to Fiji, my lopsided smile spreads across my face.

At least I was able to distract her from the painful longing that tried to creep in. Longing for the children she will never hold. Longing for the pack she can never truly be a part of. At least, not while I am in her life. And the longing for an answer that would allow her to have both, without compromising her need to keep me.

As the water for the shower begins beating down on the tile floor, I see her toss her shirt into the bedroom. I do not believe she threw it into my view simply to tease me, but surely, she must realize how it would.

She has already voiced that she plans to go to work despite my intentions of her staying home, wrapped up in the sheets with me. Still, she tempts me with the knowledge that just a few steps away, her skin shimmers with water as the steam begins to hold her in ways that I want to be.

Exhaling forcefully, I run my fingers through my hair and stand up. I suppose I should check the mail before I get myself in trouble.

The sun is bright enough to sting my eyes as I open the door and I reflexively squint. Despite the sudden, sharp pain from the sun, I manage to make out several of my neighbors waiting at the bus stop with their children.

As I make my way to my mailbox, I smile at them simply and wonder if they were out here when Krista came home. She would have noticed the kids. They would have reminded her of her own failed pregnancy.

Krista doesn't talk about her son often. It is a pain she does not reveal to just anyone. A sadness she carries with her always but has become exceptionally brilliant at hiding.

She was seventeen and had been in love, or so she thought. They had dated since they were sophomores. Now as seniors, they looked to the future; not knowing that he would not have one.

After dropping her off at her house, he was in a terrible accident. Crushed pelvis, among other injuries, but it was the rupture to the arteries around the heart that killed him.

Krista was rightfully shattered. Not only did she lose the love of her young life, but she didn't even get the chance to tell him she was carrying their child. Defeated, she was having a child while she was still a child herself. And by a boy who could no longer be there to help her.

She lived within the pack. However, because she was still human, they could not sense her pain. Despite her close family, she was alone in her devastation. They could not feel her shame and she did not want to show it to them.

Doctors were able to tell her it was a boy when she lost him toward the end of her first trimester. She had felt broken when she had first learned of her pregnancy. However, losing him seemed to awaken a torment that crushed down on her with so many conflicting agonies.

Heartbroken and wounded, she became an expert at hiding her emotions behind her carefree persona. Guilt overwhelmed her. She had wished her pregnancy away and that wish had been granted. Now she was only left dreaming of the warmth of a fragile little boy in her arms. Imagining the rosiness in his cheeks and how she might see her mother's brow in his tiny face.

Despite the lack of logic and reason behind it, there are times when she feels a lingering, incomprehensible guilt reminding her of her body's inability to carry her child.

But the most pressing guilt that plagues her is one she does not dare to speak aloud. Somewhere buried deep, she hides it from everyone, even from me. But it is there, hiding in the corners of her memories. I have seen it flicker across her face once, but only once. It is the guilt born from relief and fueled by the knowledge that while she mourned for her son, she was also relieved by her loss. She guards it from herself carefully. Afraid of what it would mean to acknowledge it.

I have been a vampire long enough to have given up my hopes of a family that might include the pitter-patter of little feet. However, she has not had as much time to process such a reality. While she smiles so easily, and her laughter is always so light, I notice her eyes seem to linger on the faces of children when we are in public. And I see the way she stares at herself in the mirror, mentally preparing, before going to yet another baby shower that isn't hers. Subtle things she hopes to conceal but are all too obvious for someone who cares enough to watch for them.

Seeing these children holding their mothers' hands while they wait for the school bus, I am reminded of exactly how much life my love robs from Krista.

But instead of confronting those thoughts, I try to distract myself from feeling guilt for something I cannot change and pull the mail from the box. As I sift through it nonchalantly, I let the futile conversations around me capture my attention.

Karen, who lives in the house next to mine, stands with her twins in a small cluster of other mothers, gossiping and snickering senselessly. Unlike the other children who prance around the small crowd, the twins are well mannered. I quite enjoy the times they have come over to use our pool. Everything is placed back where it belongs. They are polite and respectful, which are increasingly rare attributes found in children.

Ella, the smaller twin, is timid and soft-spoken, unlike her adventurous and foolhardy twin brother, Ethan. Her dark hair is pulled back into a ponytail while his red hair pokes about wildly.

"Hey, Nick," Ella calls out to me happily. Wearing her purple flowered dress, she smiles sweetly at me, waving excitedly.

Ella is not big; however, she does not let her small stature stop her from getting her way. Her angelically round face and bright blue eyes would melt even the coldest heart. And she knows how to use both to her advantage.

I smile back at her and wave as the brother runs over to me. "Look, I lost another one," he says, smiling wide and exposing his missing front teeth.

"That's great."

"Yeah, and the tooth fairy left me a twenty!" he exclaims. A twenty. Karen must have forgot to go to the bank for change again. "Mom said she would take me to the store after school."

I smile widely at his excitement. "Wow, apparently losing teeth is a lucrative business. Maybe I should lose some teeth. I could use twenty bucks," I joke.

Ethan shoots me a look of phony disbelief. "Yours won't grow back," he tells me incredulously. But that's where he is wrong. Mine would grow back.

Before, I can say anything else, his mother calls for him, "Ethan, honey, leave Nicolas alone. He's busy."

"It's fine. Really, he's no trouble," I say to her as he rushes back to her side.

She smiles at me warmly. Out of politeness, I smile back then look back at my mail pretending to be busy with something of importance for humans. As much as I like my neighbor, there is no part of me that wishes to join a flock of females for a chatting session.

As my eyes reach the first piece of mail, I hear, in tones too low for a human to hear from this distance, "I don't know how you can live next to him and stay faithful."

Without looking over, I can imagine the scene near me. The gaggle of girls, one leaning over slightly, whispering to Karen loud enough for the others to hear but quiet enough for the children to remain excluded.

I hear the smile in Karen's voice as she retorts, "He has a girlfriend."

Someone snorts a laugh and adds, "There's nothing friendly about what I'd do to him."

It is odd what people will say when they believe you are human. Because, if she knew what I really am, she would know that there is nothing *friendly* about what I would do to her either. Unless, of course, what she wants inside her is a cold set of fangs.

I continue to flip through the envelopes as another softer voice tells them, "I heard he's sterile."

"Jess," Karen scolds.

There is a small giggle followed by, "I'm just saying, you wouldn't get caught."

I can hear the fine, loose rocks along the edge of the road shift under someone's feet as they clear their throat. Only Karen would be so uncomfortable that she would feel the need to reposition awkwardly so I'm sure it is her shuffling that I hear.

The same soft voice, belonging to Jess, asks with a certain amount of humor, "Do you ever go upstairs and watch him when he's in his pool?"

There is a short pause, followed by several laughs, and I can only assume Karen smiles shamelessly at the question.

"I knew it. I so would," says the first woman.

There is a lightly embarrassed chuckle as Karen responds, "I can look, just not touch."

"Well, what if, *I* look, and *he* touches?" Jess asks with a giggle. The other women laugh quietly as she adds jokingly, "I'm serious. Joe's going out of town next week so I kinda need to know soon."

The women chuckle loudly, like they just rolled out of dollar margarita night. Even if I could not hear their conversation, they would still be making themselves just as much of a speckle.

Suddenly, I hear Karen shush them. "Here she comes."

Assuming they could only mean Krista is near, I look up in time to see her walking toward me. Holding a muffin in her mouth to keep her hands free, she buttons her work shirt over a camisole and somehow still manages to look enchanting in coveralls.

Watching her, I cannot help but to smile my most genuine lopsided smile.

When she reaches me, she takes the muffin from her mouth and kisses my cheek warmly.

"Hi, Karen," she calls as she waves at the group.

I do not see Karen's response but knowing her, she is much too embarrassed to reply with more than a simple wave back.

Krista grins at me as she asks, "Anything good?"

I smile back at her. There is never anything good about human gossip.

I pull her toward me, leaning close to her ear. "Did you know that Joe is going out of town?" I say with pretend shock and dismay lighting my face.

She drapes her arms over my shoulders delicately. "Lucky Jess."

"Lucky Joe," I correct.

Krista chuckles lightly. "Don't let those girls fill your head with flattery so much that you can't fit back inside the house," she teases.

The heat of her body warms my skin through our shirts, and I cannot help but to be lost in it. Nothing the women behind me say could ever matter. It did not matter much to begin with, but now I can barely even remember what was said. The only thing swimming through my mind is how I am entirely encompassed by her.

Her scent wraps around me, shielding me from the world around us. Her warmth is comforting, easing any insecurities about whether she would be better off without me. In this moment, I do not care if I am right for her; she is right for me. And as she looks at me, unaware of the crippling affect she has on me, I am reassured that this is the place I want to stay lost in forever. In her touch.

Placing my hands on both sides of her neck, I let my thumb graze over the soft skin on her throat as I say quietly, "Never." I lean my forehead against hers gently. "Nothing will ever keep me from you. Not even my big head."

She smiles at my jest as I rub my thumb over her cheek.

I normally choose not to use my accent; however, she does enjoy it, and, in this particular moment, I want her to know these next words are from my truest self.

Tenderly, I tell her, "God doesn't see vampires. He doesn't curse us or bless us. That's what I was taught. But when I'm with you, I question all of that. Surely, God must have seen me just once because I have been blessed with you."

I feel the heat of her skin as she blushes warmly, and I add, "There's no other explanation because I have done nothing in my entire life to earn you for myself."

She smiles softly at me as she says, "I wish I could be an open book like you. Just say whatever I think, whenever I think it. I never seem to have the right words."

"Words are useless without actions," I assure her. "You always know just what to *do*. How to bring me back to life. I wish I could do that. Do exactly what you need me to." Like being honest, for a start.

Her curl tumbles across the back of my hand as she moves to kiss my cheek warmly. "You have no idea what you do for me," she says quietly.

She stares at me, thoughts tumbling in her mind. Krista has never found the words as easily as I do. Instead, she tells me more subtly than simply speaking her affections aloud.

An observant person can hear all they need to know by watching her tenderness dart across her face in the most delicate ways. The flutter of her heart resonates with the warming of her cheeks. Her eyes shimmer, the light never catching the same facet twice.

She stares fondly at me for an extended moment. Perhaps, she considers everything, but she cannot find words adequate enough to suffice herself. And although I would love to hear what is capturing her mind, her gentle gaze and the tender touch of her fingers on my arm tells me all that I need to know.

At last, she lets out a longing sigh. "I have to go," she says with faint sorrow in her voice.

I could try to talk her into staying home. She already wants to. But obligation would pull her to work, and my pleading would only add regret to her leaving.

So instead, I tell her simply, "I suppose I should get back to work too. Especially since the Lock just moved my deadline up." I press my lips to her forehead gently. "I'll see you tonight."

Something in my words light a fire in her eyes, and she smiles widely at me. "Yes, you will. I'm sure you're going to see a whole lot of me tonight, mister," she says with a playful tap on my nose.

She watches me as she backs toward her car. Shoving the muffin in her mouth once more to free her hand, she opens the car door, smiling over her shoulder at me. She mumbles through the muffin, "I love you."

"Love you, too," I tell her as she pulls out of the driveway.

I watch her start down the road leading out of the cul-de-sac and round the corner before I let out an exasperated sigh.

Closing the mailbox door, I look over my shoulder at the gaggle of ladies standing nearby. "Hey, Karen, is it supposed to rain today?" I ask, already fully aware of the forecast.

Despite believing I could not have possibly heard their vulgar comments, Karen's smile attempts to conceal her embarrassment by pushing her hair behind her ear as she answers me, "No, I don't believe so."

I look up at the sky and squint at the brightness of the sun before telling her, "Be a good day for a swim then, yeah?"

She laughs nervously. "Yeah… I guess it would be, yeah."

One of the ladies chokes back a laugh and hides her face by pretending to scratch the back of her neck.

Smiling at their collective awkwardness, I use my mail to wave my goodbye. "Well, you tell Kevin I said hi."

"I will," she replies, anxiously biting her lip.

I nod in their general direction and mutter my goodbye, "Ladies."

Once inside, I sit down at the computer desk once more. My morning had started so promising. One monster was temporarily, yet blissfully satiated, while my other carnal desire is, if I read Krista correctly, well on its way to being appeased later tonight.

There is only that ugly stain in the middle that darkens my day. That bleak part where I agreed to go to the Lock and offered to be nice to her cretin of a brother.

However, I did agree, and now I sit here staring at this overbearing cross as it stares blankly back at me.

"Just couldn't spare me from Montana, could you?" I ask the heavy cross over me.

Staring up at the dark wood, I attempt to clear my throat of the dry, scratchy lump that is forming under its condemning glare. I swallow hard but it does nothing.

I let out a long, forceful exhale and begin typing. However, before the first sentence is finished, my thoughts turn toward Salem.

It doesn't make sense. Why would the Genesis hire out an assassination? They already employee some of the best. Casiana, who was second to Amelia, is not exactly an assassin but she is certainly more than capable. Cold and calculating, Casiana has abilities unlike a common vampire. She walks in the sun, like I can, but she is also gifted with the unique power to bewitch other vampires into a vacant, coma-like stupor and that power alone makes her the most dangerous creature I have ever encountered.

Yet even if Casiana could not get away from her duties within the Genesis, there is Mila. The most loyal follower of Lilith, Mila is an altogether harridan.

There are rumors that she too walks in the sun like me, though I have not seen it personally. Mila is not a Nexus like me. Truth be told, I am not sure what she is. An assassin, with fangs, immune to the sun, but other than that, I know very little about her. Regardless, I do know that Mila *is* a monster. A forerunner in the Genesis, she may not have been the one who attempted to kill Krista years ago, but she is just as capable and just as demented as the rest of them.

Wearing the same odd medallion, Mila and Casiana share a distinct and strange bond. There is more to them than a simple employee arrangement and much more encompassing than their mutual religion.

No, there is something else lurking between them. Something much darker. Something they keep very guarded.

Either one of them could easily handle Salem. If they wanted it quiet, they could have done it themselves effortlessly. So why contract it out? Why go through so much trouble for a journal?

And what does any of this have to do with me?

Chapter 3

Ash clings to my nostrils as the dense smoke weaves around me. I have been here before, surrounded by the embers of my home. Waiting for the inevitable. Hoping that this time the memories will not consume me so quickly. The searing of my lungs as the heat rises around me is palpable.

I know what's coming but I cannot stop her. I see Marcella step in front of the window. Lifting the gun, she stands in clear view of the wolves while remaining in the shadows, ever careful of the sun. But it is not the sun she should fear.

Lying on the floor, I am unable to do anything more than watch. Raising my hand toward her, I start to scream to her, however, no words escape my lips. There is only silence as she takes her final staggered step backward.

Tears weigh heavy as I watch her icy fingers wrap around the dagger in her chest. I cannot hear the crackling of the wood burning around us or hear the sharp inhale as Marcella gasps for her breath. The only sound rippling through the thick air is the clanging of the blade as her body collapses to the floor.

Marcella looks desperately at me, reaching her crimson-painted fingers toward me. I want to rush to her. I want to hold her in my arms as her blood pushes through the soot beneath her. But my body is paralyzed by something I cannot comprehend.

This isn't how it happened. I did hold her. She died in my arms. But that knowledge does not change what is happening now. It feels familiar yet strange. Like two memories strung together loosely. I've seen those haunted eyes before. It was the way Ann looked at me so many years ago, when her dead body lie broken on the ground.

I was unable to help her then; just as I am unable to help Marcella now.

I feel the constricting of my chest. The same crushing pain I felt when Salem had collapsed my lungs and sternum on the night he turned me. But it is not Salem I see standing on my chest. It is a dark auburn wolf. The weight of its paws presses into me. Its claws dig into my skin, while its drool drips onto my face as it snarls inches from me.

I watch Marcella as the light in her eyes begins to dim. Her blood inches toward me as she pants frantically.

Suddenly, a gray wolf pounces on her, grabbing her head in its mouth. With a quick snap of its jaws, Marcella is gone, nothing more than ash dusting his tongue.

"No!" I manage to scream as a sudden rush of strength fills me once again. Forcefully, I shove the auburn wolf back, ready to fight my way out of this jumbled nightmare.

I thrash at him wildly, but every strike seems to have little effect. His, however, do. He leaps at me, pushing me back again to the floor and again I am pinned and hopeless. Like a rat in a sinking cage, panic begins creeping in. I cannot breathe. I cannot escape. I will not survive.

*   *   *

A pounding at my door rips me from my nightmare abruptly. My black eyes shoot open as my arms lash about erratically, still tangled in the fog between my dream and reality.

Warm hands grab my face as I hear a calming voice, "Nick. Nicolas, breathe."

But I can't breathe. My chest will not expand with my ragged inhales. I can still feel his paws on my chest. I rub my hand over my skin, feeling for the indention that must surely be there, but there isn't one.

My eyes dart about the room without focusing on anything in particular as I gasp desperately. Her grip on my face tightens, preventing me from looking around and forcing me to look her in the face.

"Nick, listen to me," she says, keeping her gentle tone as another round of banging on the door echoes through our quiet home. I try to turn toward the sound, but her hands hold me firmly. Staring back at me are her soft brown eyes. They hold me, allowing me to slip further from the confusion I awoke in.

As I look at her, my muscles begin to relax, and I let my eyes change to their natural green. I am not in that burning house. Looking into her eyes, I know where I am. I am home.

"Nicolas, open the door! I need you," Roddy shouts from our porch.

Roderick? Why is he here? My head swims with the fresh feeling of dread and death from my dream so much that I cannot shake myself free.

My thoughts tumble over one another like a leaf caught in a storm, unable to grasp any appropriate response to waking up to Roddy pounding on my door. The scent of Krista's blood teases my nostrils with both the guilt of causing her pain and the burning lust that calls to my hunger to cause more. My throat rages with greed, which only flames my annoyance with Roddy that much further.

Knowing that my irritation is misplaced, I close my eyes, trying to focus on calming my hunger and easing the anger scratching at the surface, but the pounding on the door again only causes my jaw to clench.

Krista's hands are soft as she reassures me, "Don't think about him right now. Roddy can wait there for a moment. Impatiently, I'm sure. But he *can* wait."

I feel her forehead rest against mine as she takes my hand and lays it on her chest. Feeling the rhythm of her breaths grazing across my chin helps me to focus and pulls me back more firmly to reality. Slowly, the heavy scent of ash and death begins to recede into my memories once more.

"I can hear your heart still pounding," she tells me delicately. Rolling her hand along my cheek, she whispers, "Just breathe with me."

I inhale again, this time gaining some peace and sense of consciousness. This time, the smoke dissipates, and in its absence, I can smell her. Moss, crisp and fresh. Chanel No. 5, her favorite. There is something else lingering that I can't quite put my finger on, and blood. Blood, new and trailing over her skin.

My eyes shoot open once more and I glance her over quickly. "Did I hurt you?" I ask, but I already know the answer. On her arm are three thin cuts. I sigh at the sight of them.

Krista turns my face back toward hers. "It's nothing."

True, the slices are clean and fairly superficial; and it is also true that she will heal much faster than a human would. However, it is not *nothing* as she states. It is very much something. It is the very reason vampires are not meant to be awaken, particularly, startled from sleep. A vampire lost in the realms of dreams can be dangerous.

"Are you okay?" she asks warmly.

I nod slowly. Despite my still heavy breathing, I am at least in control of myself again thanks to her. She is the only person who has ever been able to comfort me so quickly and I could have hurt her so much worse. The scrapes on her arm are not very deep but they could be next time, which is something I do not wish to think about.

Brushing my thumb over her cheek, I tell her quietly, "I'm going to get you a bandage."

The pounding on our door rings once more through our halls as I stand up, letting the sheets slide from my lap.

Krista's fingers trail down my arm and hold at my wrist so that I look at her once more. Smiling, she bites her lip. "I'll get the bandage." She pulls herself up from the bed with my arm. Then standing beside me, she rests her chin on my shoulder. "You just try not to kill him." She nods toward the door.

Quickly, she kisses my cheek and makes her way to the bathroom. I briefly hear the way the cold tile sticks to her feet as I start down the hallway. Before I make it to the living room, there is another series of bangs on my door and Roddy yelling loud enough for the entire neighborhood to hear, "Nick! Wake up! I need you!"

I groan to myself. Tara better be dead. Because I am going to kill her son. And I simply do not want to see the disappointment on her face when I do.

"This better be good, Rod," I huff to him as I swing the door open.

Shoving passed me quickly, Roddy pushes his fingers through his hair distractedly.

His panicked pacing dissipates my irritation all together. "What's wrong, Roddy," I ask, but he does not hear my words.

His eyes dart but never seem to lock onto me as he stammers out, "Nicolas, I... I don't know... where to start."

"Just tell me what happened?" I try.

"Did Finn call you?" Without stopping for me to answer, he continues to sputter hastily, "No. No... of course not. He can't."

Grabbing his shoulders, I ask him firmly, "Roderick. What's happened?"

Finally making eye contact, Roddy lets out a shaky exhale as the overwhelming reality of his words flood him. "My father's dead," he says as tears begin to puddle at the base of his eyes. "And if you don't do something, my mother will be too."

Eric was a waste of life. Apparently, he was a better alpha than husband or father. For me, he was always too hard and too abrasive to be much good for anybody other than himself. But Tara, she is different. Tara is caring and strong. She balances being a leader and a friend.

I can smell the blood drying on Krista's arm as she walks into the room. Pressing the Band-Aid to her skin, she listens purposefully to our conversation as Roddy's eyes begin to drift to the side, lost in his sorrow.

I place my hand on the side of his face, forcing him to continue looking at me. "Roddy, start talking."

Krista lays her hand on my back gently, the heat of her palm easing my growing angst. Her fingers rest along the bottom edge of my shoulder blade bringing so much more comfort than one would expect from such a small gesture. I glance back at her briefly, but she seems completely unaware of how her simple touch soothes me.

With another shaky breath, he nods. "Saul, he's their beta. Well, was the beta. He, um... he challenged my dad and, um..." Roddy twists his mouth, reeling back the sadness in his voice before he continues, "And he won."

Appalled, Krista covers her mouth with her hand to conceal her sharp inhale. Challenged him for alpha. A fight to the death. Without Eric, Tara is no longer an alpha. She no longer shares his strength. Tara is weakened, stripped of her position and power, but still too proud to back down.

I do not need Roddy to finish. We all know the death sentence Tara would willingly dive into now. Tara cannot stop being an alpha. She doesn't know how to not be a leader. Being alpha is her whole life, and she would willingly give her life to keep it.

"My mom challenged Saul, Nick. She's going to die."

No, she's not. Tara is my best friend, and I will not lose her to some silly wolf nonsense. I cannot let that happen. I won't. I just need to think. I need a plan. How am I supposed to stop them all? If I kill Saul, the next beta will take his place, and so on and so forth. Tara is at the very bottom of ranks now. I cannot kill enough wolves to make her alpha.

But maybe I don't have to.

Roddy said Finn was not able to call me directly to tell me what happened. That means one of two things: either there are orders to keep me out of the loop, which is very possible, or Finn has a plan. Pack rules protect the pack. Finn cannot physically ask me to hurt any member of his pack. But he can tell Roddy what is going to happen to his mother. He knows Roddy will tell me, just like he knows that I will do everything in my power to protect her. And just like I know that Finn will do anything to protect her too.

"When?" Krista asks Roddy quietly.

"Mom didn't want to wait but Finn ordered a mandatory two day reprieve due to her being a grieving widow."

Finn ordered her to back down. Oh, I can only imagine how furious she was over that.

"Forty-eight hours. That clock has already started ticking," I tell him directly. "We need to pack a few things and get to the airport."

"Do you have a plan?" Roddy asks hopefully. Any plan is better than none. After all, this is his mother. The only parent he has ever been close to.

"The start of one," I tell him, but it isn't my plan. It's Finn's or, at least, the plan I am assuming Finn has. I mean, it is the most logical. It also allows for the least number of causalities which means very little to me, but would be of importance to Finn.

"Good because we board in two hours," he informs me.

I nod. Two hours is not a lot of time.

Taking Krista's hand, I start toward the bedroom.

"So, what's your plan?" she asks in whisper as she shuts the bedroom door.

"Basically? To not die." I open the closet but packing clothes seem so insignificant. I mean, do I really need a change of clothes when my friend's life is at stake?

"That's a good plan," she says half-heartedly.

Aimlessly grabbing, I toss a few shirts on the bed before pulling the suitcase from the shelf in the closet. "Finn has a plan. I'm sure of it. He's been in love with Tara for a long time. He's not going to just sit back and watch her die."

As I lay the suitcase on the bed and begin to unzip it, I add, "Just like the way I can't watch you get hurt over this."

Krista's shoulders slump as she tosses a shirt on the bed knowing what I am about to ask her.

"Finn's fourth in command now. That means I have to at least kill three wolves." Probably more though. It will only be three if I guess which wolves are the highest ranking in order *and* if they aren't all ordered to attack me once I kill the first one, which they will be.

Exhaling forcefully, she crosses her arms over her chest.

"Krista," I start again in a low voice. "I think you should go to your father's and stay there until this is over."

She looks up at me for a moment, gauging what I am saying.

"It's the safest place for you," I add.

"No," she says matter-of-factly. "I already agreed to stay back when you go after Salem, but that's it. You get to ask me to sit out once per decade and you've already used it up. Sorry about your luck."

Walking over, I place my hands on her shoulders. I rub my fingers along her arm tenderly. "I don't like it either, but this is going to be a mess. If you're there, in the middle of a fight like this, I'm going to be distracted. I'll be looking for you, trying to make sure you don't get hurt, making sure they don't come after you to get to me, which they will do if they're smart."

She shifts restlessly. She may not like what I am saying but I am right about this. With her there, I'm vulnerable to being injured by trying to protect her regardless of whether she needs me to or not.

She is my weakness, and she is an obvious one at that.

Sighing lightly, she forces a small, unyielding smile on her face. "Your concern is cute; but let me assure you, it is misplaced."

"Krista, I love you and I would genuinely love to have you fighting next to me." I smirk a little as I add, "After all, there is something very attractive about a capable woman."

And Krista is very competent. Prepared to kill werewolves to protect me and powerful enough to rip a man's head from his shoulders, which I would quite enjoy watching.

"But if this goes sideways,"—*and it very well might*—"I can't have it coming back against your dad's pack. But more importantly, this cannot lead back to you."

With a long sigh, she lays her hand on mine and rubs her thumb over the back of my hand. "You underestimate me."

But I don't. I shake my head to myself.

I know what she can do and more importantly, I know what she would be willing to do for me. But I am smart enough to know that she should never have to perform such dark deeds just to keep me.

"Nick," she starts softly. Moving her hands so that both are on my cheeks, she cradles my face to emphasize the importance of her next words, "*You* are my pack. And this is the family I want fight for. Trust me, I can handle myself."

I smile at her confidence. "I know you can." With a small chuckle, I admit, "I'd like to see that actually."

Smirking, she adds, "Well, then, keep watching, mister."

My fingers brush along her arm, letting the heat from my skin ease her lingering worries and tell her delicately, "Watching you won't be a problem. Truth be told, I have a very hard time taking my eyes off of you."

Blushing, she lets out a quiet chuckle. She lets me hold her, rubbing her hand along the small of my back for a moment, lost in her thoughts. I do not pretend to know what she is thinking of, but her words give me some idea, "You're not expendable. Not to me," she says softly.

She's worried. That's what is flooding her mind. She is worried about me dying in a fight and her not being there to protect me. With that, I recognize there is zero chance I am going to be able to convince her to stay. Instead, I offer a different bargain, "Krista, promise me that no matter what happens, you will not phase, and you will not help."

"Nick..." she begins hesitantly.

"You won't phase, and you won't help," I reiterate. "I need you to promise."

She twists her feet, trying not to make eye contact with me as she thinks of another way to refuse me. So, I add, "I wouldn't ask you to leave this fight to me if I thought I would fail." But that is not exactly true.

I very well might fail. My plan is vague. I do not know the layout of what I am walking into, nor do I know most of their faces, let alone their wolves' fur. I am essentially going into this far more blind as I am comfortable with already.

Sighing, she adversely agrees, "Fine. I promise I will not phase to help you. But I *am* coming."

Gently, I push her curls from her face. There are no words to express how much I love her. How much I want to keep her, or how much I fear losing her.

Like a magma flowing through my core, it's her who keeps my feet on the ground. Without her, my world would stop spinning.

But saying that after asking her to sit on the sidelines of a fight like she's a feeble, little child seems fruitless. It would seem like an apology instead of an affirmation.

So instead, I simply tell her, "Thank you."

*   *   *

Most of the flight, I have been preoccupied with the imminent brawl. Even if I somehow manage to kill the correct three wolves and only those wolves, Tara will be mad at me. She will be annoyed that I took her fight from her. She will be furious that I killed members of her pack. And she will likely be angry that I will be unapologetic about both. Still, it's better for her to be angry than dead.

Krista leans her head back on the seat as she looks out over the clouds from the small plane window. Watching her, I am unsure if she is silent because she has so many thoughts racing through her mind or if she merely knows that I do.

Her thumb glides over the back of my hand subconsciously. There is something in the way her hand warms my skin. The way her chest rises and falls, matching pace with my own as though each shared breath might carry my distress away.

I have never had someone care about my well-being more than their own before. Vampires have little use for such benevolent behavior. I suppose humans and werewolves might have more experience with this. This tenderness. This selflessness.

For a long time, it had been foreign to me, the way other creatures love. Even after ten years and despite her unflinching ability to continue showing me how merciful love is meant to be, I somehow still do not expect her expertise at recognizing the times when I simply need her. Not her body. Not her blood. Just her. Her touch, her kindness, her strength, but, most often, it is her patience that I need most.

Looking back at the real relationships I have had, and excluding the relationships that were merely physical (which honestly, are most of them), there is not one person that has offered themselves the way Krista does. Unwavering compassion for another is simply not coded into a vampire the way it is in other species.

Lifting her hand, I bring Krista's fingers to my mouth and press my lips against her skin, holding them there longer than necessary as I savor in the blushing of her cheeks that my kiss yields.

Smiling bashfully, she bites her bottom lip lightly and looks out of the window to hide her captivated grin. "We don't have to go, you know?"

"Go where?"

"The Lock." She turns to look at me as she continues, "With this, and Salem…" She shakes her head lightly. "It's a lot."

It is a lot. A lot of death. A lot of fighting. And a lot of speculative planning. Not to mention the Genesis will undoubtedly be calling on me once they hear that I went after Salem.

Furthermore, I still do not realize the plans they have for me at all. They have never made me privy to why they changed me into a Nexus. I don't even know what I promised them in order to save Krista's life all those years ago. But I do know that they will not be happy if I manage to get to Salem first.

There is sincerity in her voice. She believes that the precarious nature of the next few days might be a bit excessive, even for me. And she is willing to miss seeing the birth of her best friend's child to shield me from it. Her selfless gesture makes me smile to myself.

I look at her softly, "You would miss Montana."

"I do miss Montana," she says quietly. "I love and miss my family very much. But if you say, '*No Lock*', then it's no Lock. And that's no problem."

Tempting. One little phrase and I could skip seeing her brother and all those other damned dogs. One exaggerated fib and I could probably get out of ever going back to Montana.

But either of those would be a lie. The Lock is, unfortunately, not going to be the most complicated or perilous part of my week.

Sighing, I lean my head back against my seat near to hers. "It is a lot. But I can handle a lot. I can handle anything because I have you."

There it was. My chance to avoid her family, within my grasp, and just as quickly as it appeared, I let it slip away. However, it was worth it to see her warm smile spread across her face.

Leaning over, I give her a simple, soft kiss on the cheek. "I love you, Krista Hartley. And I would rather be trapped in the nightmare that is Lockwood Estates than have you miss your brother. Because given the chance, I will not miss," I say with a smirk.

She snorts lightly and rolls her eyes. "Sometimes you are the sweetest person," she says sarcastically. "But most of the time, you're just impossible and facetious."

"I beg your pardon, but I am never *just* anything. Well, except maybe extraordinary," I tease.

She giggles lightly in response. "Oh, you're definitely one of a kind, for sure."

Smiling softly at her, I change the subject, "Besides, I think I might need Warren's help with Salem." Shrugging, I add, "I still don't know yet, but we'll figure that out tomorrow." Provided that I am still alive tomorrow.

Krista's eyes dart to the side as she notices something but does not move her face away from mine. Her mouth twists into a grin that is meant to contain her quiet giggle.

When her eyes meet mine again, she nods toward the front of the plane. "Roddy wants you. I can see him waving like a toddler."

Without lifting my head from the chair, I roll over to peer at Roddy a few rows away. He motions for me to come to him eagerly. Rolling my head back to face Krista, I tell her with a sigh, "Give me a second."

As I stand to leave, Krista adds with a wide smile, "For Roddy? You'll need more than a second. You'll probably need the rest of the flight."

I chuckle to myself and ask her jokingly, "Now who's being facetious?"

Krista laughs quietly to herself as I walk the rows to Roddy and sit down next to him.

"Oh, there you are," Roddy starts sardonically. "We are going to come with an actual plan, right? We're not just going to sit around making eyes at your girlfriend the whole flight?"

With a light chuckle, a smile spreads across my face. "Of course. I have a plan." Well, sort of one.

But more than a plan, what I need most is answers.

Even so, there is something more important that needs stated first. Looking around, I check to be sure that Krista is distracted and not eavesdropping as I start quietly, "Listen to me. We will come up with a plan but it's my plan. This is my fight. You and Krista cannot be there."

Roddy shifts in his chair, holding back most of his rebuttal as he says through tight lips, "But this is my mother we're talking about."

"That's exactly why you can't be there. You are all werewolves." It is also why we are sitting in coach on this plane. There's not a chance, I'd put myself in the cheap seats if there weren't still restrictions barring wolves from sitting in first class.

"The other packs cannot become involved in this. Not Krista's and not your fiancée's. Too many people will get hurt."

Roddy leans back a little surprised by my knowledge of his fiancée at all.

However, before he can say anything, I get the conversation back in the direction it needs to be in. After all, a good plan means less chance of dying, which is also pretty important.

"Yeah, we'll talk about her later. Right now, I have questions about your mom's pack."

Refocusing, Roddy nods his head.

I continue, "The three wolves above Finn—what colors are they?"

"What colors?" Roddy asks curiously?

I fight the urge to groan at his lack of understanding. The question that seems to defy logic to him would be quite obvious to anyone who has ever been in a real fight. Ever.

I mean, seriously, even Luther could understand what I'm asking.

"Yes. What colors? I need to know what their wolves look like. Their human forms are of very little importance. Because when they come after me, it will not be with fists. It will be with teeth and fur."

Roddy nods again as he tries to keep up. "Okay. Um, Saul's first. He's the alpha now. He's um, pale, both his wolf and his human. His hair and his eyes are so light that they're both almost white. He's not huge but bigger than you."

Okay, well, I do not care about his human form but at least we seem to be getting somewhere finally. "And his wolf?"

"Also pale. Very, very light gray. He's kinda unnerving to look at in both forms."

"And where would I find him?" I ask coolly.

Looking at me, Roddy swallows hard as though he is either unsettled with the calculating tone of my questions or with his part of callously planning the demise of the pack he grew up with. Still, he answers just the same, "Probably at the construction site."

Construction site? I can work with that. I lean toward him to prompt him to continue.

"It's a six-story building that they're remodeling. I think it used to be apartments. Saul's the one who orchestrated getting the property so he'll be there."

His eyes drift away as he lets out a heavy sigh. "Actually, all three will probably be there. Quite a few members of the pack are supposed to be there every day until it's finished. So… yeah, probably all three."

Perfect. Altogether in one place, at one time. I couldn't plan a more perfect slaughter. Well, I could. I have. But still, this is setting up to be more streamlined than expected.

Even though I attempt to hide it, the chill in my voice still slips through as I tell him, "Now tell me about this new beta."

Chapter 4

There have been times when I thought being a wolf would mean having the best of both worlds. They live as immortals, relishing in the strengths of their wolf, yet still delight in the splendor of being human. However, they are not truly free to exploit their gifts.

And humans. I can admit that there have been times in my life where I have even grown envious of them. What passion and zeal for life one must have when there is a ticking clock driving you.

However, the more I have learned of both species, the less I would choose either life for myself. That the fervor humans should possess is more often wasted on frivolity and that the perks of being a were-wolf are suffocated by their confinements.

Vampires, on the other hand, have little restrictions. And I have even less than most.

Like what I'm doing today. A human would have no chance of surviving and a wolf would have no chance of even beginning. As I walk along the gravel road leading me to the construction site, I am certain that there is no creature I would rather be.

Around the next bend is the construction site. The construction site where I will unleash an unholy amount of carnage. No other monster can do what I am about to, I am essentially limitless.

The gravel crunches under my feet as I round the bend and get my first peek at the old apartment building. Like the pack's new alpha, the building is large but not huge—a mere six stories. Very much in its infant stage of the remodel, the melancholy building stands alone in a forest, isolated from any soul who might be able to help these doomed wolves today. The red of the bricks stands out against the dark green of the full trees behind it.

The drab rustling of the plastic hanging over the windows adds an eerie edge to the air as I approach the parking lot, taking inventory as I go. There are more cars than I was hoping to see. While some of the drivers are undoubtedly human, I can safely assume that there will be at least one werewolf per vehicle. That means at least eight wolves are within the vicinity and most assuredly will be ready to fight.

I listen closely. Most of the construction noise is coming from inside. Clanging of metal lets me know that I will run into trouble on the second floor. Still, I should prepare for wolves to be on every level.

I take a moment to scan the area one more time before making my presence known. The more I know about where the others are, the better. Unfortunately, the only two people outside and in plain view are both humans.

When they see me approaching, they stop painting the brick a dull, beige color. The younger one looks confused. However, the other knows exactly who I am. I can tell by the way her eyebrows draw together in an annoyed manner.

I smile at them both as I approach but we all know it is fake.

The woman who recognized me says to the younger man, "Go find Saul."

Yes, do find Saul.

As he trots, off still unsure of what is happening, the woman mutters in a disgusted tone, "Ugh. It walks in the sun now?"

She meant for me to be insulted but her jab is weak and falls drastically shy of her intentions.

Instead, I point to the sky, I ask her mockingly, "Is that what that bright light is?"

She scoffs at me but our conversation is over anyway. The young man jogs out of the building just ahead of Saul. Roddy was right. Saul is large enough that his punch would pack a hefty weight if we were in a bar fight. However, this is no bar, and it is not his punches that I need to worry about.

More than his size, it is his paleness that seems more intimidating. His whitish hair, light eyes, and bleached skin give him a supernatural, almost haunting appearance.

"I wondered when you would show up," he says to me. "I thought it would be sometime next week before you heard the news."

The news that Tara would be dead.

Shrugging, I tell him flatly, "I had some free time."

He takes off his work gloves as he snorts to himself. "That eager to die, are we?" He gestures around himself. "Look around, leech. You're outnumbered and you don't have allies here. Not anymore."

I look around. However, it is not at the straggling werewolves who have begun to linger into the background. No, if Saul knew me at all, he would realize that I care very little about the odds. What I am looking for is a weapon.

My eyes stop on the painted brick. I grimace slightly. "That is a very ugly color. How do you expect anyone to live happily in a building of that color?"

With an irritated chuckle, he steps toward me. "Color? Really? You came all this way and that's what you want to talk about? Interior design?"

"Exterior, actually. But no, I wasn't planning on much conversation."

"Good. Then stop talking and starting listening. After I kill you, I'm going to kill your little friend. And you—"

I cut him off dryly, "Oh joy! A monologue. Just what this moment needed."

He steps closer. Feeling his anger flex against me, I cannot help but smirk at him. This is exactly where I was hoping he would be at this point—distracted by his hatred.

"Listen here, pal," he starts sharply.

But I am done listening. He stands close enough now and is unsuspectingly blind by his fury.

My fingers wrap around the thin metal handle of the five-gallon bucket of paint at my side. In a blink, I swing the paint into the side of his head and crush his skull against the brick. Pieces of bone and flesh fleck across the fresh paint as the bucket bursts, coating his limp body in beige.

If I weren't a vampire, it would still be easy to know which ones the humans are. The humans stand frozen in shock, appalled. Unable to process what they witnessed, they are oblivious to the stillness in the air as wolves rise up inside the rest of them. I look at them, my cheeks speckled with bits of their alpha, and let my eyes grow black as a smile stretches across my face.

The blond wolf in the back is the first to phase. He rips out of his human form furiously and charges for me. The odds of my success are better inside. There, I can take them on in a more organized manner so, naturally, I run.

Rushing along the side of the building, I leap through the first window I come to and tumble onto my feet. Someone howls outside as I dash through the stacks of lumber and supplies. The heavy cry resonates through the air. My head start does not afford me as much time as I hoped, though.

I pull open the elevator doors as the wolves begin pushing into the building, and then open the emergency hatch in the elevator roof. As I pull myself up quickly, the wolves begin slamming themselves into the elevator. I scurry into the safety of the dimly lit shaft, feeling the air off their gnashing teeth push against me as they snap at my heels.

As I hurriedly climb the cables to the upper floors, the wolves' throaty snarls chase me through the shaft. Their teeth pull and scrape at the opening of the hatch but to little avail. They will not be able to follow me up here.

Their deep growls vibrate through the cables beneath my hands as the narrow space snaking the sound toward me. Claws and fangs scratch and grind against the rugged metal. With each minor bend, the cold steel shrieks loudly in protest.

Growling, their hot breath creeps its way up the shaft after me. The heavy saliva smell swirls around me, mingling and mixing with their natural wolf stench, making the tight space suffocating.

As I near the fifth floor, a dark wolf throws its head back and lets out a deep, sorrowful wail knowing that I will soon disappear from its clutches. I jump to the fifth-floor elevator doorway, landing on a tiny ledge, and pull the doors open, unsure of what I might find on the other side.

The sudden burst of sunlight pierces my eyes sharply as I stumble into the main room. The open space is large with a few ladders, some welding equipment, and several sizeable toolboxes near a pile of chains along the wall under the window.

The wolves' feet thud up the stairs swiftly to find me as I rush over to the toolboxes. Quickly, I shuffle through the tools, tossing out anything that does not look particularly useful. Caulk guns, channel locks, and vice-grips scatter across the floor carelessly. Pulling out a drawer on the toolbox, I spot two spud wrenches and pull them from the plethora of less effective tools.

The pounding of their paws on the stairs grows closer, and I can feel the heavy drumming of their feet thudding toward me. The sound of their paws just beyond the doorway resonates through my chest. Yet, even with the onslaught of werewolves coming my way, I pause, patiently holding my ground.

Raising my arms, I hold the heads of the wrenches in each hand and allow the tapered spike to lay along my forehead as I watch the door.

The snapping of their teeth is somehow louder than the door as they break through, and three wolves burst into the room practically on top of one another. The blond one finds me first and charges straight for me again. His limited experience with vampires makes him predictable and vulnerable, which is helpful.

He rushes toward me, wild and sporadic, fueled by his overwhelming malice and desperation. He does not realize how quickly I can move, and as he lunges, I shove the spike of the wrench into his ear. Rolling over his body as it droops to the floor, I use my momentum to pull the spike from his head and stake a tan wolf through the top of its skull.

It's almost unfair that they are so much more amateur than me. In the blink of an eye, two wolves lie at my feet in their human form, dead and growing colder by each passing second. The quickness of their deaths leaves an odd energy lingering in the air. It grates against me, pricking at my skin as blood drips from the wrenches onto the concrete, tapping the floor near my shoes like a clock.

This third wolf is different. It is hesitant. Letting out a low, deep growl, it looks for an opening. It is not ignorant of fighting vampires, and it will not go down quite so easily. But regardless, it will go down.

The sound of more wolves padding up the stairwell rings in my ears as they rush to join us. I do not have the luxury of time while this wolf waits to receive its backup.

Flipping one of the wrenches in my hand, I toss it like a dagger at the wolf, forcing a reaction. Jumping out of the way, the wolf uses the opportunity to lunge at me.

I leap onto its back and sink the spike of my remaining wrench deep into its chest. Bellowing, the wolf slams me against the wall, crushing the air from my body forcefully. The jolt causes me to lose my grip on both the wolf and my wrench, and it clangs onto the floor.

As I scramble to my feet, the wolf whips around and bites into my leg. Its teeth pierce deep into my calf muscle as it drags me along on my stomach. My fingers find little help as they claw at the ground. The concrete is much too soft, and my nails merely carve grooves into the smooth floor.

As the wolf backs up, it begins shaking its head, viciously flinging me from side to side. Its teeth tear through my flesh, ripping my skin with the ferocity of being tossed about. I kick at its face in attempt to dislodge its grip, but it only tosses me more violently. Blood disperses into the air with every twist of the wolf's head, splattering little plops of crimson thoroughly across the room.

The werewolf does not ease its locked jaw as saliva trails down its teeth, scorching into the crevices of each puncture wound. Clawing at the wolf's face, I grab a fistful of fur for leverage and shove my thumb into its eye socket. I press relentlessly into his eyeball until I feel the firmness of his eye give way to the soft popping of it rupturing against my thumb and warm fluid streams over my skin.

Yelping loudly, the wolf drops me to the floor. I stagger to my feet as it shakes its head, trying to relieve the pain of its new reality. Grabbing its leg in my hands, I swing its struggling body over my head and slam the wolf onto the floor, listening for the inevitable shattering of ribs and being comforted by the snaps and cracks that ring through the space.

The wolf phases back into his human form. Blood coats his cheek, pouring from his eye socket. As he struggles to cough, blood splatters over his chin from his quickly filling lungs.

The sudden, prodigiously alluring aroma of fresh blood wafts toward me as I study his failing body. He is not one of the wolves above Finn so he does not have to die. Still, I should walk over to him and finish this. A quick death is the only mercy I can show him now. However, the searing pain in my leg limits my ability for clemency and I leave him to his fate as four more wolves burst into the room.

A gray wolf springs at me. I dodge its jaws easily and grab its fur at the shoulder and hip. Using its own momentum to swing it around, I toss it into a pillar. It lets out a deafening bellow nearly covering the sounds of its ribs crunching against the cold stone. It rolls onto the floor wheezing loudly. Its raspy, ragged inhales tell me that more than one of its ribs are broken and at least one has punctured its lung.

The second, light brown wolf, snaps at me. I recognize the darker auburn wolf behind it. That one is Finn. With orders to kill me, that is exactly what he will attempt to do. However, since I need him alive and reasonably unharmed, I will simply have to avoid him until I can kill enough wolves to make him alpha.

Leaping over the brown wolf, I roll down its back and rush toward the center of the room and the wolves. As Finn pounces at me, I slide under him to escape his grasp. As he soars over me, I kick him in the chest, feeling his sternum crack under my shoe.

Finn skids across the floor, crying out, but the distress in his scream is more of frustration than of pain. It will slow him down which is what it is meant to do. Hopefully, it will allow me enough time to keep my distance from him until he can call off the attack without either of us dying.

Moving across the room quickly, I grab a piece of rebar from a small stack in the center of the room without slowing my pace. The red and brown wolves chase after me, snapping and growling erratically. Their anger ripples through the air, pricking up the hairs on my arms as I make my way to the outer perimeter of the room.

Slamming the rebar into the concrete, I wrap a chain around it several times frantically to keep it from slipping. The wolves close in on me. The red wolf snaps its teeth just as the brown wolf's paws slam into my chest, knocking us both through the thin veil of plastic covering the window.

My hand tangles in the chain as we fall, and it jerks me to an abrupt stop. The brown wolf crashes down on me, smashing my body against the brick wall while shoving my body down, dislocating my shoulder. The rough wall scrapes flesh from my cheek but it is the stretching and ripping of my shoulder muscles that forces me to cry out. My muscles spasm in protest as I dangle from my trembling arm.

The wolf claws at me as he continues to fall and lands on the unforgiving ground with a thud. Phasing into his human form, he thrashes in pain in the dirt beneath me. Reaching up with my good hand, I grab the chain and pull myself up to free my throbbing arm.

Laboriously, I twist my aching hand from the tautly bound metal chain. Wincing through the excruciating movements, I let out an agonizing scream through gritted teeth and attempt to use the pain to focus on the task of freeing myself. Holding onto the chain with my uninjured hand, I untangle myself and my arm drops immediately.

Before I can drop to myself to the ground, a set of teeth appear out of a third story window and grab the chain. With a sudden tug, the chain is dragged into the building, pulling me into the third story with it.

The room is fairly well lit but the cement dust hovering in the air makes it difficult to see. Like a thick fog settling, it graciously attempts to hide the two humans who cower in the corner. Shielding their heads, the tan wolf that pulled me in to this murky room thrusts its jaws toward me again. I swing at the wolf, driving my fist into its face and dislodging a few of its teeth. They slide into the abyss of the haze. Its teeth will grow back but not quickly enough to help with this fight any longer.

The tan wolf backs up a step to shake its snout, but that delay is a mistake. I glance around the room for anything useful, but the heavy cloud of dust only allows a vague outline of the objects in this room, even for my eyes. So, without wasting any more time, I lunge at the wolf, tackling it as a football player might, driving my shoulder into its abdomen and knocking my shoulder back into place.

We hit the floor hard enough to see another burst of cement dust displace into the air around us. It attempts to settle as I grab the hammers near my feet and slam one into the wolf's head.

The tan wolf closes its eyes tight, whining painfully as two more wolves dash in. One black with gray tips on its feet and the other faded blond color, but neither is Finn, which is good.

I rush toward the black wolf. Using the claws of the hammers, I grab the piping above me and swing myself onto the wolf's back. Wrapping my legs around its ribs, I crush the bones beneath my thighs. I slam the hammers into its head relentlessly as it yelps wildly, bucking and scratching at me. Still, I continue to pound the hammers into its head and body, hearing the snapping of bones with each blow.

The blond wolf leaps at me, knocking me from the other wolf's back. Tumbling over myself, I find my footing before the blond wolf does and I charge at it, wrapping my legs around its throat. I place a hand on both its upper and lower jaws and pull its mouth open, ignoring the way its teeth dig into my fingers and its saliva burns into my skin.

Sensing the distress of the blond, the black wolf struggles to stand but its bones are too shattered. It whines intensely in protest as it hears its pack member's jaw pop under the stress of my force. The blond wolf shrieks unbearably as the joint of its jaw snaps and unhinges. Its flesh tears as I rip its mandible from its body completely.

The blond wolf collapses in my legs and begins to tremor violently. Its body twists and twitches painfully as its muscles seize and lock, resisting its natural tendency to phase back into its human form.

I stand up, watching it for a moment as it shudders and spasms severely, writhing torturously. Placing my foot against his head, I press down until I feel its skull collapse, crunching under my weight. His body goes limp but I have no time to even wipe the fragments from my shoe.

A charcoal wolf charges in with second wolf and Finn behind it. I was hoping to have delayed Finn enough with the broken sternum to not have to fight him again, but here he is. And again, I am stuck having to be careful not to seriously hurt a werewolf as he tries to very thoroughly hurt me.

Picking up the hammers, I rush toward the wolves. I slam the claw of the hammer into the charcoal wolf's neck, tearing a large clump of flesh from its throat. Blood splatters onto the floor and disperses into the air like a fine mist. The wolf drops to the floor as I continue past the wolf. I cannot tell whether his wounds will heal or he will die. Nor do I care.

Swinging the hammer, I strike Finn in the nose hard enough to lodge fragments of bone into his sinuses. He shakes his head, snorting out blood in attempt to eject the pieces of his shattered face onto the floor. More importantly though, his preoccupation with his broken muzzle offers me a chance to flee him once again.

I dash out of the window and onto the fire escape. The other wolf, a smaller cinnamon wolf, chases me onto the metal landing. Jumping up, I grab the ladder above me and lift myself up so I can kick cinnamon wolf over the railing.

It falls to the ground but this height will not kill it. It lands on its side beneath the fire escape, still very much alive. But not for very long.

With an abrupt jerk, I pull the ladder down onto its throat with enough force to hear its spine shatter. The wolf phases back into his human form as I hear the deep rumbling of Finn's growl growing closer. I rush down a flight of stairs on the escape and jump from the second story landing to the soft ground where a cocoa-colored wolf is waiting for me.

It leaps onto my back and bites into my neck. Hot breath warms my skin as my blood trickles down my chest and paints my shirt. Grasping its fur, I drag it over my shoulder from my back, ripping through my flesh with its teeth as I toss it to the ground.

As it lunges for me again, I slice my claws across its face, flaying the skin along its jaw and across its eye. It steps back, blinking erratically from the pain and attempting to refocus its blurred vision. Taking advantage of its temporary distraction, I spring toward it. Kicking the wolf in the side with both feet, I cast it into the brick wall.

With the sound of ripping plastic, two wolves jump out of the first-floor windows and pad toward me. A few others hold positions closer to the building, waiting for a command to finish me off.

Closing in on me, the two wolves flank me from each side. One slams into me, knocking me to the ground. But I intended this. I wanted it to believe that I was unprepared.

When my hand hits the ground, I grab the rebar lying in the grass and shove it through the soft tissue under its mandible and into its skull.

In the distance, a human leaps onto one of wolves. In a blur of flesh and fur, I see the human twist the wolf to the ground. A few wolves circle them, blocking my view as the other wolves close in on me quickly.

I pull the rebar from the limp body and scramble from beneath the dead werewolf. As I get to my feet, the other wolf bounds at me. Seemingly in mid-air, the wolf transforms back into its human form. She lands with her face mere inches from mine. Snarling at me with the rebar at her chin, is Finn's ex-wife and, more recently, Saul's widow, Lydia. Behind her anger is a flurry of frustrated tears.

"Enough," I hear Finn's human voice command.

If they had been paying attention, the wolves might have noticed the relief that washes over me at the sound of his voice. It is only for a split-second though. I rein it in quickly. No wolf can know that I was counting on Finn living. I needed him to stop this. But even more so, I need him to be alpha so that he can help save Tara.

Keeping my eyes tight, I look in the direction his voice had come from to see him walking quickly toward me. But behind him, someone else catches my eye. Standing over a naked man is Krista. Her eyes are not the indulgent brown that I lose myself in frequently, but instead are crisp and blue. Even in her human form, the eyes of her wolf stare back at me.

She steps over her kill and jogs toward me as Finn pushes the rebar aside to step between me and Lydia.

"That's enough," he says to me firmly.

For show, I keep my eyes black and my voice cold as I tell him, "Tara's my friend."

Just as decisively, Finn responds, "She made her choice."

He does not believe that. He does not believe that Tara should die for her misguided choice to fight an alpha. It is a death sentence that no grieving widow should be permitted to make.

But none of the wolves can know that he wanted this as much as I did. They need him to be an alpha that they can respect and they would not respect him if they knew that all of this death stains his hands as much as it does mine.

"I need you to go," Finn says with authority. "Nobody else has to die. She wouldn't want this."

He is right. Tara would not want this. She will already be angry that I killed so many in her pack. But she will live long enough to forgive me.

Rushing over, Krista wraps one arm around my waist and holds the other up to Finn as though to block him. "We're going."

She leans her weight into me to nudge me but I stand fixed for a moment longer. Looking at me, she repeats more sharply, "We're going."

I do not take my black eyes from Finn as I tell him with insincere venom in my voice, "For now."

Krista leans into me again and I give into her weight as I step back. We walk across the yard quickly as though we are concerned that Finn might order an attack from behind or change his mind about letting us go. But that is not a real concern. Finn is not a danger. He is an accomplice and with him as alpha, the wolves that scowl at us as we leave are no more threatening than pussy cats.

We make our way toward a drug store a couple of miles away. I try not to limp as the pain of saliva burns into the bites on my leg and shoulder. But the further we go, the more the wounds constrict and tighten. If I don't wash out the saliva soon, the bites will scar.

I am grateful that we don't talk much. It helps me use my energy to hide my pain. Besides there isn't much we are permitted to say anyway. The risk of lingering ears somewhere along our route overhearing that Finn is not the innocent savior they need him to be is too great.

The pack is unstable and primed for another munity. They need to believe that Finn is a strong leader. That his actions were for the benefit of the pack, not simply that he was willing to sacrifice as many as it took to save the woman he loves. They need to trust that their lives are just as valuable as hers. The truth of his betrayal would fracture the pack irrevocably. Not to mention, within a pack, treason is punishable by death.

Once we arrive, Krista gathers a few bandages for some of my larger wounds. I make my way to the restroom and begin filling the sink with water. It will not matter if the water is hot or cold. Once it is blessed, it will burn just the same.

As the water pours into the sink, I pull my shirt off carefully. The drying blood from the scratches on my back sticks to the fabric, causing it to pull at my skin. I grit my teeth tightly to keep from groaning as my flesh reopens and fresh blood trickles down my spine.

I shove the shirt in the bottom of the sink to plug the drain. Leaning my head to the side, I attempt to get a better view of my neck. The bite is larger than I expected and the edges are still rough and uneven. It will not heal properly until I clean out the salvia that is searing deeper with each movement.

Luckily, the lacerations on my back, though they are deeper, they are not from teeth but from claws. Those will heal nicely without the scorching water I'm about to endure.

A quiet knock at the door pulls my attention from the mirror as I turn off the water. Unlocking the restroom door, I let Krista inside. Her arms heap with a plethora of supplies that she struggles to keep from dropping due to the precarious way she stacked them.

A small smile slinks onto my face as I watch her but she is oblivious to it as she fumbles in and sets the pile of various gauzes and tapes on the counter.

"I wasn't exactly sure what you might need," she tells me gently as though the volume of her voice might somehow cause the salvia to burn into my wounds more.

Boiling into my tissues, the werewolf salvia constricts further into my skin. If left to fester inside me, it would scald my muscles, seething in around them and strangling their mobility with its flames. It would leave my body scarred inside and out, and warped with pain that would be forever unyielding.

Without asking if I need her to, Krista begins helping me undress. I could do it myself but, my throbbing shoulder sincerely appreciates being spared unnecessary movements at the moment, so I do not stop her. As I loosen my pants, Krista rubs her fingers over my skin, softly tracing my bruising.

"It looks worse than it is," I half-lie. Some of the bruises and cuts will heal fairly quickly but the bites that chewed through my neck will be much slower to heal.

The bruising along my back is mostly from the violence that took place to my shoulder. The muscles holding my shoulder blade had ripped beneath my skin when I got caught in the chain. That dislocating pull of my shoulder is what had caused the dark bruise spilling down my back.

The scratches that run deep into my flesh, scraping into the bone in some places, are not so terrible. Despite how they appear, they will not last.

Krista helps slide my pants down, not realizing that the blood from those gashes has begun to congeal into the jean material. I only wince slightly as my pants pull at my wounds and somehow, I manage to keep Krista from seeing how much it aches me.

Moving my hands, making a cross above the water. I whisper the prayer I have said more times than I care to, blessing it and sealing my impending pain.

I stare at the water for a brief moment, knowing the pain that awaits me in the seemingly benign liquid. With a heavy exhale, I meet her eyes in the mirror. "You don't have to watch this."

There is honesty in my words that she cannot deny. Watching me pour holy water over my already burning flesh will not be a pleasant sight.

Her fingers trail over my arm tenderly, as she slips a clear plastic cup into my hand. Reassuringly, she whispers quietly, "It's not me I'm worried about."

She presses her soft lips to my uninjured shoulder, despite the drying blood there. Her tender touch brings comfort but does not remove the dread that is attempting to settle in me.

Resting the cup on the edge of the sink, I look at the cool water, knowing the fire it possesses. As much as the salvia burns into me, this will be worse.

Dipping the small cup in the water, I pour it over my neck, letting the water scorch deep into my flesh. Careful not to crush the porcelain, my hand grips the edge of the sink. My body longs to scream in protest but the blaze trailing over my skin takes my breath and only a sharp inhale manages to disrupt the still restroom air.

Pressing herself into my back, she wraps her arms around my waist. Not concerned about getting herself wet, she holds me tightly as I pour another cup of fiery liquid into my neck wound. To her, the water feels like cool, like any tap water might feel to any normal person. But to me, it twists into each nook of my charred flesh.

Just beneath my ear, I can almost hear the tissue fizzling deep beneath the skin in opposition to the blaze as it cauterizes my already blistering skin. I let out a restrained groan through tight teeth as the flame smolders over me, pushing tears to my eyes. My body rocks back and forth in hopes of dispersing the agony.

My breaths grow sharp and tremble like with my hand that braces against the sink edge. Krista leans into me more, letting her body rock with mine and longing to relieve some of my distress with her hold of me.

Careful not to break her embrace, I pour the water on my leg, flushing out the rest of the salvia and replacing it with the flame of a liquid torch that hisses into my skin as though it is peeling my flesh beneath.

The severe pain makes it difficult to focus on anything other than the way the water blanches my skin. My knees grow weak, forcing me to lean my body against the sink for added support. My muscles contract, my body trying to expel such a curse from my flesh.

Krista holds me, supporting me almost completely, and helps me sit down on the floor. I lean against the metal wall of the restroom stall. My fractured ribs shift under my skin. However, the pain of my unstable ribs pale in comparison to the flames sweeping along my skin.

Keeping my eyes closed, I shudder against the cold stall. But it's not the coolness of the metal nor the tile beneath me that has my body quivering. The remnant of the water still sizzles along my skin as I rest my head back against the stall.

The worst part is over. The accursed holy water is finished for now and I can begin imagining the flames dissipate, departing my body with each breath. In and out, over and again, like a wave washing over me and leaving me worn but not beaten.

Krista wraps my leg wound with gauze. I assume she does this simply because she does not know what else to do. There is little she can do for me in this moment but her compassion for me urges her to do something, anything, no matter how fruitless it may be. My wounds need no bandage; yet, her delicate touch is comforting. Besides, the gauze might help block some of the air that only fuels the heat of my scorched flesh.

"You could have gotten hurt back there," I tell her softly. I roll my head toward her so I can see her avoid looking me in the eyes.

"But I didn't."

"You could have. I thought I told you not to help," I say with more crispness than I mean to.

Krista looks at me sharply and pulls the gauze tight to my leg causing me to flinch.

"That's not what I meant," I say reflexively.

"Good." She smiles lightly. Looking back my leg, she continues to wrap as she responds, "You did tell me that, but you also said you weren't going to die. And to be honest, that looked kinda iffy for a moment."

She raises her eyebrows, waiting to see if I contradict her but I don't. She is right. It did look questionable. Going into a fight relatively blind is never ideal and there were considerably more wolves than I anticipated.

In the lack of my response, she adds, "Besides, I said I wouldn't phase and I didn't, so…" She shrugs with a satisfied smile.

Thinking back, she never promised not to help, only not to phase. She chose her words carefully and I took the bait. Clever girl. There is little point in arguing with her anyway. Not only will it not change anything that has already happened, but it will also not keep her from attempting something similar in the future. You cannot argue with a woman who is as equally smart and stubborn as myself. That much I have learned.

I watch her as she tapes the wrap on my leg, securing it. Her shirt hangs heavy, wet with the water and my blood from holding me while

I cleaned my wounds. My blood is swirled with the water in an odd pattern, like a macabre tie-dye.

There is a quietness to her, but it is not from serenity or peace. It is weariness that settles into the corners of her eyes that weighs her down. And I know that it is not the fight that exhausts her.

It is that werewolf. The one who was lying naked at her feet. The one whose death is replaying in her mind. I am well versed in managing the simultaneously overwhelming and depleting rush of emotions that swill inside after you take a life, overlapping spells of both relief and grief. However, this is a new experience for her. The reality of killing another werewolf is not one she has ever foresaw or prepared for.

Pushing myself from the metal wall, I lean forward enough to rub my hand over her fingers on the gauze, offering only minimal comfort. Nothing I can say will make this better. Nothing will take that memory from her mind. And nothing will take away the guilt.

Words are not needed. They are not useful at easing the edges of this type of grief. So, I do not try. Instead, I tell her softly, "Thank you."

My words pull her from her mind, and she looks over at me as I add, "For not listening to me. You very well may have saved my life."

And perhaps she did. There is no way to know for sure now. Besides, at a minimum, she did spare me from more bites and pain, and right now, she needs to hear that her actions were the right ones.

"How did you know it was him?" I ask her. Out of all of the werewolves present, how exactly did she choose the alpha?

A small smile lights her face briefly as she says, "Oh, he had a tell."

"They all had tails."

She chuckles to herself but I can hear the pain still lingering in her voice, "Not a tail. A telltale sign. For him, it was something in his stance. It isn't haughty. It's something else. Something that screams, *leader*. Every alpha has one. And it's easy to spot once you've seen enough of them."

A telltale sign. Well, that would have been considerably helpful for picking an alpha out of a crowd.

"I have seen it in you, too," she adds matter-of-factly.

"I have the tale-sign of an alpha?" I chuckle disbelievingly. There is little chance that I could ever have made a good alpha. I am far too selfish for that.

"Sure. Behind all that arrogance is a man people inherently want to follow. There's a natural leader inside of you."

I snort to myself. Just because I'm not a follower does not make me a leader.

"Then why don't *you* listen to me?" I jest.

"Because you're not my alpha," she answers with a light giggle.

Krista slides over closer to me to cover my neck wound. Her fingers are light against my skin and I smile at her lovingly.

Her cheeks flush slightly as she smiles back at me. She pushes my chin away, turning my head so she can access my neck better.

Gently she leans me forward, off of the wall, and wipes the remnants of the harsh water from my lacerations on my back.

"Do you think Tara will fight Finn for alpha?" she asks quietly.

I think if it comes to that, Finn would rather submit and be killed by the next in line than attack Tara. After all, this isn't the first time he has helped in the slaughtering of a pack to protect her.

I chuckle to myself lightly. "Finn has no intention of fighting."

He intends to propose. I watch Krista put together what I already have. Finn's marriage to Tara will restore her rightful position as alpha and without any additional bloodshed.

Krista's eyes light up with her words. "Marriage. You think he will?"

"I know he will." At minimum, Finn has been in love with Tara for decades, probably much longer. And although this is not how he envisioned it, I am very certain he has thought about this moment many times before. The moment where he can confess his feelings and ask her to be *his* alpha.

"What do you think she'll say?"

I don't think Tara really has much choice. "She'll see the opportunity to become alpha again. This time with a nicer husband."

Tara knows Finn well enough to know that he will not expect her to be anything more than an alpha unless she chooses him for herself. He will court her before asking her to be his wife in any way more than legally. In fact, Finn will likely be elated to finally have the chance to prove his worth to her.

"Does Tara love him back?" Krista asks as she tapes the gauze on my neck.

"I think she could. In time."

Tara doesn't need to love Finn to marry him. The only thing Tara has ever needed in her life is to be alpha. She barely cared for Eric any more than any other member of her pack from what I could tell.

What Tara did have for Eric was respect. After all, Eric was a leader by nature. And leading is something that Tara has always been enamored by. Eric truly did put the pack before himself and Tara, which is something Tara always felt was honorable. Even though, it always seemed to agitate me.

Finn, on the other hand, is quite the opposite. Finn is enigmatic and understanding in ways that Eric could not fathom. But the biggest difference between Eric and Finn is that Finn is willing to sacrifice his own desires, and even his own pack, to ensure that Tara gets everything she needs. While this may not make him the best suited alpha, it will help him to be the type of husband Tara will inevitably fall for.

"Tara's always been fond of Finn so it's merely a matter of seeing that he not only has merit but also heart. I think she'll find it difficult not to fall for him and I think it will happen much quicker than she imagines possible."

Noticing that Krista's hands are not working on my dressing any longer, I look over at her and see her smiling warmly at me.

She looks very much like she did the first time I saw her. Moving my hand to her cheek, I hold her face delicately and rub her cheek with my thumb, savoring the tenderness in her eyes. As the light catches the copper flecks in her irises, her smile pushes her cheeks upward but cannot hide their sparkle.

She looked at me like this before she knew what I was and even before I knew what she meant to me. That first night, I saw a future that didn't belong to me but never suspected that in that instance, she saw it too.

Perhaps if we had realized the significance of our attraction, we would have driven away, never coming back to face the consequences of our love.

But regardless of what I might change or not change about our first night together, I am grateful that her love burns just as warmly as it ever has.

Pushing her curls behind her ear, I whisper to her, "Finn will be good for Tara, just like you are good for me."

She looks at me softly and rests her chin on my shoulder, letting the heat of her skin ease my aching joint as her fingers rub along my forearm, tracing over the dried crimson.

Her eyebrows come together curiously as she reaches toward me with her other hand. With a faint smile, she wipes a bit of something beige from my temple. "Is this paint?"

Paint? Oh, probably from smashing Saul's head. "Yeah."

Grimacing, she rubs the dry fleck of paint between her fingers. "It's an ugly color."

I snort, trying to keep my laughter minimal and keep my ribs from shifting with my lungs.

Without asking why I find her comment so comical, Krista stands up and reaches her hands down toward me. "Come on. We can't stay here too long."

She is right. The longer we stay, the more attention we draw from the locals, both human and not. After tearing through a wolf pack the way I just did, attention is not something I need or want.

Krista helps me to my feet then leaves me alone in the restroom to dress myself as she pays for the supplies we used. I groan lightly as I slide on my pants, but my shirt causes the most pain. My ribs shift under my skin and my shoulder protests as I raise my arm to pull the tattered shirt over my head.

Once I manage my clothing, I find Krista at the register. The cashier, a young girl with far too many piercings in her face, stares at me with wide eyes as I approach. She does not stop scanning items as she poorly attempts to watch me inconspicuously.

Leaning on the counter, I wait for her to make eye contact with me then flash her a smile, knowing that the white of my teeth must contrast drastically with the blood drying on my face.

Krista smiles innocently at her. Her German is smooth and flawless as she lies effortlessly and tells her, "Cosplay."

She looks at me for a moment longer with crossed eyebrows but as her eyes drift back to Krista's trusting smile, the tension in her face melts away. With a light exhale, she nods and replies with her German accent, "Cool."

Cool. There is nothing cool about being tricked so easily. If this girl had any clue about the world around her, she would be able to recognize that the bits of brain on my shoe that used to belong in a person's skull. A living, breathing person.

Pathetic. It is no wonder why humans are so easy to manipulate when they keep themselves so completely unaware and naïve.

I could show her the dark parts of the world that eludes her. The fire in my throat begs me to. I would heal faster; I would feel stronger. It would be easy.

I watch the veins in her neck, just beneath her sheer skin, so pale that I can see them clearly as she talks to Krista. They beckon me. My hunger lashes my throat, whispering sweet promises of the quenching relief her blood would offer.

I clear my throat but it does nothing to remove the fiery lump forming there. It would be easy. Just grab her. Take what I need. There are no witnesses. Nobody to hear her cry. Self-gratifying murders make very little sense to werewolves, but Krista would not stop me from killing this frivolous girl.

I could earn her forgiveness. I could explain my compulsion. The darkness in me, that greedy hunger that rips through me and this pathetic human in its path. The insatiable emptiness that consumes me, warping me from the tender man that she loves into a rapacious beast bent on grand destruction with seemingly little repercussions.

I could explain it away. Tell her of how the pain makes my control unstable, that I could not stop myself. I could tell her that I *needed* to.

Krista lays her hand on mine, pulling me from my thoughts like a wave sweeping shells from the beach, tumbling bits farther away until they recede from view. Her warm touch steadies me. The fire raging in my throat protests her intervention but her calming touch is there before I could ask her. It is almost as though she could sense me subconsciously reaching out to her, begging her to help steady me.

"Keep the change," she tells the cashier as she pulls me toward the door.

As we walk across the parking lot toward a blue Audi S4, I say sheepishly, "I wasn't going to."

"I know," she says simply.

But she does not know. And to be fair, neither I do.

As Krista opens the car door to get in, I ask her, "Where did you get the car?"

Smiling widely at me, she shrugs. "I have friends."

I smirk to myself. But this is from my friend. This is Luther's car.

While I would not have always thought so, Luther has proven to be a reasonably, good friend to me. And despite hating werewolves in general, Luther has an undeniable weak spot for Krista simply because I do.

Currently, he is living in a group home almost a hundred miles from here so it wasn't much effort to send his car. However, Luther would have sent his sheep a thousand times that distance to help me.

I will never admit it aloud, but he is a better friend to me than I have ever been to him.

"Really? Scheming behind my back? And with Luther?" I tease.

Playfully, Krista rolls her eyes. "Get in the car."

I let out a stifled moan as I slide into the passenger seat. The movement pulls at the wounds on my neck and unforgiving seat pushes against my ribs.

Krista looks at me questioningly as to whether or not she should drive slowly to spare me some amount of suffering, but I shake my head. No, I want the distance between us and that pack more than any relief a slow drive can offer.

As Krista pulls onto the road, I lay my head against the cool window letting the pain of my aching body hold me silently. There has been a body in this car recently, I can smell it. Death, blood, and fabric shampoo. Fabric is a mistake for vampires. But of course, Luther would not have leather or even vinyl seats. He is, after all, always the amateur.

*   *   *

Even with the door open, the steam from the hotel shower clogs the air in the small bathroom as the insufficient vent fan rattles in attempt to keep up with the humidity. The water that ran over my skin was hotter than usual but it did little to distract me from the blaze scorching up my throat, begging me to quench it. I will have to make a point to hunt when Krista falls asleep.

Standing by the sink with my towel wrapped around my waist, I wipe the steam from the mirror. I attempt to clear my throat and watch with my green eyes as my tongue rubs over my fang. The rough, jagged edge grates against my soft tongue. Leaning closer to the mirror, I rub my finger over the broken fang. Just the tip but it will need to be pulled so a new fang can replace it.

Later, after I'm done hunting, I will search Luther's car hopefully, for a pair of pliers and take care of this tooth. But only after I hunt. A broken fang might not puncture the skin as effectively, but it is still better than none. And I don't plan on waiting the entire day for my fang to regrow so I can hunt appropriately.

I look in the mirror, tilting my head to the side for a better view. The lacerations that tore through me from claws are healed, just faint red lines as though they were drawn on my skin. My bones that were crushed and the ligaments that were torn may not be completely restored yet but they are mending well. Even the wounds that had werewolf salvia in them have sealed, but not much more than skin deep. The muscles under the flesh are tender, bruised, and painful to move. However, by morning, there will be no traces of a fight at all.

"Phoenix called," Krista starts from just inside the room. "She gave me an address that I assume is for Salem but she didn't say much else."

It is for Salem. I can guarantee it. Phoenix is not a friend who calls to have a simple chat.

"I don't think she likes me much," Krista adds.

She doesn't. Phoenix tries not to tell me as often as she thinks it but she genuinely cannot fathom my feelings for a wolf.

"Phoenix doesn't like anyone who isn't paying her to." I laugh lightly to myself.

Krista does not laugh. The room is quiet. Even the rattling of the ceiling fan seems to fade as anxious tension begins to replace the steam in the air around me.

I step into the doorway to see Krista sitting cross-legged on the bed with a faraway look as though she didn't hear me at all. Wearing just a t-shirt, she hugs a pillow against her as though it is somehow holding her thoughts together as she glances off to the side without focusing on any object in particular.

I know what plagues her mind. It is Salem. I watch her for a moment without disturbing her until she finally glances over at me. She stares at me with concern in her eyes and forces a small smile as though that would convince me that she is not worried that she saved me from one fight just to watch me die in another.

Salem could kill me but I'm not afraid of him. I have fought him before. And despite knowing he is an equal adversary, that he is just as strong as me, just as skilled, and that any bit of bad luck could give him the upper hand, Salem is, after all, *just* a vampire.

Instead of lingering in her anxieties that I know I cannot take away, I change the subject altogether.

"Is that my shirt?" I ask her impishly.

Her unease melts from her face as a slow smile spreads. Notoriously bad at packing, Krista has a habit of forgetting the most basic and essential items. I cannot express the vast quantity of hotel toothbrushes we have accumulated. It is almost like collecting spoons from every state except these purchases were necessary and not worth displaying.

"I was in a hurry," she says flatly.

Maybe so, but that is not why she forgot. She is simply too disorganized to pack a bag without a list and procrastinates too much to make one even when there is time.

Smirking, I tell her, "Take it off."

Her eyebrows come together incredulously so I continue, "I didn't say you could borrow it so…" I gesture with my hands in a lifting motion. With a mischievous smile, I raise my eyebrows suggestively. "Take it off."

"No," she says with playful defiance. She shakes her head at me and asks bluntly, "What am I supposed to wear?"

Grinning widely, I shrug. "Guess you should have thought of that before you packed like a toddler," I jest.

Lightheartedly, she tosses the pillow at me, hitting me in the chest. "Be nice or next time, I will remember to pack pajamas and they will be flannel and they will *not* be flattering."

Chuckling lightly, I nod and put my hands up in a surrender. But in all reality, there is very little that would not look flattering on her.

I lean toward the mirror once more and run my tongue over the foreign chipped edge of my fang. I hear her soft footsteps coming toward me.

Standing behind me, she wraps her warms arms around me, leaning her body into mine. I glide my fingers along her forearm as she nestles her ear into my back and lets out a quiet sigh.

"What are you doing?" I ask softly.

"Listening to the heart that holds mine," she says gently.

Her words force my lopsided smile onto my face and I squeeze her hand against me.

Moving deliberately, she slides around me and into my arms to stand facing me. There is sorrow hanging behind her copper eyes, despite the way she tries to hide it.

Her fingers trail up along my arm to my neck, letting her fingers glide over my sealed but tender wound. I hide the way I want to wince but she can see it in me still.

She starts to pull back her hand but I tell her, "It's okay. I'd rather have the pain than miss your touch."

Wrapping my arms around her, I press my lips to the top of her head and hold them there longer than necessary, wishing my lips could take the worry from her mind.

Then, leaning back enough to look into her eyes, I tell her softly, "I promise, I'll be fine." I lightly shrug. "I've had worse."

"I've seen you worse." Her eyes drift away as she adds quietly, "But you've never went up against Salem already this weakened."

No, I haven't. And he could win. She is not wrong about that. This journal could be a colossal waste of time; an unnecessary risk without any real benefit. There is a chance that the journal may not have any answers of any value to me inside.

The gaps in my past were always carefully painted over with lies. They make any thoughts of my future hazy and unclear, like a mirage that I can see but may not be there when I reach for it.

However, for the first time in centuries, I do have a future worth seeking answers for. As those thoughts tumble about, I feel her warm fingers skim along my cheek.

With softness in my voice, I tell her quietly and, more importantly, truthfully, "There are times when I look at you, and I wish I were a werewolf, or even a human, but I'm not. Fact is, I'm not really sure what I am. Or why the Genesis wants me. But I do know that this is the closest I have ever come to getting any real answers. This isn't a fight I can simply choose to avoid."

My words seem to relax the tension that had been building in her shoulders. "I know." Her fingers float over my arm, stopping to hold my hand in hers. "And I'm not asking you to."

She looks at me purposefully. "Nicolas, I killed a man for you today. There is *nothing* I am not willing to do to protect you."

There is storm of emotions she must feel about killing him that I know I cannot grasp. Her father, her pack, her entire species betrayed in a single act. The fear that she could have lost me. The guilt in knowing that she would not change his death. Her duty to me cost her something today that she can never get back.

Surely though, she is also aware of how much pleasure seeing her standing over his dead body brought me. The animal in her eyes. The power she possesses, fierce and controlled. The thighs she wraps around me held down a beast while she snapped its neck in her delicate hands. Beautifully brutal. It's enough to spark a second, more urgent desire to sweep through me, whispering for me to touch her, to feel her.

Reaching up, I twist my finger around the curls near her chin and let my eyes roll over her face, taking in the softness of her skin and the sweetness of her small smile. She believes the words she says. Completely trusting. Completely relaxed in my embrace.

Unguarded and exposed, she is capable of such decisive violence yet stands deliberately vulnerable, purposely stirring the voracity in me. Surely, she can feel it. That hunger rippling in the air around us, tingling along my arms, pricking at our skin, beguiling us to close the narrow space between us.

She feels my craving for her, thickening the air. I know she does. It's what forces her to swallow hard as it encourages her heart to pick up its pace. It's what has her breaths growing heavy.

She watches me from the tops of her eyes as she pulls her hair aside, exposing her neck, offering her tender skin to me. "Let me help you heal."

Not a chance. I am aware that I need to feed. That fight took more from my body than I had anticipated. It needs replenished and the demand it creates is not a patient one. This is when a sheep comes in very handy but Krista is no sheep. And I will not use her as such a demeaning role.

I shake my head. "You don't know what you're offering." It is something I cannot undo, cannot unsee, and a taste I cannot forget. She cannot deny my words and she does not attempt to.

"I know the risks," she replies but she is not taking about any risks to herself.

It is not that her blood does not tempt me, but it does. It is inviting, calling to me, telling me I can have both, flesh and blood, simultaneously even, teasing the man in me with the delight in caving to my monster.

However, the fire in my throat pales to the craving boiling beneath my skin and there is another desire I choose to pursue. One I want more. More than blood. I want to taste the salt of her skin. I want feel her body beneath mine. I want to become wrapped in her savage strength.

She slides her hand to the base of my neck, letting her thumb glide over my jawline. "It's not *my* pain that I worry about." Leaning closer, her lips brush over my ear as she whispers, "It's okay. Just for tonight, let me be everything you need."

With her cheek next to mine, I let the heat of my breath graze over her ear as I whisper back to her, "You already are." Everything I need and more than I deserve.

Kissing her ear softly, I feel the chills form on her skin. I drag my fangs over her skin from her ear toward the base of her neck, encouraging her heart to pick up its pace and her breathing to grow rough and heavy.

Tilting her head back further, she lets out a deep exhale that tells me her eyes are closed. As she runs her hand through my hair, I know I could bite her. She would let me. I would feel her soft, fragile skin snap against my fangs. Her body would waver as my teeth slid inside her. But that is not what I crave most. Not with her.

My fangs stop on her neck precisely where I would bite her if I chose to. Instead of fangs, I press my lips to her skin causing her to suck in a sharp breath.

Placing my hand gently along the base of her head, I bring my lips just in front of hers and let my gluttony for her creep into my words, "I'd rather taste your flesh."

She stares at me intensely for a brief moment as her breaths grow more determined and her eyes no longer choose to hide the swarming of euphoric chaos spiraling around us and threatening to drown us both.

Pulling my face to hers, she then kisses me with a longing behind her lips, telling me that she needs to feel my body entwined with hers as much as I want to feel hers. I slide my hand under her shirt to the small of her back, pulling her against me and feeling the heat of her body seep through the thin fabric between us.

Her teeth drag over my bottom lip, biting lightly and pulling hard enough to pluck at my yearning for her. Tracing my skin with her fingertips, she trails a path of fire along my back. The remaining pain I had moments ago is buried deep in a remote part of my mind where it hides from the dark lust raging in me now.

Her lips glide along my neck to my ear, letting her hot breath simmer over my skin as my aching for her pushes my heart to pound in rhythm with hers.

My hand glides along her ribs to her hip once more, stopping to twist around the side of her panties and keep my face near hers as I ask, "Did you pack extra?"

Slightly confused, she replies, "Yeah."

Smiling impishly, I rip the sheer fabric and toss her panties to the floor.

Placing her hand on the side of my face, she laughs lightly. "Cute."

I nod. "I thought so."

Grabbing her thighs, I lift her off the ground and set her on the sink, knocking the plastic hotel cups to the floor. I guide her knee up along my ribs as her lips move with mine quickly, full of passion and vigor.

Her legs wrap around my hips, using her foot to push my towel enough for it to fall under its own weight. She gathers her stolen shirt in her hands and pulls it up over her head, tossing it to the floor. The sound of it plopping down on the cool tile echoes in my ears as I slide her to the edge of the sink and her breath catches abruptly.

The aroma of her perfume that clung to my shirt becomes lost the small bathroom. The sticky humid air is already tainted by the scent of the other wolves in this mediocre hotel and something else that I do not care to waste any effort on right now. There are more pressing matters.

My tongue flows along her throat and up to her chin, naturally urging her head back to let a light moan escape into the air. Kissing softly, I slowly glide my lips down over her body, savoring the smoothness of her skin.

Her simple touch drives a frenzy that rises inside me. I close my eyes, letting it take me as my eyes shift to their deep, carnal black. I slide one hand on her hip, curving my fingers around her frame.

The steamy air moistens her skin that warms beneath my lips as I press my lips on her delicate neck. A small, broken gasp escapes her, causing my body to buckle to the greed that has been building within me.

Caressing her tongue with mine, I feel her heart pounding against my chest, reverberating a heat through my body. My hand slides over her ribs and along the curve of her breast. Despite there being no space between us, she pulls closer into me somehow, pressing her breasts against me. The heat of her body burns into me, radiating a fervor of desire through me as her body trembles under my touch.

Her flesh flushes as my kisses move past her breast, pausing to press my lips to her navel. The heat of her skin, fuels the torch that sears from the very core of my being. Trailing further, I grasp her butt and pull her hips to my face.

With a quick inhale, her hands clutch the edge of the counter as she arches enough to comfortably toss her head back. Her dark curls stick to the steam on the mirror as she gasps for unobtainable air.

My tongue dances over her, increasing the ferocity that has acutely grown with my every touch. Her hands slowly slide along on her tingling skin, swimming in the raving uproar rushing uninhibited throughout her body. Her hands sweep over her breasts, stopping to caresses them gently before continuing on like a snake, swerving and winding over her every curve.

Her legs tighten and compress against my head, muffling her moans from my ears. Her fingers push through my hair as her hips rock into my lips. Subconsciously, her fingers flex in my hair, pulling painfully as her body tenses with each breath she holds.

Her body shudders beneath me. There is an urgency filling the small bathroom that has my fingers coursing along her thigh, persuading an eager greed to bolt through me, and coaxing her fingernails to dig into my shoulder as she lets her hunger flood every ounce of her body. Her feet press into the muscles in my back, harder with each scream that rushes out of her.

Pulling at my hair, intentionally this time, she entices me to rise. Her eyes are wild with a savageness I used to think was reserved for ravenous creatures like me. She crushes her lips to mine as I slide my hand to her butt and drive my hips into hers. Inhaling sharply, she claws her fingers in my shoulder, cutting into me harder than she realizes but the pain only intensifies my need for her.

Her hand wraps around me, pulling my body to hers. I kiss her with a fire that has been stoked and flutters in the air between us, pricking at my skin as a constant reminder of my vigorous appetite for her. I trace my tongue over her lip and her body quivers, exciting an eagerness for the scorching of her fingers lingering on my skin.

Leaning against me, she bites into my shoulder, not hard enough to break the skin but the pain sends a fluttering of flames from my core radiating throughout me. The softness of her hair as it brushes over me, bouncing with each rock of her hips, leaves a sizzling shiver in its wake.

Captivating and alluring, her silky skin lures me to become inescapably lost in her embrace as she holds her body against mine. Her legs tighten around me, pressing her knee into my injured ribs as my hand slides along her thigh, but the pain does not hinder my pleasure. It merely causes my breath to catch. My sharp breath rolls over her neck, cooling the light perspiration collecting there and sending a shiver coursing through her body that makes her grasp me even more firmly.

Her feet lock themselves together behind me and pull me deeper with each thrust. Her uneven breath grazes over my skin, beckoning the blaze deep inside me to rip free. Broken and jagged, her shaky breaths send a pulse of heat charging through me as I brace myself with my hand against the mirror. The steam squeaks under my hand, forcing my attention for a moment to her hazy reflection.

Her flawless skin begs to be spoiled by my touch. The paw prints sailing along her spine call my name, forcing a possessiveness to my kiss that sends her heart racing. Her body rolls into mine, multiplying the lust plowing through me.

I kiss her fiercely, letting her feel the need behind my lips as her fingers glide over the ripples of my abdomen, dragging a searing flame along my flesh.

My grip on her tightens as my breaths quicken. Her fingers press into my back as she moans loudly. Loud enough for any wolf on this floor to hear us. And I hope they do. I hope they know what I do to her. What she does to me. Surely, their small brains can recognize why their wives do not make the same sounds.

Her head tosses back, her eyebrows tight with rapture for me. Her fingernails dig into my shoulder and her thighs tremble against my ribs. Her desire, her pleasure amplified by the risk of losing me earlier today, urging her to pull her forehead to mine as her body contracts around me. The ecstasy washes through her like swells of waves in a storm, hungry and dangerous, as she screams, unable to contain it.

Little bits of blood pool around her nails as they pierce my skin with the rush of frenzied elation. Her hot breath dissipates into the steam inside the bathroom, leaving no traces of the exhilaration that surges through her body, exciting every nerve in its path.

Her skin quakes lightly with delirium as another sharp gasp escapes her body. A bead of her sweat rolls down her neck, rushing its way toward her breast as though it might be able to quiet the fire pulsing through her.

Her body, ruffled yet beginning to simmer down, relaxes against me as she attempts to slow her breathing. Her fingers flow over my chest as her eyes open slowly, her breath warming my skin.

Gently, I trail my finger along her brow and down her cheek, pushing the curls from her face and look into her brown eyes, wild and uncaged. So beautiful. So powerful. Utterly impeccable. She is undoubtedly the sum of my existence and she is mine. All of her. All mine.

I press my lips to hers once more softly. Then moving slowly, I kiss her gently on the tip of her nose. Delicately, I stroke the backs of my fingers down her arm, calming her excited skin and letting her savor in her moment.

Her fingers glide along both sides of my neck and hold my head as she looks at me breathless, still panting mildly, and nods.

Pressing my lips to her neck, I kiss my way toward her ear, feeling her flesh heat under me. Her fingers entwine in my hair as her heart begin to race yet again. Taking hold of her, I firmly pull her hips into mine once more.

Chapter 5

The colored lights flash with the bass of the music, adding to the energy in the room. I feel the beat resonating in my chest as though it is forcing my heart to match its tone.

But I am not here for the music, or the lights. I'm not even here for the alcohol behind this counter. I am here for her.

The bartender sets her drink down on the bar. Feeling my eyes on her, she smiles bashfully. "Are you gonna order a drink, or are you just going to stare at me all night?"

I shrug. "I'm pretty picky about my drinks." But she already knows that. Krista knows me all too well.

"So, option B then? I can work with that." She laughs.

She slides the glass toward herself, leaving a wet trail. Condensation rolls over her fingers and drops, but I do not watch it splatter on the floor.

My eyes only see the way she licks her bottom lip, preparing to taste her drink. It glides across her soft lips, tempting me so much more. As she raises the glass to her lips, the pounding in my chest thumps like a drum sounding into the deepness of night.

Her eyes watch me over the rim of her glass. She knows I cannot look away and relishes in it. She knows that I belong to her alone. I am her captive.

As she begins to lower her glass, I slide closer. I reach for her drink, moving it aside, while my other hand cradles the back of her neck, pulling her ear to my lips.

"Are you going to dance with me? Or are you going to keep pretending you don't intend for me to hold you tonight?"

Blushing, she answers by taking my hand. She guides us through the crowd of humans. A few notice her wrist-band that identifies her as a werewolf. Some take a step away, disgusted, but that does not deter her. Pulling me on the dance floor, she wraps her arms around my neck.

Her fingers trail through my hair as she watches me. Her eyes roll over my face, examining every small bit of me as though it is the first time she has ever held me. Her body moves with mine, in sync, as one, as the rest of the room simply melts away.

She buries her face into my neck, leaning her body against mine. The scent of her envelops me and I'm lost. Lost in the slow smile that spreads across my face, forcing my eyes shut. Lost in the way her smell calms me, pulling me from my monstrous impulses and closer to being the man I once was. But mostly, I'm lost in the flood of consciousness of her hair brushing over my shoulder, her hand gracing my skin with its smooth touch, and the way her body leans into mine, coaxing me to give into this new forever with her…

*   *   *

My mind wanders away from my memories and back to reality as I trail my fingers along the stony wall that surrounds the Lock. Lingering in my more pleasant memories, I had avoided thinking about the memories that this place actually stirs on my walk here. Memories of a tumultuous unmasking of my true self and of the pain caused by watching my mother be ripped from my life.

I make my way toward the security booth near the entrance. The rocks are rough and damp with dew, giving the air around me an earthy smell that is comforting, much the same way Krista's own wolf scent is.

Without any real neighbors, the Lock is quiet and peaceful. A perfect place to slaughter without witnesses.

At least, that's what a group of nomads thought when I killed them here, in this very spot, just outside these gates. My eyes drift to the cemetery across the street, where the nomadic vampire was pulled under, the holy ground swallowing her whole.

That was the night Krista's pack discovered exactly what I am and their very nice security guard was replaced by this rather wretched one. It was the night they discovered monsters do exist and, that sometimes, they just so happen to date your daughter.

When I approach the booth, I fake a smile and the chubby man behind the glass slides the window open. "Hi, Frank. It's been a long time."

"Not long enough, Nicolas," he says unenthusiastically.

I scoff lightheartedly despite his lack of humor in his words. "Right."

Leaning on the counter, I tap the little dancing hula lady just inside the window. She rocks back and forth on the counter. It is predictably tacky in the most cliché way.

As I cross my arms and lean on the edge of the sill, Frank groans audibly.

"So, anyway," I start with a false cheerfulness. "Krista probably told you I was coming. So, if you would just press the button and open the doors, I'd very much appreciate it."

Exhaling forcefully, he sets his coffee mug next to his thermos, which I assume is brimming with even more stale coffee.

"She did. But Bryant told me to make you wait out here. He said they're having a meeting this morning and he would come and get you himself when they're done."

I bet he did. I'm not feeling very patient, though.

"Come on, I just need to pop in there for a bit. I'll go straight to Warren's, I swear," I tell him with a forced nicety to my voice.

"Yeah, no, I don't think I can," he replies condescendingly. "And I don't think I would even if I wanted to. Which I don't."

My smile fades. It would be so easy to reach in that tiny little booth, grab his flaccid, little body, and creep into his feeble, doltish mind. Killing would be more satisfying than enthralling, but enthralling would be so much easier to explain.

It doesn't matter anyway, I have a better idea. Well, maybe not better, but a more amusing idea anyway.

"You're a difficult man to like, Frank, but all the same, I wish you luck."

His face crinkles together in a half-disgusted confusion. "Luck with what?"

With a light chuckle, I tell him, "Stopping me, of course."

The muscles in his face fall lax with the reality that he will fail to keep me out and he will have to report that failing to Bryant.

I do not wait for him to say anything or even attempt to move, even a flinch. I smile at the distress my words cause him for a mere second before I run to the stone wall. Kicking off of it, I land with my foot against the security booth and again kick off, bounding between the building and the wall, ignoring Frank's obscenities from inside the booth until I land on the roof of the security booth. Leaping onto the top of the wall, I perch myself on top with a wide grin.

Frank scrambles out of the back door of the booth just in time to see me smirking down at him. I place my hand near my forehead as if to salute him but instead of a salute, I merely present my middle finger to him before rolling off of the wall backwards in a flip. I land on my feet facing the wall that now stands between Frank and me and hear him shout, "Son of bitch!" and the slap of something smack the ground, which I assume is his hat.

The radio crackles and I hear Frank mumble to Bryant that I'm inside the Lock. Bryant responds dryly, "Just leave him. I'll look for him when we're finished."

Satisfied with myself, I stroll away. The streets are fairly quiet as I make my way toward Warren's house. Several rows over, I can hear the sounds of children playing, the creaking of a swing, and innocent laughter. But the houses nearest me are silent. I can feel them watching and occasionally, I see someone. Maybe human, maybe not. They pull their blinds down to hide me from the world inside the safety of their homes. And cannot blame them.

I am, after all, their natural enemy. And I did kill several members of this very pack just a decade ago. It was basically self-defense, so for the humans, ten years may seem like enough time to forgive my actions. Especially when I had found myself in such an unfortunate situation. However, when it comes to their pack, werewolves are slower to pardon and even less inclined to forget.

Their disdain for me is one of the reasons I slept in a motel last night instead of with Krista where I belong. My dreams are the other, more concerning, reason. I mean, truthfully, their hate alone would not keep me from Krista. It never has before. But my dreams are more dangerous than mere hate.

All vampires sleep. Not all dream. It isn't very common but, when they do, it is usually a memory. My dreams, however, are not like most. My dreams are a prison; a nightmare of memories blurred together with fears that paralyze me. My dreams plague me, they press into me, stealing my breath. The dark stains of my past mix into a nightmare in such a way that waking is not enough of an escape.

My only saving grace is that Krista is able to soothe me with her soft voice, drawing me from the shadowy realm that traps me. Her eyes, gentle and brown, cradle me, helping me slip from the chaos of my mind and back into this world. Back to her.

Still, it is dangerous for her to be near me when I awake from such a slumber, and given the events of the past days, I could not justify the risk. Each time I smell the hint of her blood stinging the air, a very culpable knot sinks into my abdomen. Nothing about wiping blood from an injury I inflict shows how much I care.

Besides, the last thing I need is to wake up provoked and ready for a fight inside the walls of the Lock.

Climbing the steps to Warren's house, I look across the street at Mitchell's home. Still the same tan color it was all those years ago when I came to see Krista. Before any of them knew what I am, before Krista left with me, and before Warren moved in with Simone.

Back then I drove a little blue convertible which ended up completely totaled, at no fault of the wolves. But before that, we had spent the whole night together, talking and dancing under the moon. And when she kissed me, just outside these walls, the heavy wooden gates no longer separated her kind from mine.

The memory of it pulls a lopsided smile onto my face as the door swings opens.

Smiling back at me, despite the exhaustion scrolled on her face, Simone tells me happily, "Nick, come on in." She steps aside in the doorway. "Everyone is next door. Probably talking about you."

"Well, I'm sure that's an interesting conversation," I tell her sarcastically.

Mitchell's home is the most logical place to host a meeting like this. It's private enough that only those participating in the discussion will be privy.

Bryant's house is located on the opposite end of the complex so it makes sense that he would come to his second and third in command instead of asking them both to drive to him.

And Warren's house is simply not the most suitable for such a potentially heated debate. Wolves are dumb but they're not stupid enough to intrude on a pregnant woman's home by disturbing her day to sleep in.

Taking both of her hands in mine gently, I kiss her cheek causally. "You look lovely, Simone. As always."

Rolling her eyes, she retorts, "You flatter. As always." Then with a light giggle, she adds, "My ankles are so swollen that they don't even resemble human anatomy anymore. I can't breathe when I lie down. There are feet in my ribs as we speak and I waddle now instead of walking. But thank you, just the same. You're very sweet."

But I'm not being sweet. I mean it.

She does look rather swollen, not just her ankles, but her face as well. But in its fullness, her face is flushed with a delicate pink color. Her hair shines brilliantly, full of life and health. The way she shifts herself to alleviate the pain in her ribs, no groan, no whimper, only a forced exhale, accentuates her strength.

True, a pregnant woman smells atrocious to a vampire, especially this far along. The way the mother's blood mixes her child's is off-putting early on, but becomes quite repulsive with each passing day. Still, this natural defense to keep predators like me at bay only makes it easier for me to not think of killing her.

So, in its own way, even her stench is pleasing.

"No, really. You look radiant, Simone. I mean it, pregnancy suits you."

She cannot help herself but to blush.

I nod toward the kitchen. "Do you want me to finish your pancakes? They re burning."

"Oh, shit!" Simone rushes into the kitchen and I can hear the clanking of the metal pan hit the sink as I follow in behind her.

Standing by the sink, Simone pushes her hand through her hair frustratingly. Her round belly looks so much more pronounced with the way she leans her back against the edge of the counter.

"It's like my brain is asleep all the time," she says quietly.

"Well, I can't help with that but I can give your brain a break and take over breakfast." She smiles softly at my offer as I slide out a chair. "Come on. Sit."

"Thanks."

As she sits down, I tell her, "If you like, I can make a mean crepe."

She plops her feet up on an adjacent chair. "Jacks won't eat it. The name sounds too fancy."

She giggles lightly at her own words as I agree, "Pancakes, then."

Just then, a scream comes from the hall but it is not the sound of fear or pain that I am familiar with. It is the joy only a child finds in waking each day that fuels his screeching.

"Speak of the devil," Simone jokes.

The little blond boy rounds the corner and his face lights up. "Uncle Nick!"

I kneel down as Jackson rushes toward me. The small six-year-old's resemblance to Warren is uncanny, almost as though he created his own doppelganger.

His body slams into me as he wraps his tiny arms around my neck.

"I missed you, too, buddy," I say, squeezing him.

Jackson smiles widely at me. "Hey, do you want to go camping with us this summer? I already asked dad; he said it was okay."

"Camping?" Yeah, no. Camping, the way humans camp, is not my idea of fun.

"What a great idea," Simone says with amused sarcasm. "I was going to go but you definitely should. It could be a guy's trip instead. Just think of all the fun you would have." She smiles at me deviously.

I glance over at her, pretending to be more annoyed than I am. It will be harder than that to get me on a camping trip with canines, even if it is Warren.

"As much as I'd like to, I'm not going to ask your mom to miss out on all the fun." I smile flatly back at her and she giggles to herself.

"I'll tell you what," I start. "The next time I'm here, I'll bring my telescope with me, and you and I will seek out some new constellations for your book."

Jackson's wide eyes. "Do you still have that journal with all the constellations we found last time you visited me?"

With a nod, Jackson rushes off calling back to me, "I think I know where it is."

As he scampers down the hallway, I turn back to the stove and begin mixing the bowl of batter that Simone had started earlier.

"You're good with him," she says softly. "It's a shame you can't have any of your own."

No, it isn't. Vampires are sterile by design. We are not meant to be parents. Too many unpredictable situations that lead to death. And typically, that death isn't ours.

Instead of telling her all the doom and gloom of the reality a vampire would face by having a child, I say simply, "Nature would disagree."

"Mm," she says as she shifts, incapable of finding a comfortable position. "You could adopt."

I tried that once. In Alaska, I attempted to keep a human girl who went by the name Punzi. My adoption was… well, I like to think of it as denied.

I wanted so badly to keep the little orphan that I foolishly led her straight to the very people who ended her. Their actions are their own and they alone are accountable for them. But I led her to them and the guilt of that is mine to carry.

I flip the pancake in the pan. "And risk murdering an orphan? Have you no heart?"

Snorting, she rolls her eyes at me. "You wouldn't kill a kid."

But I would. And I have. I know the pleasure of their blood, delicate and light. Untainted by the ever-constant aging and declining

KATHRYN HORSLEY | 105

health, it is sweeter and richer than an adult's ever could be. It is as though you can taste the very innocence and purity in them.

Even my name, Nicolas, was stolen from a child. I took his life and his name but he gave me back so much more. I watched his eyes lose their light; watched as a gray pallor took over his skin and his fingers grew cold. It wasn't until I felt compelled to visit his grave that I even learned his name. He gave me back a piece of my humanity. He gave me back my ability to regret.

That was long ago. I have taken great lengths to make sure he was the last child to die by my fangs for pleasure. But there have been others, out of necessity.

I will always be a vampire. That means, there will always be that deep-seated temptation just waiting to catch me off guard. As much as I want to restrain myself, I will always be a risk.

I set the plate with a steaming, mediocre, box-made pancake on the table near her and force a smile. "You've never seen me step on a Lego." I lean toward her. "Pretty sure I'd want to kill somebody over that."

Simone laughs, "You and me both."

I hear the footsteps on the porch before the door opens.

Warren steps inside and smiles widely at his wife. "Good morning, beautiful."

She smiles back at him and replies, "Good morning," as he walks toward her.

Stopping behind her, Warren rests his hands on her shoulders and kisses Simone on top of the head. "How are you both this morning?"

She rubs her belly intently. "We had a rough night."

Warren twists his mouth briefly. "Hm, well, I'll take Jackson with me then so you can take a nap later."

Simone rubs her fingers over Warren's hand on her shoulder as she looks up at him. "That would be great," she says lovingly.

Wait, no. Warren can't be doing anything with Jackson later. I asked specifically for Warren to come with me to kill Salem. He is the only wolf here I would want to ride in a car with and the only one I trust to have my back.

Warren simply smiles at her softly before he calls down the hallway,

"Jackson come and eat your breakfast. You're going with me to the shop."

"The shop?" I ask incredulously.

However, before I can voice my concerns any further, Warren nods his head to the side, motioning me to follow him. "Let's talk outside."

Great. Good news is never delivered after saying, *'Let's talk outside.'* Still, as Warren starts toward the door, I follow.

Jackson trots into the kitchen in such a rush that I have to step aside to keep him from running into me.

"You're leaving already?" Jackson asks me disappointedly, holding a little, navy-blue notebook in his hands.

"Yeah, but just for a few days. And then I'll be right back. I just have something I need to do first."

"What kind of something?"

Warren looks back at me with Jackson's question and gives me a stern look as though I would not naturally understand that I cannot tell a six-year-old that I plan on ending a vampire's life.

But knowing my limits, does not mean I cannot be somewhat truthful. Besides, Jackson is the son of a werewolf beta whose pack tolerates a vampire tagalong. He hasn't been exactly sheltered.

Bending down to his level, I tell him, "I'm going to have a good, thorough conversation with a very bad man." And that conversation will be spoken almost exclusively with the language of violence. "And I'm going to make sure he stops being bad and starts being good." Good and dead. "But, Jack, you do not need to worry about people like him. As long as you are within these walls, you are safe. Bad guys are afraid of werewolves like your dad."

With a light chuckle, Warren jokingly jabs at me, "The smart ones are."

Choosing not to acknowledge his teasing, I stand up. "I'll be back in a few days but until then, I want you to be extra nice and help your mother. And... if you can do that, I will make sure you get a whole ten dollars when I get back. How's that sound?"

Jackson's eyes light up at the idea. "Deal," he chirps, grinning excitedly as he runs off toward the table where his lukewarm pancakes wait.

I walk toward the door that Warren holds open and stop in front of him. Looking back, I wave. "Goodbye, Simone."

"Bye, Nick. We'll see you in a couple days," she calls back to me.

Then looking back to Warren, I sigh. "Alright, come and break my heart. Let's get this over with."

Warren half-smiles at my joke as we walk onto the porch where Bryant waits for me. Great. Even better.

"So…" Warren begins hesitantly but does not beat around the bush as he continues. His words spill out of him quickly. "I'm not going with you to kill Salem. Simone needs me here. She's due any day and Jack is so young. Right now, she needs my help for normal day-to-day things. I can't just leave her alone. Not right now."

I shake my head as he is talking. I have already considered this. I wasn't planning on leaving Simone alone to take care of Jackson when she is so far along in her pregnancy. Krista is her best friend and more than willing to help her for a few days.

But before, I can say that aloud, Warren adds, "And, yes, Krista could stay with her but then there's also no guarantee that I would be back before Simone delivers. And Nick, that is non-negotiable. I have to be here."

I press my fingers along my forehead as though they can somehow push away the tension that is forming. I understand his need to be here for the birth of his child; I truly do. But I also understand that he is still my only real choice for a partner in this. And understanding a situation rarely makes accepting it easier.

Warren adds, "Somebody else will go with you, but not me. Not this time."

Not this time? This is the only time I have ever asked anything at all from any of these canines, and apparently, it has been a waste of time.

That's what I want to say but I don't. This is not what I wanted to hear. It is not even close to the realm of possible responses that I was hoping for. Still, I attempt to bury my frustration with the situation.

"Who are you proposing?" I ask bluntly.

Warren looks at Bryant, reluctantly. "Um… well…"

Who could be that bad that Warren would not readily tell me? I mean it's not like they are ignorant enough to put me in a car with someone like Mitchell.

Bryant cuts Warren's lingering answer short, "Warren, why don't you check on Simone. I'll take it from here."

Relief washes over Warren's brow and his shoulders relax as he hurriedly dismisses himself. "Sure thing."

Warren has never had issues being direct and straightforward with me. Yet, he slides past me and disappears into the house as though he can't stand the very thought of being out here when I figure this out.

Warren isn't a coward. His evasiveness can only mean one thing. I shake my head fiercely.

"No," I say as the door closes behind Warren. "Bryant. I'm not taking him," I tell him harshly, unable to hide my frustration. "I mean, you can't really be serious. Mitchell? Do you want us to kill each other? Is that the plan? Because that's what will happen if you put us in a car together."

Bryant shifts in place, thinking of the words he wants to use. "I think it could be good for both of you."

"On what planet?" I ask, trying to keep my voice level. Despite not being overly loud, my British accent weaves into my excessively critical tone, "It's bollocks, Bryant. No dimwit on this entire Earth could possibly think this is an ace of an idea. This is Mitchell we're talking about. *Mitchell*. He killed my mother. I kicked his puppy. We hate each other."

Bryant stands quietly, letting me process all the thoughts he has already considered. "You didn't kick a puppy."

No, I didn't. But that is not the point. Point is: I cannot possibly be stuck in a car with Mitchell. Just forget it. Forget the whole lot.

"Thank you, but no thank you. I'd rather go alone."

"I'm sure you would. But I'm offering Mitchell."

I can ask a vampire. It would mean going after Salem during the night. That would not be ideal but it would be better than relying on Mitchell.

Bryant leans over as though he can sense the direction my thoughts are taking me. "Salem will be more vulnerable during the day. You need a werewolf so you can use the daytime to your advantage."

Yes, that is why a daytime attack was the plan, but Mitchell was never part of the plan.

With a heavy sigh, Bryant rests his arms on the railing of the porch, looking out toward the houses across the street. "Nicolas, why do you want to marry my daughter?"

Taken aback by the sudden shift in conversation, I simply stare at Bryant. Why wouldn't I want to marry Krista?

I have told him a thousand times; Krista is my entire world. Far too important to remain simply a girlfriend. The frivolous nature of such a temporary term does little to express my limitless devotion to her. I may not be perfect at proving it but her wants far outweigh my own.

Bryant interrupts my thoughts, "I'm serious. Krista is a werewolf and there is no changing that. She always will be a member of a pack, even if it isn't this one. Not one pack out there will ever accept you. None. Not the way you are. You're not only a vampire but you're resistant, smug, standoffish, confrontational, obnoxious, pompous, querulous—"

I cut him off, "I get the point."

"I don't think you do," he continues calmly. "In a pack, personal feelings are irrelevant. If you marry her, you will be a member of this pack, like it or not. Everyone, that includes you, has to have everyone else's back. We protect each other regardless of whether we like them or not."

Or loathe them, apparently.

"All for one and one for all? Like a bunch of musketeers?" I ask sardonically.

"Yeah, like musketeers so that would make me the king," Bryant continues, unruffled by my contemptuous remark. "What you mistakenly perceive as power is actually responsibility."

Bryant looks over at me with a tightness in his eyes. "I have to see the bigger picture and make decisions for the whole pack. Everyone, wolf and human, obeys those orders, and not just that ones they agree with. Every member of this pack has a part to play."

He pauses to let those words sink into my mind before adding simply, "If you truly love my daughter, I suggest you learn how to play your part."

I huff quietly to myself. The whole concept of accepting Bryant's authority is repelling. Obeying is not my forte. It never has been. Not even when I was a human. Especially not blindly following suggestions that are as provoking and preposterous as bringing Mitchell along with me.

Leaning against the column, I let out a heavy exhale. I drop my head back on the wooden pillar. Exhaustion is not a feeling vampires are accustomed to. We do not fatigue the way humans or even wolves do.

However, the very thought of Mitchell coming with me to hunt down Salem stipends my energy in an unfamiliar way. It is not exhaustion I feel creeping in. It is the deflating, pending gloom of surrendering to Bryant.

"We're going to kill each other," I tell him grievously, trying to keep the defeated tone from showing in my voice.

"No, you won't." Bryant leans against the railing, rubbing his hands over themselves. "Krista told me that you promised to be on your best behavior this trip, and I can trust you to honor your promises to my daughter, can't I?"

I do not respond as I do not believe his question warrants an answer. Of course, I honor my promises. Well, I try to anyway.

"And despite not being all that pleased to hear that he would be accompanying you on this little excursion, Mitchell has already been given similar orders," Bryant adds.

I scoff. "You could have just given him orders not to kill my mother and we could have avoided all of this to begin with."

"Perhaps," he somewhat agrees as he looks out at the houses across the street again purposefully. "Sometimes, I forget how rash Mitchell can be."

I shake my head to myself. Rash is an understatement. He killed Marcella for no reason other than to get to me. She never even looked him crossly. He just showed up, burned our house, and killed her without ever thinking twice.

"But ask yourself, Nicolas. If you were in his position, what would you have done?"

Bryant knows what I would have done. Once I have made up my mind, nothing can stop me. I would you have avenged the violation against my sister. The difference is, I would not have stopped with just one wolf. I would have slaughtered the whole infernal pack.

"You don't need to answer that," he tells me. "Because, regardless of what you would or would have done, this is where we find ourselves today."

With a long exhale, Bryant continues, "Besides, it's not like you will alone. Your little friend, Roderick, wants to go with you."

I groan. This cannot be happening. I cannot let Roddy come along this time. He won't be able to do what might be necessary. But instead of saying that, I redirect, "I'm not waiting for Roddy. I want to leave immediately."

"Well, good news. He's already here."

I look over sharply at Bryant but he mistakes my concern for confusion. "He arrived very early this morning and told me all about what happened with his mother over the past couple days."

I sigh. I bet he did. I bet Roddy talked and talked and talked about every single detail that I was not planning on sharing with Bryant.

"He told me about his father dying." But he didn't say that neither of us will miss his father much. Or that his father was harsh or about how much we both hated him. "He told me about his mother's challenge for alpha." Which was completely unnecessary. Tara is the only wolf in that pack competent enough to be alpha. She should have never had to make such a challenge to begin with. "About how you came to save her."

Looking over at him, I ask flatly, "And about all the bodies I left behind?"

Nodding, he smirks irritably at me. "Mm, hm. He even told me that you brought my daughter along and she killed a man with her bare hands."

The air inside my lungs dissipates in an instant. I have nothing. No explanation, no apology that will suffice.

"Bryant…" I start, but my words fade quickly.

"Oh, trust me, I have my own thoughts about that," he says, hiding the contempt in his voice, "but we're not getting off topic. I have a point to make so let's just focus on the matter at hand for now, okay?"

Bryant turns to face me, clasping his hands together in front of his chest as though they help him gather his thoughts. "Nicolas, I don't like you. I never have. But my daughter seems to. That means we have a shared interest in keeping her happy and safe. I need you to be able to look past yourself and become more like the pack creature I believe you can be."

Look past myself and see what exactly? A bunch of obstinate, snarly mutts watching my every move. Simply waiting to tell me how many things I need to change about myself completely to even hope to belong on some mediocre level. No, thank you. I'd rather live with Luther again.

This particular pack is like an anchor that only serves to weigh me down. Despite that fact, it is clear that I have two options: take Mitchell and Roderick, the last two people I would have chosen for such a task, or go alone. And I honestly do not know which would be worse.

I close my eyes, letting out a long sigh. "I don't know how to not hate him," I admit quietly.

"I would expect that," Bryant says gently. "But that's because you don't *really* know anything about him."

Nor do I want to.

"And he doesn't know you. You're both stuck in the same moment. Unable to move forward. I think you could both use a new memory to build from."

A team building exercise for Mitchell and myself. What an absurd idea.

"I can hardly wait," I mutter sarcastically.

Bryant smiles to himself. "Well, Mitchell isn't thrilled either but he did go to fetch the car like I asked him to. You're both just need to trust me with this."

His use of the word 'fetch' brings a slight smile to my face even though I don't believe he meant it the same way I heard it.

The sound of the tires crunching the small stones along the edge of the road pulls the smile from my face. Here it is, the car that will be my prison for the next few days. I will have to ride in a car next to the man I hate, on a mission to kill another man that I equally hate. Ridiculous.

Bryant's hand plops on my shoulder. "Nicolas, I wouldn't send Mitchell if I didn't think it was for the best."

There is nothing I can say that will make any difference so I simply nod. Not a nod of agreement because I do not agree with the decision he has made. But my nod is one of conceding.

The stubbornness that thrives in Krista, she clearly gets from Bryant. I can see it swimming behind his eyes, waiting for me to yield and surrender to his test.

Because it is a test to see whether I can bend and bow like the wolves here do. Vampires are not inclined to groveling, we do not beg, and we certainly do not bow. But I already know that I must. My next steps are going to feel completely unnatural. Disarming, even.

Sighing, I push my fingers through my hair as though I can brush away the burden that this will be. Bryant isn't offering a guarantee that doing this will grant me his blessing to marry Krista. But I want it. I have wanted it for years. And this is the first time he has even hinted that he might consider allowing me to be a part of his pack.

It simply comes with the price of enduring his son for a few days.

And if I truly consider it, his request simply comes down to a matter of priorities. Am I willing to sacrifice my pride to gain a wife? Of course, I am. I am here after all; in this hellhole of a wolf's den, begging like a pup for an extra bone.

Bryant has seen my willingness to put Krista ahead of myself. Surely, he has. But what Bryant wants is for not only Krista, but her entire pack to come before me. If I truly want her in my life, the pack must always come before me. That's what he wants me to understand. That's what this little field trip is supposed to teach me.

Fine. I can play your game. For now.

I push off of the porch column. "I suppose that's my ride."

Bryant agrees casually, "I suppose so."

I leave him on the porch as I walk toward the car. Mitchell's family surrounds him, flocking to him as though he is leaving for college. Renee, his wife, nods her hello to at me as I get closer to them.

I smile at the way their youngest child, Gideon, wraps his arms around Mitchell's waist tightly, full of love and admiration. Full of the loyalty that should be shared between a father and son. Not at all similar to the way I would have hugged my own father. There was no loyalty shared between us, and his love for me was born only out of obligation.

Being only five years old, Gideon's arms do not quite reach. His fingers desperately clasp onto one another so he can squeeze his father harder despite the inadequate length of his arms.

Molly, however, stands alone in a typical teen fashion, refusing to participate in such a grossly pathetic display of intimacy as a group hug. So, she waits, her face frozen in a bored expression, for her turn to hug her father and wish him luck as instructed.

However, her disinterest in the send-off shifts when she sees me. Smiling wide, she waves at me fanatically. "Uncle Nick, hi!"

Smiling back at her, I wave to Molly as I approach Krista.

"She missed you at her birthday," Krista reminds me.

"Yeah, I know. I'll have to make it up to her when I get back. Maybe take her to the mall and let her pick out something."

Krista chuckles to herself. "Oh, I bet she'll pick out a lot of somethings. Uncle Nick's wallet tends to get very deep when he feels apologetic."

I laugh to myself because she is right. I do owe Molly an apology and I will most assuredly attempt to buy her forgiveness.

Wrapping my arms around Krista's waist, I nod toward the people and the car. "Did you do this? Was this your idea?"

She shakes her head. "No, I'm not that cruel."

Then, from several feet away, I hear Mitchell mumble low enough to keep the kids from discerning his words, "Well, it sure as hell wasn't my idea."

I keep my eyes flat but Krista can still see my irritation. There is no reason for such an asinine nitwit to use such language. Normally, it would be fine, however, there are both women and children present. Such crassness is disrespectful, at a minimum.

"Your brother is a cretin. If you ever start to doubt how much I love you, I want you to think back at this very moment and think, *wow, look at what Nick did for me. This fantastic man locked himself in a car with an imbecile for days, crying himself to sleep, dying a little with each passing second. And he endured all of it, for me. I am without a doubt the luckiest woman on earth."*

Krista laughs. "Yeah, that's pretty much exactly how I will remember this."

She smiles with a softness in her eyes that silences the voices around us. Regardless of how little I have done to deserve it, she still looks at me with the same fire that she had when she kidnapped me from a fair. That night I tossed my keys in her hands, not realizing that I had already given my heart to her just as freely.

At the time, I naively thought it was the moon and her carefree nature that added so much vivacity to her, but I was a fool. It was me. And still is. It was the zeal of finding her 'one' that filled her that night. I know this because it is the same feeling that endures in me still.

"Listen, it's only a few days, and when you get back, if you want to, we can skip out of here early," she offers softly. "I hear Fiji is nice."

"I like Fiji."

"Yeah, me, too." Her fingers stroke my hair, mimicking the gentleness in her voice. "I'm thinking... huts on the water, sand in uncomfortable places."

I smile as she echoes my own words from days ago back to me now. "Yeah?"

"Yeah."

It may not seem like it to an outsider, but her offer to leave early is a sacrifice. Too many days are spent without her family. Too many nights running in the moonlight with strangers. She is afforded little time with the people she belongs with, yet she is willing to lessen her time to give me more.

It is her delicate balancing of two conflicting worlds, the way she makes it all seem effortless, that makes me desire to be better than my nature.

Stroking her cheek with my fingertips, I lean my forehead against hers, letting myself inhale the sweetness of her scent and longing to hold onto it for the days to come.

"There are not enough words to express how much I love you," I tell her quietly.

Words are rarely enough. Love is not simply a noun. It is about actions not merely the feelings driving them. I will get in this car. I will suffer through taking Mitchell and Roddy with me. For her. And I will return to find that she is equally willing to leave all of them behind. For me.

Roddy walks passed us toward the car. With his impeccable timing to ruin the most tender moments, he calls loudly, "Alright, let's get this show on the road."

Leaning closer to Krista, I whisper, "And *that* is the cherry on top of this whole operation."

"You love Roddy. Besides, he could be a buffer," she tries.

I nod. "A buffer that stands between me and my sanity, perhaps."

Watching Mitchell walk toward the front passenger side, I attempt not to be petty as I call out, "Shotgun!"

His face scrunches up, disgusted. "What are you, twelve?"

"I'm old enough to understand the rules of shotgun. I called it; now sit in the back," I snap.

"Whatever." He rolls his eyes as he reaches for the passenger door.

No. I called it. That seat is mine. Fueled by a rising heat inside me, I rush toward the car. Leaping onto the top, I sail across the roof on my side to beat Mitchell to the door. As I slide off, I plant both feet into his chest, knocking him to the ground as I land seamlessly.

"What the hell?" he snaps angrily.

Without responding to his childish pouting, I slip into the front seat and slam the door shut as he scurries to his feet.

Partially embarrassed and mostly just furious, Mitchell slams against the car door with both palms. "You bastard!"

I smile at his outward display of frustration. "Oh, come now, my parents were married," I jest, simply to dig at his anger a little more.

Renee grabs Mitchell's arm, pulling him toward herself. "Three days. Don't let him get to you. This will all be over before you know it."

"That's easy for you to say. You aren't the one trapped in a car with him," he mumbles quietly to her. Then with a gentle kiss on her cheek and without any more grumbling, he gets into the backseat where he belongs.

As Krista walks around the car toward us, Renee points at me through the open window. "You will bring him back to me."

"In a bag?"

She looks at me sharply but she is not serious. Deep down, Renee knows I don't have much choice. "Don't test me," she says sternly.

I raise my hands in a fake surrender. "Just had to clarify. It was valid question."

The corner of Renee's mouth quivers as she holds back the small smile that fights to be free. Attempting to hide it from me, she walks away, shaking her head to herself lightly.

Krista leans onto the edge of the windowsill. "Was the front seat really worth all that?" she teases.

Smirking, I explain, "The rules of shotgun are finite. And without enforcement of such rules, we are no better than savages. So yes, I do feel good about doing my part to maintain a structured society."

"Ah, yes, the good ol' shotgun kerfuffle leading us all to our demise. Thank you so much for preventing the collapse of society. My hero."

She trails her finger along the ridge of my nose from between my brows down to the very tip. Then taking my face in both of her hands, she kisses my forehead, holding her lips to my skin longer than usual. When she leans back, her eyes are tight with concern. "Make sure you come home."

I take her hand from my face and hold it near my heart. "I will always find my way back to you." So long as I am alive. "Always."

Her fingers drag from my hand as she steps back from the car and we begin to drive away slowly.

Leaning back into the seat, I let out a quiet, forced exhale.

"It's only a few days, Nick. We'll be right back," Roddy says, misunderstanding my reservations.

It is not the days away from Krista that vexes me. While not ideal, a few days is not the type of distressing situation that would weigh on me so heavily. My real agitation stems from the extra two warm bodies in this car.

Mitchell, for obvious reasons, brings with him a certain set of obstacles. The constant bickering he will provide me with will surely serve as an irritant and distraction from staying on task. That is, if I can avoid killing him now that we are alone and unable to escape one another.

He is an added complication. Now, not only must my plan include eliminating Salem and claiming the journal, I must also keep Mitchell alive despite the distraction of his heart beating.

Roddy will do very little to ease the tension. I doubt he knows how to defuse the situation, and could potentially make things worse. However, he will offer plenty of chattering background noise with his pointless dialogue.

Roddy is the more likeable and less annoying of the two. However, he is more of a burden to bring on this particular venture than Mitchell. And since I would prefer Mitchell to stop breathing altogether, preferring him to Roddy speaks volumes.

Roderick is in no way prepared to face a vampire. Particularly not this vampire. And I do not want to face his mother if I put him in Salem's path.

As the gates open, Roddy asks optimistically, "Right or left?"

"Head toward 93-North. We're going to Prairie City."

"Prairie City? How's it going to take three days? Prairie City isn't that far from here."

No, it isn't. We will be in Prairie City, Oregon, before dinner. But Prairie City is not where Salem is hiding.

"My plan calls for three days. Prairie City is merely our first stop. Now drive."

Chapter 6

Salem. That wretched name has been etched into my mind since I first learned it. Marcella loved and taught him just as she had me. With trainer after trainer, she ensured that she did not have to watch either of us die like she had with her human son, Noah, all those years before.

It was Salem who stole my human life and delivered me into a world filled with venom. And it was Salem that Marcella decided to abandon after she secretly requested him to turn me.

Why she decided to forsake Salem for me, I may never understand completely. However, she did forsake him. She asked him to unknowingly create his replacement then deserted him in the night as though she had no other choice.

In my earlier years, she could have tried to persuade me to forgive him instead of fostering the hate I feel for him now. It worked for herself. Hiding her part in my creation for centuries, she made sure that I loved her far too much to walk away. And that worked. When I finally did discover the truth, I was angry but forgiveness for Marcella was never truly far from grasp.

However, she did not help Salem in the same way. Marcella encouraged my disdain for him even before I had learned his name. She never spoke a word of kindness or understanding for his actions, despite knowing his intentions were only meant to gain her good graces.

The truth was always very simple, she knew could not keep us both. The more I hated Salem, the more I would cling to her. The savior who swooped in and rescued me from the nightmare I did not realize she helped create.

Salem may have been her son before me, but he was never her favorite. I was always the preferred son. Chosen because I resembled Noah. That's what she told me, time and time again. However, I wonder now if that is even true. How much more did Marcella purposely avoid telling me?

I had my chance to ask her, seek out my answers, but I let that chance pass me by. Part of me did not wish to know. Did not want to risk losing her to something as insignificant as the truth. I would have kept any lie to have my mother back.

But now, Marcella is dead and her secrets may be lost with her. Our time cut short. By Mitchell.

Bringing Mitchell on a mission to kill Salem is about the worst idea ever. However, the Lock wolves are too brainless to recognize that a murderous adventure is not the time and place for a family bonding session between beasts.

It is as though someone decided that I cannot have Salem without being punished first.

A month ago, I could not foresee that I would get the chance to face Salem. But if I had, I certainly wouldn't have ever fathomed that Mitchell would ride alongside me. But there he is, in the backseat, watching out of the window while Roddy drives us closer to Oregon and unknowingly further from Salem.

And Roddy. Poor, clueless Roddy. He has no idea that he will not be going with us on this little adventure. That my true intentions are to leave him behind, in Prairie City and in the safety of exclusion from our trip entirely.

Looking over at him, I see a wealth of inexperience in calculating, planning, or even assisting in an ambush of any type. He has no real encounters with vampires, outside of me and my family. And certainly, none with vampires who intend to kill him.

He is in no way prepared for this. That is why Oregon is such an integral part of my plan. It a simple drive of only a few hours. Close enough for his bride-to-be to pick him up wherever we decide to ditch him along the way.

I watch him for a moment, drumming his hands on the steering wheel, naïve and carefree in a way I have long since forgotten.

"So," I start. "Tell me about your fiancée."

His face lights up with a wide smile at my mention of her. "Lindsey," he informs me, nearly blushing.

Seeing him so absorbed by the very thought of her, so lovesick he cannot hold back the delight in his demeanor, makes me smile to myself. "How did you meet?"

"At a ComiCon convention. In San Diego."

"Really?"

"Yeah, I was there to get Mark Hamill's signature on that *Joker* movie poster I have, and she was there dressed as Lady Galadriel."

"The elf from *Lord of the Rings*?"

"Yeah," he agrees eagerly, pleased that I knew the reference. "I tell ya, when I saw her…" He clicks his tongue. "Man, that was it."

"Love at first sight? Just like that?" I raise my eyebrows skeptically.

"Yeah, just like that," Roddy insists, then shaking his head, he asks me incredulously, "Don't you believe in love at first sight?"

I'm not sure what I believe. I know I didn't. Until I met Krista, love at first sight sounded a lot like infatuation laced with luck. Not love.

But after I saw Krista at that gas station, there was no going back. I was utterly lost in an instant. There was no tomorrow without her. And no reason to deny that I already belonged to her. In that brief moment, every fiber of my being had become woven into hers.

Roddy does not wait for my answer, "I mean, didn't you tell me that you fell in love with Krista the first time you saw her?"

I laugh to myself. I did tell him that. "That's different."

Roderick scoffs. "How?"

Glancing at him with raised eyebrows, I tease, "Well, for one thing, I was already attracted to women."

And Roddy was not. I spend years covering for Roddy. Lying to Tara nearly cost my friendship with her all together.

Roddy chuckles and nods. "Touché."

I understand the compelling pull of an immediate, all-consuming attraction. Pursuing Krista was reckless and stupid. Neither of which, I am prone to being. I didn't have a choice. I was utterly unable to stop myself. Krista was and is the only direction I am able to travel.

But Lindsey is different. She's the partner his wolf has chosen. The Roddy I know would have chosen differently.

I rest my head back on the seat and say gently, "I am thrilled that Lindsey makes you feel so happy. I really am. I just hate thinking that you are going to spend your life denying yourself simply because your wolf has other plans."

His shoulders relax as he exhales softly. "Ah, Nick," he starts in a voice tainted with pity for my inability to comprehend. "Bonding isn't like that. I'm not denying myself. My love for Lindsey is as real as anything I've ever felt."

Love is a compelling and fickle state, a convoluted labyrinth of complexity. Yet, somehow, the werewolves have managed to complicate further it by adding a third party into the equation and allow their own wolf to have a say in the choice as well.

I've never had to question my own feelings like that. Even the most emotions have always been *mine*.

"There are some big advantages to being bonded, you know? I will never love anyone as much as I love Lindsey. And she will always feel the same way about me." Roddy grins wildly, like a boy in junior high. "I mean, I never have to worry about getting divorced. Who can say that these days? That's just how bonding works."

The entire concept of bonding, not being able to control who you decide to spend your life attached to, is difficult for me to wrap my head around.

I shrug lightly. "I guess I just never realized how persuasive it could be."

Roddy says matter-of-factly, "That's because you're trying to separate me from my wolf and you can't do that. We're not the same but we're not separate either. It's not like I consciously handed over control of my love life to another person, some stranger I've never met. This is my wolf. It's not a part of me. It *is* me. It's hard to explain but my wolf isn't a separate being with a separate mind. It's just a different state-of-mind, a different version of myself."

Two entities in the same being. Two essences occupying the same space. That I can understand. It is much like the way my monster lurks inside me, trickling down into everything I do.

However, the demon in me is not driven by improving oneself in totality or stature. Instead, its only motivation is the pursuit of greed. My hidden beast does not refine; it maims and kills, and it relishes in it.

Misinterpreting my silence, Roddy stammers, "I mean, if you're worried that Krista might find her mate, don't be. Bonding isn't rare but it isn't common either. I mean, the likelihood of that happening is super low—"

I place my hand on his shoulder to interrupt him before he continues to sputter any further drivel and smile softly at him.

"I am not worried." Actually, I do worry. Especially now that I know just how powerful bonding can be. If bonding can sway Roddy so much, then there is nothing I can do to prevent Krista's wolf from finding someone more fitting.

"Good. You shouldn't be. She is crazy about you. I mean, I don't get it."

Mitchell pipes in from the backseat, "Me neither. He's a pretentious little prick, bent on a self-gratifying existence."

His words grate against me but it is not the words he says that irritates me so much; it is merely the sound of his irksome and asinine voice.

I smile sarcastically at him. "Maybe we bonded. Maybe you'll be stuck with me forever." I don't really believe that but watching the heat rise to his face makes it worth saying.

"Wolves do not bond to humans, and we certain don't bond to vile little vampires," Mitchell snaps with a testy tone.

"Just because nobody has, doesn't mean it can't happen. Nobody has ever tested that theory, have they?"

I turn around in my seat simply because it will stoke his temper more. "Besides, I have done a lot of other things with your sister."

Mitchell shakes his head, nearly growling, "You did *not* bond with my sister."

A smile at how easy it is to press his buttons. Deep down though, I'm sure he is right despite how much I enjoy irritating him. Bonding does not make any logical sense for a vampire.

Everything in a vampire's nature is about control. Controlling emotions, situations. Control is how we stay alive. Lose it and you sentence yourself to death. So, the entire concept of handing your control over to a beast you keep inside absurdly goes against every fiber of being a vampire.

Roddy grabs my arm from the back of the seat, pulling it around so that I must turn in my seat to face forward again as I chuckle to myself. "Okay, Nick, that's enough. Let's stop poking the bear with a big stick."

Continuing, Roddy attempts to turn the conversation in a less heated direction, "Can we just focus on a topic that has nothing to do with vampires, or Mitchell, or Krista at all? Yeah? Maybe something like my upcoming marriage? Or the price of chalupas? Anything where we can all agree to not disagree for a few hours, please."

Agree to not disagree. The only way to do that is for Mitchell or myself to never speak again. And personally, I am more than fine with not speaking to him for an eternity but Mitchell is still fuming in the backseat and his anger refuses to let his tongue rest.

"Wolves won't bond with someone unless they can provide something they need within the pack, like children or power." Mitchell leans back confidently. "You have nothing to offer my sister or her wolf."

Nothing. Absolutely nothing that would benefit her wolf or the pack. But I can provide Krista with a level of happiness her pack has never offered. Simply pointing that out, however, will not smear that smirk off Mitchell's smug face.

Instead, I turn again in my seat. "I may not be able to produce offspring but there is something I do give her. All the time, almost every day, in fact, and she loves it. It's my big…" I smile, accentuating each word. "Fat…" My words burn into his mind like an ember. "Bank account."

Deliberately stoking his temper, I raise my eyebrows.

Roddy laughs nervously. "That's not funny, Nick."

It is funny though.

Not to Roddy, who worries that my words will ensue a fight while he is driving down the road. And certainly not to Mitchell, who scowls at me, plotting a thousand ways to murder me, all of which he is too inept to complete.

But it *is* funny.

Still steaming, Mitchell settles back into the seat without interrupting his glare. He does not need to speak; I can feel his hate. It is the same hate I have felt many times before. He isn't the first werewolf to despise me. And he won't be the last. Not if I can help it.

Krista tells me that the animosity I receive from the wolves is an exception. That it's not typical werewolf behavior. She claims that the werewolf community is fundamentally quiet and gentle, like a sound of light rain.

To me, that simply makes them comparable to a dreary and tiresome thing. She uses the fact that humans tend to become more hostile around me as well as evidence that I am the common denominator. Like something innate about me makes others wildly defensive, as if I exude some kind of warning of the horrors I can inflict.

I admit, she does make a decent case. However, I'm not so sure about that theory. I think, maybe, just maybe, what makes others so petulant and contentious is that they can sense that I realize what simpletons they really are.

My phone rings in my pocket, distracting me from the ever-stifled air inside the car. Roddy leans over to peek at the caller's name on my phone as I press the button to ignore it. I am not ready to speak to Tara yet. Or listen to her explain to me why I should not meddle with her pack affairs. And there simply is no chance I am allowing her to unleash a verbal berating on me with Mitchell within hearing distance.

"You gotta answer it eventually," Roddy says simply.

"Not today." I already know the conversation awaiting me. She's furious. Angry that I got involved in a situation she wants to pretend she could have handled alone. But she couldn't have and we both know it.

"You know she's pissed at you."

"When isn't she?" I jest. But, in all seriousness, she is annoyed with me rather often. I supposed that is to be expected when a guy like me keeps a female wolf as a best friend.

"I didn't have much choice," I say gently. Looking in the mirror, I can see Mitchell watching the road pass by quietly, steeping in his fury.

Roddy huffs to himself. "I'm not questioning your motives here. I'm perfectly happy with the outcome. My mom is alive because of you. And that's not the first time I have been able to say that."

Roddy looks at me but the kindness in his eyes is not much more than camouflage. Behind his relief and elation that his mother is safe, is a deep well of guilt and regret. It was he who brought death to their door quite literally when he took me directly to those who had to die in order for Tara to live.

He used to belong to the pack he betrayed. The same pack that his mother mourns today. I took that from them. A part of their pack and a part of his innocence. And no matter how much it was necessary, the slaughter of his fellow wolves weighs on Roddy. But he will never dare say that aloud.

With a small smile, he steers the conversation to his mother. "But"—he shrugs—"you know how she is."

Proud, and stubborn. Yes, I do know. I know that she doesn't like for me to get involved in her pack dynamics. Normally, I do keep my distance from it. But this… this was too much to leave to fate.

Tara is a far superior alpha to anyone in that pack. Her position should have never been questioned. It's their idiotic rules about a woman's status coming directly from her husband. It's absurd and out-dated.

There is no reason she should have been in that predicament in the first place. "I think her anger is misguided," I mutter quietly.

It's not that she has zero reasons to be angry with me. I did murder several werewolves that, until a few days ago, she was responsible for. But the fact remains that I had to intervene for her simply because she was restricted in saving herself. That is where her frustration should be focused.

Roddy's eyebrows come together with confusion, trying to discern the meaning behind my words.

So, I clarify, "Your mother will disagree but the concept of power and status being obtained only through your husband is ridiculous."

I shift in my seat so I can face Roddy better. "Her role was robbed from her, and she was placed in a weakened state at the very bottom of the pack. And if she wanted any of it back, she is expected to fight without any hope of winning. Why? Because she suddenly was single? Don't you think that seems a bit crude?"

Roddy's shakes his head, fumbling over his words, "No, I mean… I do. It's just… When you say it like that, then yeah, it sounds wrong."

Roddy adjusts his grip on the steering wheel awkwardly as though he is worried his answer will not suffice the explanation. "It's not something we can change. It's not like a rule we just made up to be douche-bags or 'keep women in their place' kind of nonsense. It's like the way we have to take orders. It's just out of our control. It's something that just *is*."

A disgusted groan rolls from the backseat. "It's because we're not humans; we're animals," Mitchell says in a gruff voice.

With a heavy sigh, Mitchell sits up and leans against the back of our seat more laboriously than necessary. It is not the movement that distresses him. He is dog, sitting up is not a trick he would find difficult.

More so, it is the necessity of explaining this to me simply because Roddy is incapable is the real burden.

"In certain species, males are more colorful, more robust, etcetera. Their entire purpose is attracting a female. Proving that they have the best possible genetic code that a woman would want to pass to her children. And it's the females who get to choose any partner they want. They don't need presentation. They're already enough the way they are. Wolves are sorta like that."

Thankful to not be the only one chiming in, Roddy glances at Mitchell in the rear-view mirror. "Yeah, like that kind of."

However, Mitchell ignores him and continues to focus on me. "We don't have horns or feathers. All we have to offer is our position within the pack. To share in our strength."

"So, you strut your power around like peacock? Emphasis on being a cock?" I jeer.

Roddy's laughter erupts out of him but he quickly manages to gain his composure and his face falls flat.

Mitchell, however, does not find me as funny and narrows his eyes in annoyed disgust. "My point is that women have nothing to prove to us. Female werewolves risk their very lives to continue our species. Childbirth is quite literally life or death for wolves."

I would rather swallow my own tongue than agree out loud with Mitchell. So instead, I sit quietly waiting for him to finish.

Mitchell continues, "If they had enough authority to fight in battles, they would and our entire species would die out. When it comes to battles, we fight, and we die for them. Because we're disposable—they're not."

I smirk as I tell him, "I'm glad you realize how disposable you are. But frankly, the rest of it sounds like a great sales pitch. I mean, it's not like women can't have power. It's that they only gain it through marriage or by bonding. It doesn't make sense for power to be dependent solely on their relationship status."

Mitchell smiles as though my question is foolish. His arrogant little patronizing eyes burn into me, but he speaks before I can interject, which is probably a good thing.

"The power they assume with marriage is meant to level the playing field within the marriage, not the pack. It makes both parties equal so nobody can exploit their ranking."

He snorts a sort of laugh to himself as he continues, "It's not about power, it's about checks and balances. When I married Renee, I didn't lift her up so she could become third in command. She rose to assume the same authority as me so we could be true equals within *our* marriage. If our marriage dissolved, there would be no reason for her to be equal to me. She would need to be equal to her next husband. We're not humans. Their rules don't work inside a pack. Werewolves aren't created equal. There's a hierarchy, but every position is important. When we speak of superiors and inferiors, we're talking about positions within system—like a boss or a manager. It has nothing to do with a person's value. Krista is my inferior, but she is not less of a werewolf than me."

Every position has its place, has its duty. Every member is valued. So on, and so on. All of that sounds like a lot of tripe you would hear at a pointless three-hour meeting.

Those rules are meant for whelps. They will never apply to me or to Krista by proxy. Those kinds of rules have no place with a vampire.

"When I marry your sister, make no mistake that there will be a superior," I tell him bluntly. His eyes flutter with annoyance as I expect them to. After all, he is so easy to antagonize.

Before he can mutter any useless dribble, I add, "In every way possible, your sister is better than me. I will never be her equal, no matter how much I try."

His eyes soften, blinking quickly as he processes words he did not expect to hear. Quietly, he lets out a quick puff of breath with his disbelief.

"Well," Mitchell starts quietly. Relaxing some, he lets his shoulders drop slowly. "That's something we can both agree on."

Mitchell leans back, wiggling down to rest the back of his head on the top of the seat. With a deep sigh, he closes his eyes and relaxes his body.

Waiting for sleep to take him, he clasps his hands over his lap and lies still with his neck exposed, full of misplaced trust. The passing trees cast a flickering light over his skin and I watch the movement of his throat as he swallows.

I could have my claws in his throat before he could even think to flinch. I could watch the life leave his eyes, and feel his blood paint my flesh. I could cleanse the world of his uselessness.

But like the trees, I let this moment pass by. I turn around in my seat and away from the temptation behind me. Resting my head back, I look out of the window. If I am quiet enough to allow Mithell to fall into a slumber, I will be granted some small form of escape by his silence. The more time he spends asleep, the less taxing this trip will be for the both of us.

Besides, the less talking we all do, the less I need to worry about discussing the trip details and letting it slip that Roddy will not be joining us for its entirety.

Instead, I watch the world pass by my window. Sleepy towns with humans scurrying about like ants in the sand. Thick trees and fading mile markers watch silently as the bustle of cars rush past without ever appreciating the beauty that lurks here.

The miles pass quietly before I notice Roddy's mouth twisting as he chews on his lower lip, lost in anxious thought. He rubs his hands over the steering wheel, adjusting his grip aimlessly.

Softly, I break the stillness that has been comforting me for miles, "Roddy, I know why I've been quiet." I smirk, nodding toward the backseat where Mitchell is resting his eyes. "I've been trying not to wake the beast." Mitchell scoffs at my words but does not move from his relaxed position. "But this isn't like you." I turn toward him in my seat. "Is there something on your mind?"

Sighing, he shrugs. "I don't know. Just thinking, I guess."

I could leave it here. If he wanted to talk, he would. And I certainly would prefer to pass as many miles as I can in silence, but Roderick has never been shy of speaking. His preference for conversation, even tedious conversation, is why I must persist.

"I haven't seen you this nervous since you were a boy all alone in a field and happened upon a vampire." It was the night I met him and Roddy had nearly fell over with fright. "You know you can talk to me, right?"

Roddy nods understandingly but still hesitates before sputtering out, "Um, well, it's Lindsey. She's great. She's perfect, actually. And I just want to be great for her. You know?"

Do I know what it's like to feel as though the love of your life could do a thousand times better yet simultaneously grateful that she hasn't figured that out? Yeah, I do.

"Well, you're bonded, right? So, that should bring you some comfort. I mean, not even you can screw that up, Rod." Lindsey will love him no matter what he does.

"Mm, hm," he agrees. Roddy rubs his hands around the steering wheel anxiously as he continues, "It's just that there will be so many things that I am not familiar with. The closer I get to the wedding, the more I worry that I might not do the right things. And I want to know that it's me that makes her smile, not just our bond, you know?"

He looks at me as though I am going to ask him to elaborate but instead, I just stare back at him, waiting for him to divulge more in his own time.

"Did you ever worry about dating Krista?" Roddy asks.

Worry would've required some bit of consideration of consequences, which I did very little of. I was so sure I could stay away from her after I saw her at that gas station. But then she walked into my house and my resolve collapsed. That was it. There was no turning back, no stopping myself, and no reason to trouble myself with potential outcomes.

I smile to myself thinking of it. "I had very little reservations. I was completely swept up, like I was caught in a current after a storm. Naturally, there was some concern about telling her exactly what I am, but that worked out fine. I'm sure that, whatever your concern is with Lindsey, it will work itself out too."

Roddy smiles to himself. "Yeah, you're probably right," he mutters quietly. "It's just… Can I ask you one more thing?"

"Would I be able to stop you?" I jest.

He grins wider back at me and shakes his head. "Lindsey wants to wait until we're married to, um, you know."

I cannot help but to chuckle lightly to myself. This is not the direction I thought this conversation was going to go when it started.

Before I can respond however, Roddy continues, "Which is fine, that's completely fine. That's not the problem. Um, the issue is that I've not… had much… experience with females, in general. So, um…"

With a light sigh, he adds, "I mean, Krista's a werewolf and you're a vampire. Didn't you worry about what it might be like with Krista the first time?"

I shake my head. "Whoa, whoa, whoa."

Nope. We are not talking about intimate details between Krista and me. Not with Roddy.

But he does not hear me over his own nervousness. "You didn't know what it might be like, or if she might bite you, or whether she might phase. Because that would've been weird—"

"Stop right there." I cut off his pointless rambling. "First of all, I respect her too much to discuss such things with you. Secondly, I will not discuss this when her brother is in the backseat."

Despite such conversation being a sure way to stir up the anger in this car, this discussion is not happening.

"Thank you," Mitchell says dryly without opening his eyes.

I let out a long exhale as I gather my thoughts. My romantic interactions are not necessary for what he is asking.

"Look, I understand that you're scared. Being unsure of what you're about to walk into, everything foreign, everything new, I get it. It can be overwhelming."

However, the most frightening part for Roddy will likely be the number of rom-coms he will endure to appease Lindsey.

"But Roddy, you're a werewolf. You have advantages here. Use them. When the time comes listen to the subtle things. The pace of her heart beating, the temperature of her flesh, things she can't fake. You can read those things like a book to know exactly what she wants. So do that. Read your wife."

Mitchell opens his eyes and pats Roddy on the shoulder with a humorous smile. "And for crying out loud, Rod, if you think you might be illiterate, let the poor girl lead."

Roddy half-smiles at Mitchell's teasing and nods to himself. "Yeah, right. Easy-peasy."

His eyes catch an approaching gas station in the distance and he shifts in his seat, happy to change topics. "Hey, we need to fill up. You guys want anything?"

"I need to stretch my legs," Mitchell says as Roddy pulls next to a pump.

As Roddy gets ready to pump the gas, Mitchell gets out of the car, groaning lightly and stretching his arms. Apparently, being cramped in the backseat is too much for such a pathetically pampered princess. He stands next to the car pulling his arms over his head and side to side.

He would never be able to handle traveling in a coffin. This car might as well be a cruise. A cruise that is apparently still too much for such a delicate doggie.

Roddy leans down to look through the window at me. "Hey, do you have a charger? My phone is almost dead."

I smirk to myself. "Yeah, I do." I do have a charger for his phone even though I do not use the same type. I have it because I am used to packing for Krista, who cannot pack to save her life. That simple thought of her flitting through my mind pulls at the corners of my mouth until my lopsided smile presents itself.

Stepping out of the car, I go to the trunk and unzip my duffle bag. Mitchell swings his arms from side to side, twisting his torso in attempt to loosen his back as I sift through my clothes. Pushing items aside, I reach for the cord in the bottom.

"Ooh, what's this?" Mitchell asks provokingly as he snatches the ring box from my bag.

A heat swells inside of me. Reaching into my bag is damning enough, but it is the item he grabs that pushes my piqued defensiveness to boil over.

"That's mine. Give it back."

I reach for it, but he pulls his hand away like a child playing keep-away at recess. But we are not children, and I am not playing.

"I said give it back," I say through gritted teeth.

Roddy steps toward us nervously. "Hey, guys. Come on, not here."

"Just a minute. I want to see it."

But it is not his to see. It is mine. My mother's ring and the only possession I have from before I was a vampire. It's the only part remaining of the woman who gave her life for mine. A woman who knew me only moments but loved me with enough strength to hold me for a lifetime.

And that ring belongs on the hand of the woman I want to spend that lifetime with. That ring is my past and my future melting together into one.

Mitchell opens the little cherry box to look at the ring I have carried with me for centuries, knowing full well that it is meant for Krista.

With a smug, little laugh, he mocks, "What, no diamond?"

The anger that has welled up inside bursts out like an explosion refusing to be contained. Quickly, I grab Mitchell by the throat and slam his back against the car, rocking the car with the impact.

"Give it back," I say with a low growl rippling through my words.

"Hey, that's enough, guys," Roddy tries, but the shakiness in his voice is more grating than helpful. "People are looking," he adds, but I do not care. Let them look. Let them watch me rip this pretentious little werewolf's head from his wretched body. Let them be horrified yet unable to look away as their screams fill the air and his blood puddles under their shoes.

"Go ahead. Squeeze a little harder, you fucking wasp," he prods me with a strained voice. I would love nothing more than to appease his request, but I know why he says it.

He needs me to. He needs me to push him past the orders Bryant gave him so he can attack me back. He needs to believe that I truly will kill him.

My grip on Mitchell's throat tightens until he is barely able to speak. "You mean, leech?" I respond callously.

"No, I meant wasp," Mitchell says in a broken voice. "An angry, aggressive, little asshole. Only good for following back to its nest so you can set fire to the queen."

A low growl rumbles through my body, as his reference to murdering my mother begs me to crush his larynx.

"Like I said a pointless fucking wasp."

His body trembles lightly beneath my hands as it aches for the oxygen it cannot grasp fully. "Do it. You know you want to," Mitchell chokes out.

Oh, I do want to. I want to feel his life fade beneath my hands. And hear his last wheezing breath attempt to escape through a labyrinth of mutilated tissues.

I want to give him the satisfaction of fighting me and lavish in the joy of watching him fail. I want to leave his limp, useless body on this pavement to rot.

However, there is something bigger than him that restrains me. A promise to let him live. A promise, that right now, I very much regret making.

This isn't about what I want. Not yet.

With a quick, stern jab, I pound my fist into his stomach. Mitchell jerks forward reflexively, despite the pressure it adds to my hand on his throat and his grip on the box fails.

It falls toward the ground as I expected it would. Without removing my eyes from his face, I catch the ring box in my free hand, still holding his throat against the car with the other.

Leaning toward him slightly, I whisper to him in an unnaturally cold British voice, "Touch it again, and I'll remove your hand."

He does not respond, which is for the best. I do not want his provocation. Not when I am already so willing to end him. I push off of the car, adding pressure to his neck as I shove myself away.

As I walk toward the trunk once more, I shove the ring box in my shirt pocket. I grab the charger and shut the trunk, tossing the cord to Roddy. He clumsily fumbles to catch it.

Roddy stands near the pump quietly, relieved that the dispute dissipated before it could escalate any further.

Without any words, I get into the car and slam the door shut. I do not look at Mitchell, but he is there, in the backseat, trying not to gag as he struggles to regulate his breath through his tender throat.

Leaning my head back against the headrest, I exhale forcefully in hopes that it might somehow release the desire to jump into the backseat and silence the heart that still beats there.

"So..." Roddy starts awkwardly trying to smooth the air. "Nobody wants anything from the store, right?"

Mitchell shakes his head.

"Okay," Roddy says with a fake cheerful tone meant to ease the tension inside the car. "How about you?"

Without looking away from the window, I tell him flatly, "They don't sell my snacks in there."

"Right. Okay then. I'll be right back." Roddy pats his hand down on the windowsill, unsure of whether he should leave us alone or not.

When he opens the door to the gas station, he looks back at us as though he expects to see us burst into flames. As though neither of us in this car as the restraint to manage our rage. But the simple fact that I have not killed Mitchell yet should say a lot about my ability to restrain myself.

Taking the ring box from my pocket, I roll it over in my hands, reminding myself of exactly why that mutt is still breathing at all. I close my eyes as I attempt to focus on her, let her ease the waves of anger that are rippling from me.

Hearing Mitchell slide forward in his seat and lean against the back of Roddy's chair, I glance over at him sharply.

He stares at me with disgust, but his words are softer than his appearance, "Okay, maybe I shouldn't have—"

I cut him off abruptly, "If you think a crowd in a parking lot is what stops me, you're wrong. I care very little about spilling their blood alongside yours simply to quiet your insolence. So, stop talking and just listen." *Or stop breathing altogether. That would be better.* "As much as I would enjoy hearing your painful attempt at an apology that you don't mean, there is a much more pressing matter to discuss."

His eyebrows come together curiously. "Okay."

I look at the convenient store, quickly assessing Roddy's location at in line and the remaining time available, which isn't much.

"We need to ditch Roddy. Either in Prairie City or before."

"What? Why?" Mitchell asks, confused.

Roddy hands the cashier his debit card, leaving mere moments before he will leave the store and be within hearing range of this conversation again.

"I don't have time to explain it to you." Not that I would expect such a thick-skulled cretin to understand regardless of the time invested in the explanation. "Just trust that it's for the best and leave it at that for now."

Standing at the counter, Roddy smiles wide at the cashier at what I imagine is some dimwitted small talk that only he would find entertaining.

Mitchell says nothing as he mulls over my words. It could be trap. Get him alone. Just the two of us. It would be easier to kill him without a witness to counter my version of events. And though that is not my intention, Mitchell cannot possibly know that for sure.

Against his better judgment, Mitchell agrees without knowing the full purpose behind my request. Nodding slowly, he sits back in his seat. He stares out the window as though the tension in this car had kept us both quiet while Roddy was out of sight.

KATHRYN HORSLEY | 137

"What's wrong with right now?" Mitchell asks matter-of-factly. "Is there a reason we're waiting until further down the road?"

Now would be fine. But unfortunately, Roddy has the keys and hot-wiring the car takes more effort and time than is necessary for such a straightforward task as leaving someone behind. Waiting is simply the prudent decision at the moment.

"Now is good, but the keys are in Roddy's pocket. I'm not reaching in after them. But, by all means, knock yourself out," I say cynically.

Mitchell smiles slowly as though my words inadvertently struck him as a challenge.

The door at the gas station chimes as Roddy walks out onto the sidewalk, none the wiser to our conversation.

Mitchell leans forward to tell me quietly, "Watch and learn."

I chuckle to myself. Like he could teach me anything. He is nothing more than a puppy still barely able to yip.

Getting out of the car, Mitchell calls, "Hey, Roddy, I changed my mind. Would you mind grabbing me a coke?"

Roddy raises his hands in confused disbelief as he adds sarcastically, "Sure, it's not like it is literally just as easy for you to go in the store as it is for me. But okay, yeah, I'll go back and get it."

"Thanks, man. I owe you one."

Roddy nods, rolling his eyes as he turns back to start toward the store again.

"Hey, Rod, toss me the keys and I'll move the car so we're not blocking the pump." Mitchell holds out his hands to catch them.

With an exasperated sigh, Roddy digs in his pocket and throws them to Mitchell.

Nice. I will not be saying that out loud, but it was. A clean, easy con. Effective and yet simple enough that even an imbecile like Mitchell could pull it off effectively.

Mitchell hops in the driver's seat grinning proudly as he turns the ignition.

A small part of me does feel bad for Roddy. Inside buying a coke for his friends. He will come to out to find those same friends missing from the parking lot. He will be hurt; but he will be alive. And for now, that will have to do.

"Guess this means I can sit shotgun now," Mitchell states chipperly.

I chuckle lightly to myself. I suppose it does.

Chapter 7

Nature has a way of gifting prey with the ability to sense an attack. Coded with the ability to detect specific stimuli, prey can recognize and escape a predator that it has never even encountered before. But not humans. Humans did not receive such a luxury.

Their judgement is poor, often clouded by naivety. Without any real threats for generations, humans have grown lax. They lost their ability to spot the beast behind the curtain.

A kind smile is all it takes to put them at ease, convince them to trust you. Kindness is, after all, one of their easier attributes to mimic.

Predators, like me, can feel their lack of natural apprehension and we exploit it. Even before I cause them so much fear, I feel their vulnerability calling to me. It trembles through the air like fingers stretching out across the room, inviting my monster to come out and play.

Surrounded for centuries by an exposed, powerless populace, I have grown accustomed to weeding out the weak.

For instance, this girl outside this diner, sitting on the curb, waiting for a ride. Alone. She radiates hopelessness. She whispers her longing to become a statistic, just another unsolved case. Her death would be simple and quick, effortless and, to most people, meaningless. It would be weeks before anyone looks for her. That is, if anyone ever bothered to at all.

But her familiar plucking at temptation is not meant for me. She is not mine for the taking.

I watch the couple sitting across from us, middle-aged, normal people. The male is wearing jeans and a red t-shirt, nothing suspicious. His dark hair is short and neat in a manner one might imagine an account-ant would wear. He smiles softly at his wife as he wipes his glasses with the bottom of his shirt.

His wife smiles back as she sips her sweet tea. She sits across from him in the booth with her legs crossed and wearing floral leggings and a loose, oversized pink sweater. Just a normal couple traveling. They could be driving to see their daughter graduate college or out seeing the wonders they've waited their whole lives to see. Nothing dangerous.

Convincing as they are, their unremarkable appearances are de-ceiving. Once you've been a predator for as long as I have, you can recognize the monsters among you.

When they watch the girl with the guitar, they say very little that is not in hushed tones, hunger seated in their eyes. The girl is not mine because she already belongs to them, to the darkness they let envelop them.

My phone rings, pulling my attention away from the couple. Look-ing at the caller ID, I press the red X to ignore Tara once more. I will call her when I am home. When I can assure her that going after Salem is a beneficial task. Then I can also disclose to her what my discoveries are from the journal, if there are any to be found.

Surely, any lasting anger she might have for me will effectively be cooling by then. Plus, our talk will go smoother if I allow enough time for Roddy to tattle on my leaving him behind and sparing him from the fight ahead of us now.

I look up at Mitchell as he takes a bite of his hamburger. Sauce drips on his hand like a barbarian and I groan at what a disgusting creature I have been saddled with.

"So, are you going to tell me why we just bailed on your friend? Or are you just going to keep me in the dark until you decide to leave me alongside the road too?" Mitchell asks with a mouthful of burger.

Leaving him by the road would be nice. Leaving him in a ditch that is particularly septic with no breath left to escape his body and smell-ing of decay would be better.

"Roddy can't do what I need him to." Warren could have. He would have seen the logic and obeyed because he's good at that. But not Roddy; Roddy thinks too much with his heart.

"And what exactly do you need me to do that he couldn't? Because honestly, I'm having a hard time understanding why of the two of us, you ditched Roddy instead of me."

"I need someone who can leave me to die," I say bluntly.

Mitchell chuckles lightly, clearly thinking I am joking. Then, realizing that I'm serious, Mitchell's face grows solemn. His mind tries to make sense of my words as his hands subconsciously lower his burger to the plate.

I clarify, "I need you stay outside while I fight Salem. He only needs to get the upper hand and then he could destroy us both. If it looks as though I'm not going to win, I don't want you to try to save me. I want you burn the house, even if I'm still in it."

Mitchell leans back against his seat and lets out a huff of air as though he does not have the adequate words to convey what he is thinking.

Continuing, I use Mitchell's own words to explain, "Vampires are wasps. Greedy, aggressive, little assholes whose sole purpose is to cause pain, right? Well, it is your job to stop a menace like Salem. If I fail, you cannot. Mitchell, I need you to do your job. Burn that nest to the ground,"

Despite his earlier words having stirred my contemptuous anger, he was correct to compare me to a wasp. Not the way he meant it, but wasps are voracious predators, much like me. And in that way, it was a fitting comparison.

"Salem cannot escape," I tell him matter-of-factly.

His voice is lower than I expect, almost as though he is uncomfortable with the idea of engulfing me in flames and deserting me. "That's not really how you get rid of a wasp nest."

I am aware of that. He is dodging but I do not have time to beat around the bush.

Clasping my hands together calmly on the table, I attempt to make this clear to him, "I need to know that Salem will not live to see another day. That no matter what happens, I need this to be finished. If I can't beat him, you definitely won't."

With a long sigh, Mitchell shakes his head. "I don't like it," he mutters to himself mostly.

"Do you think I do? Look, ideally, none of that will come to fruition anyway. Ideally, Salem dies, I survive, get the book, and go home. That's the plan." Well, it isn't as much of a plan as it a wish list. But still. It's what I have.

I look again to the parking lot and watch the girl with the guitar, sitting on the stoop. Her blonde hair catches the wind, urging her to rock her head to free her face from the strands. Her fingers are busy with the strings on the guitar playing some delicate, lingering song that trickles into the crisp air.

"You cannot try to save me because Krista should not have to lose us both," I distractedly mutter nearly to myself as I watch the girl.

Unknowing of what awaits her, the girl is young enough that I assume she ran away from her home. And though, I have no way of knowing what she ran from, I do know what is coming for her now. I know the beasts that are brewing inside that quaint, suburban couple.

"Maybe we just shouldn't go. I mean, is Salem even worth dying for?" Mitchell asks quietly.

My eyes snap back to Mitchell, who seems more concerned with this than I expected him to be.

"No, he isn't. Salem is simply the cherry on top. The journal he stole could be though. There could be answers that can separate the Genesis from Krista; and yes, that is worth the risk."

Protecting her is the only thing of any real consequence. She is my only real weakness, and they will exploit her if they need to. I have to know what they truly want from me. It's the only way to get ahead of them. If there is a way, I need to know how to stop them.

"Make no mistake. The Genesis is like a plague, infecting our lives. That journal just might hold the antidote. So, yes, I will face Salem," I tell him.

The longer that den of demons is in our lives the less likely we will be able to escape them completely. I need answers to protect Krista from the fallout they will surely bring with them. Marcella knew enough to hide me. Perhaps this journal will tell me why.

Sighing, Mitchell puts another fry in his mouth, but my eyes are focused behind him as the seemingly harmless couple rises from their seats.

They leave a wad of cash on the table, adding a substantial tip. It's a guise I often use myself. A good tip ensures everyone remembers them as the type of customers they are trying to pretend they are, quiet and easy to please. But that is simply a well-played façade.

"I'll be right back," I tell Mitchell. "I need to get something from the car."

He looks at me suspiciously as though I might leave him stranded at this diner, like we did Roddy. And I admit, the thought has crossed my mind.

However, Mitchell says nothing. He only watches me as I exit the diner and walk around the corner of the building where several cars are parked.

I walk past the row of cars and find the man from the diner sitting in a white sedan. Judging the fade on the gloss of the paint, I would guess that it's a 1988 Toyota Corolla. It is the perfect disguise. Single-handedly, the most nonthreatening, benign blemish in this parking lot. No person would look twice at such an insignificant item. It is not memorable in any manner.

It helps them to blend in with normal, benevolent humans. It helps them cover their crimes, but it will afford me the same favor.

Scanning the parking lot, I see the woman, smiling and making small talk with the girl. I do not need my sensitive hearing to know she is inviting the girl to ride with them. A ride that will cost so much more than a smile.

The man watches them in the side mirror. Completely absorbed by the girl, he fails to see me kneel beside his tire.

I let one fingernail extend while I pretend to be tying my shoe. Pressing my nail into the sidewall of the tire, I create a small puncture. That is all that is necessary for now.

I don't want the tire to go flat here. There are far too many witnesses. But I do intend for it to go flat somewhere down the road, forcing them to stop. Expecting to change their tire, they will pull over in some remote place far enough from here that nobody will hear their screams.

Standing up unnoticed, I walk back to the diner as the woman escorts the girl toward their car. I do not look at them as they pass. I don't want their attention. I simply, inconspicuously, go back inside.

I slide back into my booth and wave at the waitress. "Check, please?" Looking at the confusion on Mitchell's face, I tell him, "You can eat in the car, right?"

"What's the rush?" Panic washes over his face and he leans toward me and whispers, "Did you kill somebody?"

I scoff. "No." Not yet. Shaking my head. "I'm smarter than that. In case you missed it, we happen to be on a timeline. And now, it's time for us to move on."

Mitchell lets out a long sigh as the waitress slides the bill on the table. "Will that be all, dear?"

Looking at me, Mitchell asks me sarcastically, "Can I at least get a box?"

Like a child pouting, Mitchell is too self-absorbed to see that another is about to have a much worse day than him. And maybe, just maybe, his lunch isn't the biggest issue here.

I force a smile at him then glance at the waitress. "Could you bring us a box, please? Oh, and a bib too, if it's not too much trouble."

Finding humor in our bickering, she bites her lip, holding back a small laugh. "No trouble at all."

Mitchell, on the other hand, does not find me funny. Chewing hard with annoyance, he tosses his fry onto the plate and shoves his food away. "Fine, let's just go."

Refusing to acknowledge his petty behavior, I say simply, "Thank you."

Shaking his head, Mitchell slides out of the booth as I throw a fifty-dollar bill on the table to cover the check and tip.

Mitchell grabs his burger from his plate defiantly. "I'm taking this."

I chuckle to myself as we walk outside toward our car.

"That's a hell of a tip you left back there," Mitchell says, nodding toward the diner.

I took in a long, heavy breath, holding back my thoughts. He speaks the same way he smells: foul and repulsive. Nothing about him makes me want to continue the conversation.

Besides, being a hardy tipper needs no real explanation. Especially not to him.

As I open the driver's door, Mitchell tells me over the roof, "You're not trying to buy penance for your crimes, are you? Because I think that would be the most pathetic thing I've ever heard in my life."

Only a complete imbecile would assume something so ignorant. Heavy-handed tipping is a habit born out of necessity. Humans trust money; they're loyal to it. Humans can be bought.

Starting the car, I explain, "Tipping well has many benefits. But I would not expect someone so feeble-minded to realize that atonement isn't one of them."

The flash of a smile and a little bit of green paper goes a long way in getting anything you want. If we pass through this backwater town again, that waitress will remember me. She will go out of her way to help me with anything I might ask for, because she misguidedly believes my gratuity is due to kindness. When in fact, her good opinion of me was purchased.

"Okay," Mitchell starts. "But really though, what is the deal? I mean, I've seen the trips you take my sister on. And you don't have a job so how the hell do you spend money like it's endless?"

Laughing lightly, I retort, "I have a job."

"No." Mitchell chuckles. "You write articles for a sci-fi magazine occasionally. That's not a job; that's a hobby."

I laugh aloud, genuinely tickled by his presumption.

"I mean, seriously, do poor vampires even exist?" Mitchell jokes. "Because the certainly don't in the movies."

Of course they exist. Granted, they won't survive very long, not without increasing their currency. It is far too expensive to hide the way we must.

Feeling more at ease with our conversation than usual, I force my guard down enough to allow myself a bit of openness with him. "Do you actually want to know or are you poorly attempting to insult me in some strange, convoluted way?"

He thinks for a moment before answering, "I would like to know actually."

"Okay, well, if a vampire is in a pinch, we can always murder or enthrall someone so we can rob them or get their bank information. That's easy enough." And I am not above either of those. We've all done it from time to time. "But eventually, most of us settle into some type of money-generating system, something that has a lot of cash coming and going, so it won't draw people's attention, like real estate."

If I wanted to elaborate, Mitchell would be astonished to learn how much property is owned by vampires. When all you have is time, you learn how to wait for properties and gobble them up like a glutton.

"Me. I focus on art. I know how to hide there."

"Art? You don't strike me as an art guy," Mitchell inquires.

I shrug. "Marcella taught me what to look for but I'm not as good as she was. She was genuinely impressive. She naturally had an eye for it." And a knack at enthralling to buy low then enthralling again to sell high decades later.

Watching her move pieces like a game of chess, I witnessed the most conning performer I have ever known. "I once saw her buy a painting for a couple hundred dollars and sell it two hundred years later for just over forty million."

"Million? As in, six zeros?"

The shock on his face pushes me to laugh lightly. "Seven zeros if you count the one next to the four, but yeah, million."

"Geez," Mitchell says in disbelief. "I should have gotten into art."

I chuckle to myself. Mitchell would never make a good broker. He isn't personable or intelligent enough to compete with the sharks he would find lurking there.

Marcella, on the other hand, was one of those sharks. Literally blood-thirsty, she was a powerhouse. Fearless and bold, she shot like an arrow for the highest price, and she was ruthless if she thought she might receive anything less.

She was so cut-throat that she kept an entire warehouse brimming with artifacts and priceless pieces of a human world long gone. Like ghosts locked in the dark, her collection waits to be sold piece by piece by me, the sole heir to her life's work.

Not to say that I have been greedy with the money. I have contributed heavily to Luther's bank funds. The only reason Marcella left all of the assets to me is because others would not pace themselves. I have spent countless hours helping Luther get his footing in the real estate business, and I must admit that he is becoming quite good at it.

Humans actually enjoy his stupidity. They find it endearing in a relatable way. Before much longer, he will not need me at all. Luther will finally be the self-sufficient vampire I never expected him to become.

I am almost proud. Like watching a weed spurt from a compost pile. It might only be a weed but it's better than staring at rotting trash.

"I can't believe Krista didn't tell me any of this. I have asked, you know? She just avoids answering," Mitchell says, more to himself than to me.

That's because my secrets are mine. And my business ventures shouldn't matter to pack at all.

"There are lots of things she doesn't share with you."

His eyebrows come together, knitted tight with concern. "Like what?"

Like the fact that she overlooks my murderous outings each month while she chases the moonlight. That she will not ask about the couple I'm following even though she would know or about what I will do to when I catch them. Because, excusing the murder of calculating humans, who are not victims at all, is hardly difficult once you've grown accustomed to carnage.

I'm not going to tell Mitchell any of that. But I do have a story for him just the same, one that will hopefully guide this conversation in the direction of my choosing.

"Do you remember when we lived in Chicago for about a year or so?"

Mitchell nods, unsure of where this change in conversation might lead. But regardless of what he might suspect, he is wrong.

"Well, Krista told me that she didn't like her boss but never said much else about him. But something felt off, like she was hiding something. So, I decided to check it out."

I watched her for days before I noticed the pattern that should have been so very obvious.

"It was the owner. He wasn't there every day, but when he was there, the guys she worked with were careful not to leave her alone with him. And then one day, he came in unannounced and there she was, alone in the garage."

He saw her. And I saw him. The real him…

*   *   *

His gaze rolled over her body, absorbing her every curve, and locking her image in his mind for later. He smiled at her, but she did not smile in return. Angst lingered in her eyes as they tracked across the room. I could feel her unease inching under my skin like a thorn beneath my fingernail.

He rubbed his fingers along the fender of the car she stood next to, but it was my anger that he unknowingly stroked.

The streaking sound of his fingers against the cold metal cut into the tense air of the garage. "Beautiful work you do here. That body looks fantastic." Walking toward her, he dragged his hand along the little red Pontiac.

Feeling his eyes trace her, Krista crossed her arms over her chest, uncomfortably concealing herself. "It was just a minor collision, not a lot of damage."

I could have killed him. I wanted to. Like a hunter, my eyes were fixated on him. Every beat of his heart, I could see pulsating in the veins of his neck. I could hear his breath potently push into the air, polluting it with his vile presumptions.

The only thing that held me in my place was that I could feel her. She did not need my help to nullify the situation. Not yet. And my presence would only expose what I am to her co-workers. Wolves too, they wouldn't understand how a creature like her could keep a monster like me. She would lose her job, her friends, and the respect of the wolves who ran with her.

So, I waited, knowing full well that my time alone with him would come.

Stopping in front of her so close that she had to press herself against the car simply to avoid touching him, he asked her insinuatingly, "How about that rear? How does it look?"

"It wasn't damaged," she replied uncomfortably.

"Untouched? That's a shame," he whispered.

I wanted it to be the last thing that he said. I wanted to rip his larynx from his body, longed to feel his blood course over my flesh as I showed him what a truly frightening creature can do to such a revolting man.

He raised his hand to rub her arm and the intensity of my rage stirred inside of me, coaxing my eyes to fade to black. Her words, however, stopped him and me both. "Touch me and I'll break your fingers."

My anger would have to wait. She did not need me to intervene. Not in this moment. In the shadows, I waited, thinking of what my time with him would look like. Whether it would be here or at his home, during the dark night or the false safety of day. I did not know yet; but one thing was certain, my vengeance would be slow and unescapable.

There was no hint of uncertainty in her voice but still, he snorted to himself. "Oh, you poor, little bitch. If you even try, I'll have your ass thrown in jail. People don't look kindly on wolves who are violent toward humans. Who knows, maybe a couple of nights in jail would do you some good. Maybe adjust your attitude a little."

With confidence, he let the backs of his fingers graze her shoulder. Grabbing him, Krista drove her knee into his groin and he buckled over.

As his hands clutched his injured manhood, Krista leaned close to his ear, saying with heat simmering over her words, "Call the police, little bitch, and I'll tell your wife that you fantasize about fucking a dog."

"Kris, you have a call!" a man yelled from the office. But there was no ring of phone. The call was merely a ploy to put some distance between her and their crumpled boss.

Confidently, she walked toward the office, not letting her boss see any concern she might have for being fired because ultimately, it would have been worth it.

As she approached, the man near the office apologized quietly, much too quietly for the boss to hear him, "Sorry, I didn't know he was coming in today."

"It's okay, Jason," she dismissed as she passed him. "Really, I'm okay."

Krista disappeared into the office as Jason stepped into the garage. He attempted to sound friendly as though he didn't know what just transpired. And despite the tightening of his eyes, Jason's tone hid the fact that he would've liked to strangle that vile man as much I did…

*   *   *

"What did you do?" Mitchell asks.

"I went home." I didn't even tell Krista that I was there.

"Seriously? You didn't, like, punch him in the face or anything? 'Cause I even wasn't there and I want to punch him," Mitchell snaps.

I did far worse than punch that prick. "I was patient." Love is patient.

Mitchell shifts in his seat, invested in where my story is going.

"I followed him for a few nights. Then one night, he parked his car in a shadowy area near the lake. That's where I caught up to him." That's where I confronted the anger he stirred in me. That's where he begged for the mercy I was unwilling to show him. "I made sure the hooker he was with died very quickly, but he did not have that same luxury."

Her neck snapped before she could register that my hands were upon her. However, he screamed into the night as I dragged him from his car, careful not to leave any evidence of a kidnapping. No blood, no footprints, no traces of any kind.

I took him far enough from the city to eliminate any concern of being heard. I bit him in the leg, ripping my teeth through his thigh, and then I set him free. I let him limp as he ran; pretended that he might have a fraction of a chance.

I could have stopped him from screaming altogether. That would have been simple but I wanted him to know what was coming for him. I wanted to hear his fear escape when he could not.

Wiping his blood across my brow, I let the contrast of crimson against my pale skin bask in the moonlight. I was a frightful looking thing as I chased him in the darkness, making the most unholy sounds. Each time that I caught him, I tore into him more, like a feral cat with a plump, soft house-mouse.

Once he had lost so much blood that I risked him slipping away from me into a state of shock, I gutted him like the pig he was. Pulled his intestines onto the cold ground and left them for the wild vermin to devour.

The scent of blood was heavy as I ripped muscle and flesh from his bones. I tossed chunks of flesh into the lake. I ground his bones into powder in my hands and scattered it along the shore.

Finally, I lay down in the puddle of his blood until it grew cold beneath me. Watching the stars above me in the still night, peace washed over me. The smell of death cradled me, lulling me with its innate comfort. My mind was quiet against the sounds of animals scavenging through the soft tissues on the ground, the only remaining pieces of such an abhorrent human.

"Does Krista know you killed him?" Mitchell asks, pulling me from the serenity the memories of that night offer me.

When Krista came home from work, she slapped the newspaper on the table, half-frenzied. "*Did you do this?*" she asked me. She wasn't angry or accusatory; she simply needed to know.

I stopped stirring the sauce I was making for dinner to pick up the paper. The title of the story read: *Man Wanted for Questioning.* But that was as far as I got before she poured the details of the article out before me.

Her boss was missing and was the sole suspect of the murder of a prostitute. Believed to have killed her in his car and fled on foot, he was considered armed and dangerous. These were just some of statements that came spilling out of her.

She looked at me, longing to know the truth and asked again, this time slowly enunciating each word, "*Did you do this?*"

She wanted to know the truth but not all of it. Looking at her evenly, I told her directly, "*Whatever happened, your boss has no one to blame but himself.*"

That was all I said about it. Ever.

And that was all I needed to say. Krista's eyes grew heavy with the weight of tears. A wave of solace rippled off her as she wrapped her arms around my neck, holding me as though the very heat of her body was thanking me for something she dared not admit aloud.

Expecting Mitchell to understand any of her response is futile. Instead, I tell him, "Your sister is not easily fooled. But that's not the point. I need you to understand that just like that hooker, sometimes there are collateral losses. There will be people that I kill on this trip, and they will not all be vampires. You need to prepare yourself for that." It is statistically impossible for Salem to be the only causality. Mitchell may as well get comfortable with the idea now instead of getting in my way later.

"You mean humans?" Mitchell stares at me, waiting for me to clarify but he already knows that is exactly what I mean.

"It's unavoidable, Mitchell. Some people contribute most by leaving this world and sometimes other people just happen to be there when it happens."

"No. Not humans. I won't do it," he says bluntly.

"Then, you should be relieved to hear that I don't expect you to. I do, however, expect you to stay out of my way when I kill whom that I deem necessary."

Mitchell shakes his head, thinking for a moment before he responds, "I can't do that, Nick."

"Nicolas," I correct him calmly. Only my friends call me Nick and Mitchell is not my friend. "And your opinion in this doesn't matter because your dad left me in charge of this, so…"

"He absolutely did not put you in charge, *Nicolas*," Mitchell interrupts cynically.

Bryant may not have meant to, but he certainly did.

"Did he or did he not give you an order not to kill me unless you, yourself, feel threatened?"

His bottom lip quivers slightly. "That's not the same thing."

"And you're not supposed to fight me at all unless I attack you first, right?" I add.

Mitchell repositions himself in the seat uncomfortably. "Right, but…"

With little to debate, I finish his thought for him, "Which means, as long as I don't come after you directly, I can execute my plan and anyone else I feel like. And you can't lay a finger on me to stop me. Is that or is that not how that works?"

I can see it settle into him, the reality that essentially, I am in charge. He may not want to sit by willingly, but he will have to sit by. There will be no stopping me, with or without his compliance. His mind works hard to think of something to use as a rebuttal and comes up with utterly nothing.

Mitchell glares at me for a long while but at least he is quiet. The warm sunlight does little to soothe the reality of what kind of brute sits next to him.

However, it is another more bleak reality that holds his tongue. Creeping into him with the quiet roaring of the tires on the pavement is the grim realization that this trip might force him to become a monster as well.

Mitchell just stares at the floorboard, unwilling to admit that deep down, a small part of him agrees with me. I saw it in his eyes only moments ago, the satisfaction that her boss's death was brutal and slow.

Up ahead, the white Corolla slowly comes into view. Just as I hoped, they were forced to pull over due to a blowout of their passenger front tire. Once the air pressure became too low and the sidewall could no longer support the weight, it flexed beyond its limits, exploding their very hope at surviving this day.

Mitchell spots them ahead of us, stranded by the side of the road. Only the couple are visible. Not even a glimpse of the girl who had stowed away in the backseat.

The sudden distraction compels him to break his silence by muttering, "I wonder if they need help?"

Inside, I smile. How completely perfect. I didn't even have to bring them up. Mitchell has given me the cover I need to pull over without raising his suspicions. They will be dead before he can even exit the car to save them.

Perhaps after I explain the girl with the guitar, he will understand. But frankly, I don't care if he ever does.

"I'll check it out," I tell him as we slow down.

I pull along the edge of the road just past their car. Just for show, I sigh heavily as I exit the car, pretending that stopping to help them is a burden.

Walking toward them, I smile innocently at the man as I get closer. "Need any help?"

The man looks up from the jack as he raises the car to replace the shredded tire. "No, thank you. We've got it."

Ignoring his refusal, I continue closer. "Are you sure? I'm pretty good with cars."

The woman steps between me and the car to block me from coming closer. "No, thank you. We're good here."

I look around her for any evidence of the girl but there isn't much. Her guitar lays in the backseat with the pick still wedged in the strings but there is no sign of her that a human would find easily. But I am not a human.

Listening intently, I can hear the girl's heart beating, calm and even. She is likely sleeping quietly inside the trunk, like a makeshift prison that helps stifle the smell of trickling blood.

Nodding toward the guitar, I walk past the woman. "That's a nice guitar."

Irritably, she again rushes between me and the car before I get to the back window. "It's a present for our daughter," she says sharply.

"How lovely," I say flatly.

The woman grabs my arm, gently trying to guide me away from the car while her husband watches me intently.

"You know, it's funny," I start. "But that guitar looks just like one I saw earlier. A girl had it. A little blonde girl."

The woman forces a low chuckle. "What a nice coincidence."

I plant my feet so she cannot move me further. "Is it though?"

Her eyes flash to mine, calculating how much I already know. Behind her, her husband places his hand over a crowbar ready to eliminate the risk of me exposing them both. But I am not a victim that will fall so easily.

I let a cruel smile spread across my face. My eyes glaze over into a shining black abyss as a preview to the hollow darkness that is coming for her.

Before she can even flinch, I grab her head, bashing her face into the window. Glass scatters into the floorboard and backseat like rice at a wedding. Her body goes limp in my hands but she is not unconscious, merely unable to react to my actions quick enough to even tense her muscles.

Blood trickles down her face as I toss her to the ground next to the car like a dirty rag. Moaning, she holds her face, trying to comprehend what is happening and what sort of beast lingers near her now.

The man jumps up with the crowbar in his hand. It is possible that he is defending his wife, which would probably be the only honorable thing he has ever done in his entire, miserable life. However, it is equally likely that he is merely concerned with saving his own life. Even that is futile, however. His life will be coming to an end promptly.

Letting out an angry scream fueled by raw rage, he charges toward me with the crowbar raised and ready to unleash a volatile assault. Nevertheless, I move much faster than him and his reign of violence will never get the chance to touch me.

Opening the passenger door into his path, I slam the door into his body, stopping him abruptly. I grab his hair and pull him through the busted window. The protruding fragments of shattered glass scrape across his belly, tearing deep grooves of broken flesh along the windowsill. Blood wafting into the air around me, a blaze of flames awakens in my throat.

Pulling the man's head into the door jam, I slam the door closed. The clicking of the latch is nearly lost among the crunching sound as bits of his head scatter onto my shoe. His skull collapses around the cold metal as it gives way to the force of the door.

His wife scrambles to her feet, screaming at the sight of something she cannot comprehend. Her husband hangs from the window, bits of brain and skull splattered inside their bland and unassuming sedan.

Shrieks emit from her as the sounds of her fear flee from her body. My dark eyes follow her as she runs toward Mitchell, who hurries to exit our car.

I warned Mitchell not to stop me, but he obviously refuses to heed my advice. Now the memories of this day, the visions that he cannot unsee, will belong to him.

The woman's steps are loud, her feet pushing desperately into the dirt and fine rocks along the edge of the road. Yet, there is no escape for her. I slide the metal lever from the jack and throw it toward the woman. It flips through the air, tumbling end over end until it strikes her, stopping her in her tracks.

As rod lodges into the back of her skull, the sharp end forcefully protrudes from her mouth, spattering blood across Mitchell's face. She drops to her knees for a brief moment before she collapses forward onto the ground, forcing Mitchell to shuffle his feet backward to avoid her body touching his sneakers.

With a shaky breath, Mitchells tries to register what he just witnessed. He looks at the blood sprinkled over his shirt and on his trembling hands, muttering breathy incoherencies to himself.

I walk over to the woman's body. Without saying anything to Mitchell, I place my foot on her head. The squelching sound of blood and tissue pulling against the rod as I slide it from her skull makes Mitchell cover his mouth in revulsion.

"What the fuck is wrong with you?" he shouts at me angrily.

Tears grow heavy in his eyes as the swirl of emotions twist throughout him. It occurs to me that this may very well be the first time he has seen humans killed in this manner. I remember my first time; it was very conflicting.

Then again, I was not third in command for a werewolf pack. You would think he would be able to handle more than this.

"I meant it when I said I wouldn't just sit by and watch you murder people," he yells as he tries to grasp at some bit of reality. He still has no understanding of why I killed them at all. They seemed like such ordinary people.

Witnessing a death of this brutality might feel like an unreal moment for him. But I have very little compassion for his whimpering, and I do not care enough speak to him like a delicate, fragile flower.

"You weren't sitting. You were standing," I tell him sarcastically and start back toward the couple's car.

My words stir his anger further and he snaps back at me, "This isn't a joke. You killed those people after I told you not to."

As I walk past the car, I step over the man's limp body and reach through the open window into the backseat to grab the guitar.

"I wasn't asking your approval. I'm not a wolf, Mitchell. I don't need permission. I gave you a warning that I was going to kill someone. That's more than I give most people so consider yourself lucky."

I continue past the dead body to the trunk as Mitchell follows after me, shouting in angry disbelief. "Lucky? I am wearing little bits of bone like I've been fucking bedazzled. I have someone's spinal cord in my mouth!"

I simply stare at him. Nothing he is whining about warrants a response. I am a vampire, doing exactly what vampires are called to do. My only error here is that I have involved myself in a human matter. Inherently, I should have ignored the girl and let them keep her. It is not my place to stop a human beast.

Being a vigilante only draws attention to oneself. And not the type of attention that will keep a vampire alive. I should have waited for my own victim, and not gotten involved with theirs. In fact, I don't fully understand what compelled me to help at all.

Mitchell, though, does not realize why we are here. And he certainly does not realize the risk I am taking by offering this girl some small amount of grace.

I lean down near to the trunk lid. Her breathing is heavy, completely unfazed by the chaos outside of her prison. Most likely, she has been sedated, and that works nicely for me.

One less witness to worry about.

Mitchell will not accept words as easily, so I do not offer any. I simply use the lever to force the trunk open and lift the hatch, exposing the girl.

Her blonde hair covers part of her face but even Mitchell can see enough to recognize her. Despite the dirty red hand towel tied around her eyes and the duct tape over her mouth, Mitchell *sees* her.

His body recoils from the trunk, flinching as it releases his anger and confronts a new wave of conflicting emotions that flood in.

"I know her. She was playing music outside of the diner," he sputters to himself. Reaching into the trunk, he pushes her hair from her face delicately. He asks me quietly, "How did you know she was here?"

Because I, too, have kept a girl in a trunk before. Not for the same purpose they had for her but for something else. Something just as frightening; something that would end her life just as quickly.

Laying the guitar next to her, I tell him matter-of-factly, "We need to go."

Leaving the trunk lid open, I walk back in the direction of our car.

Calling after me, Mitchell scurries to catch up. "Wait, we can't just leave her here."

But that is exactly what I am going to do. "Someone will drive by soon. They will call the police and get her to safety," I explain without slowing my pace toward our car. "We cannot be here when they do."

Mitchell grabs my arm as we reach own car. "I won't just leave her here."

I roll my eyes at his peevishly childish behavior. This is, after all, simply ridiculous. Surely, even his small brain can grasp the fact that staying here is a completely moronic idea.

Huffing loudly, my annoyance with him rolls through my muscles, begging me to grab him by his throat and toss him into the trunk of our own car. I do not have time for this.

"Fine. Stay," I tell him, letting my impatience paint my words. "But I'm leaving and you can explain to the police how a *vampire* killed that couple *before* sundown. And they will completely believe you. Oh wait, no they won't because vampires don't exist. You will be arrested, and you can rot in jail for those people. And I can finally be rid of you. So go ahead, stay, be my guest."

He stares at me, disgusted that I am right. There is no way for him to explain any of what the police will find here.

With a frustrated sigh, he walks to the passenger side of our car. Glaring at me from across the car, "You are a colossal dick."

Wow. Just wow. Impressive insult. I've never been more offended in my life. That is, except by every other person who has ever tried to insult me. Ever.

"Very original," I tell him dryly.

I slide into my seat as Mitchell gets in the car. Still fuming, he slams the door shut behind him.

"Do me a favor, if you're going to try to offend me, actually *try*. Be creative. Add some flavor to your jabs."

Annoyed, Mitchell shakes his head at whatever juvenile quip is racing through his mind. "Like you can do any better," he mutters to himself quietly.

He did not mean for me to hear that final remark. He didn't mean to throw out a challenge, but I can do better. Quite better. And with very little effort.

I start the car. However, instead of driving away, I turn toward him in my seat and tell him the most honest thing I have said to him this entire trip.

Keeping my tone even, I say, "You could have stopped me from killing them. That is, if daddy trusted you enough to let out your leash a little bit. But he doesn't. It's Warren that he trusts. Warren isn't even his real son, but he's still his favorite. And if Bryant could have had it his way, Warren would be his *only* son. You're not the one who truly belongs at Bryant's side. You're just the useless mutt he bred into the world."

Too stunned to formulate words, Mitchell stares at me with his eyebrows crossed as I pull our car back onto the road.

Enjoying the dumbfounded look scrolled on his face, I smile nonchalantly at him before he can put his words together. "You see. Expletives do not *dig* the way an insult should. So, go on, try to provoke me but be creative with it. Really dig into me."

With a smirk, I taunt, "I double-dog dare you."

Mitchell huffs irritably. "Fine, I will." He shifts in his seat, thinking of what he wants to say.

It takes him longer than I expect but finally he begins, "You're a cockroach that never dies when it should. But one day, I will kill you, and I'll cut you from stem to stern. Chop you up into little pieces and hand-feed your dick to the crows. That way, you would never be able to stitch your mutilated body back together."

Alright, that's not the worst I have heard. I mean, I did live with Luther for a long time. Plus, Mitchell's comeback only had one expletive, so I have to credit him for trying.

Still, I tease, "So, let me get this straight. Of all the ways you could kill me, you would choose the one way in which my penis ends up in your hands. Is that right?"

Scoffing, he turns back in his seat. "I said I'd feed it to the birds, moron."

"It's still kind of a weird thing to say to the guy who's dating your sister. That's original, at least. And the crows were a nice touch," I continue to goad.

"Whatever," he mumbles, looking out of the window. "Prick."

As I look at him, I can feel his anger rippling against my skin like the edge of a small puddle after casting stones. With the edge of his palms resting on his knees, he keeps his fingers spread so that the bits of the woman's flesh that had splattered on them does not begin to dry and stick together.

It is not a good idea to push someone who is so desperately trying to hold themselves together. Not a good idea, but against my better judgement, I push anyway. "If you're done pouting, there are wet wipes in the glovebox."

Looking at me sharply, he snaps, "No, actually, I'm not done. You know what my problem is."

Do I have to pick only one?

"You murdered those people by the side of the road for some girl you don't even know. Which is whatever. But Molly, my Molly. She asked you to come to her birthday party and you couldn't even show up. Murder is okay, but birthday parties, that's crossing the line."

The sudden shift in conversation takes me aback. I was not expecting it and am left scrambling for an adequate rebuttal.

The only thing Molly has ever asked of me was to show up. "I had my reasons for not coming."

"Yeah, I bet you did. Work? Got it, sure. I bet your hobby-job really gets in the way of the things you want to do when you *want* to do them."

But I did want to be there for Molly. I did. I just couldn't. "You have no idea what you're talking about. It makes you sound like a fool."

"Well, enlighten me then. What was so important that it was worth breaking my little girl's heart?"

Not a little girl, she is sixteen years old but reminding him that she is growing up isn't going to help the situation.

Quietly, I mumble under my breath, "Not more important. Simply more paralyzing." And nothing is more paralyzing than guilt.

"What?" he asks incredulously.

Mitchell has never had to face the kind of regret vampires bury inside. He has no idea what it looks like. But maybe he should. Maybe I should let him take a peek into what it costs to be able to kill so freely.

"Look, I've killed a lot of people and I learned a long ago how to put that guilt in a neat little box and toss it into some abyss in my mind. Killing strangers is easy. But when you know the victim, guilt can creep inside and settle in for the long haul. You can't shake it once it's there."

It is easier to simply hide from it. Especially with children. Images of their faces find a way to sear into your mind so that even closing your eyes can become a burden. "I have to find a way to shut the guilt out. Because it will consume me and take me down a darker path than I am already on."

Sometimes that is as simple as relocating. Other times, it means eliminating the reminders, even if they are still breathing.

"Your Molly reminds me of someone I knew once. My neighbor. Her name was also Molly, and maybe that's why she reminds me so much of her." I liked her. She was a sweet kid. "But she saw too much and I was asked to take care of that."

I let the sadness seep into my voice so Mitchell can hear the heartbreak behind the words. If I do not show my vulnerability with him now, he will never hear the sincerity that he desperately needs to hear. "And I did. We were in her truck and I snapped her neck with my bare hands. I can still feel the tears that ran down her face, warming my skin."

It wasn't just the girl, though. Her mother's death is mine too. Her mother moved back to Maine to face her grief; but eventually, she ended up sitting in her parked car with the engine running inside the garage until she drifted away from her pain.

That's on me too. I was the one who took her reason for living.

Mitchell's eyebrows come together with confusion but not about what I am saying. My words he understands. How he should feel about them is what conflicts him.

"She was sixteen, just like your Molly, so this birthday was especially hard for me. I couldn't turn off that guilt, and I couldn't face it. I'm sorry that your Molly was hurt by my not being there but I didn't know what else to do."

Strangers are easy. Their faces blur together. But familiars are haunting. I pretend that I don't see them, but they're there, lurking in the shadows, waiting for the opportunity to reveal my ugliness to me. Like a mirror, reflecting the worse parts of myself.

Their guilt is suffocating.

Mitchell's face softens as he processes my confession. Almost as though a small part of him pities me and the life I must live, he sighs quietly.

As unnatural as it feels for him to hold some bit of compassion for me, his words are gentle. "I didn't know any of that," he says as though is attempting to apologize without saying sorry.

Of course, he wouldn't know any of the things I carry with me. It has never before seemed beneficial to be upfront with Mitchell about murdering a child.

He looks out the window and mutters quietly, "Great. I'm not sure how you managed it, but now I feel like the ass."

I smile to myself. He is an ass, but I suppose it would not help to point that out right now. Besides, for this brief moment, he almost seems tolerable.

"Well, I just killed a couple on the side of a highway, so I'll give you a reprieve on feeling like the biggest ass in the car."

Without looking back at me, he scoffs. "Thanks. I appreciate that."

Driving quietly, I glance at him after several miles. Deep in thought, he keeps his fingers near his mouth. His thumb rubs over his bottom lip and his eyebrows draw together. He looks much the same way Krista does when she is contemplating some ambiguously amoral thing I have done; weeding out her feelings before she compromises them.

Like I do with her, Krista would want me to tread lightly with him now—let him ease into the blending of two worlds. She would want me to have patience with him like I do with her.

Patience is a struggle for me to have with him though, despite my seemingly immortal existence. Still, I suppose that as long as he is attempting to coexist with me, I should grant him the same tolerance. Or, at least attempt to.

Reaching in my shirt pocket, I pull out the ring box and hold it out toward him. "Would you like to see it?"

He looks at it cautiously but does not reach for it. I smile, amused at the idea that perhaps he is afraid that I will truly will rip his hand off for touching it.

"It's not a trick."

With a half-smile, he takes the box. Opening it carefully, his eyes roll over the ring as though he is attempting to sear the image of it into his memory.

"What kind of stone is this?"

"Amazonite. It is the stone of hope." Which is exactly what she brings into my life. "Hope is an all-consuming light in a dark world. That's what she is to me. My light. The beacon that pulls me from my realm of shadows."

He smirks at me. "Did you steal that line from a movie?"

"No," I scoff to myself. "Hope is as fundamental to life as Krista is to me. No movie can capture that."

He studies the teal stone for a moment longer before he states, "I've never seen a stone like this before."

Probably not. It isn't common enough to pick it up from the jewelry store in the mall. I had to find a designer who specializes in unusual gems to have it set the way I wanted. And after a small bit of enthralling, that same designer gave it to me for a great price.

"Well, she isn't like any girl I've met before."

Mitchell lets out an exasperated exhale, trilling his lips lightly, not wanting to utter the thoughts that are forming but feeling obligated to say them anyway.

"Okay," he starts reluctantly and without even a hint of enthusiasm.

He shakes his head as though someone's voice is arguing with him in his head. Then letting out a sigh, he adds, "I've always had people to lean on. That's one perk about being in a pack; they help carry your burdens. But you. Your whole life is heavy and horrible, and it's chock-full of secrets. But you can't hide from us, not if you want to marry my sister. If you marry her, you're going to have to let people in."

Mitchell hands me back the ring box as he finishes, "This pack, this family, it's bigger than just any one person. It's bigger than me and it's a lot bigger than you."

The rift I have caused in their family is big, too. So big, that many of his werewolves left the pack when Bryant granted me amnesty. And much too big for any of them to want to help carry my burdens. They would rather watch me buckle beneath the weight. And who can blame them? The damage I have caused within their pack is irreparable.

I allowed Krista to care for me before admitting what I am. Let her invest her heart in mine without allowing her to make that decision based on facts. It was not fair to her. And it was not fair to them. I fractured all of their trust.

What's worse is that they know I do not care. I would do all again. I would repeat my lies because it secured her affections.

Because I need her.

When I am with Krista, I do not miss Ann. I do not dream of my human life because I no longer crave it.

All I want is to hear my name in the whispers of Krista's smile. I want her warm hand to reach for mine in the dead of night. I don't know why she can make me yearn for her the way she does. But I do know that no other person in nearly six hundred years has ever made me ache for them so completely.

And I know that if I must wait another six hundred years to keep her, I will do so tirelessly.

I shrug dismissively. "Well, I doubt Bryant is going to give me his blessing anytime soon. This whole sharing our secrets and brotherly bonding is probably something neither of us need to worry about just yet."

Mitchell is quiet as though he does not want to tell me. "You know she doesn't need to have his permission, right?"

He isn't telling me anything that I don't already know. It lingers in the back of my mind constantly, urging me to skip the formality altogether. But this isn't about ease. It is about respect.

Byrant's for me and mine for his.

It is about proving to him that I am not some thief in the night, stealing his daughter and dragging her into a cold, hollow world. It is about showing him that I need him to acknowledge I am worthy of her, even when I am not. I need him to sleep without worrying about the monster sleeping next to her. And accept that while he loved her first, I will be her forever after.

"I do know that, but I want it. And so does Krista." She pretends that it doesn't matter, but she craves his blessing, not as her alpha, but as her father even more than I do.

"Well, how many times have you asked?"

For his blessing? "Oh, I'd say, every six months or so for the past seven years. Give or take." And every other time I have seen him in person.

Seventeen times, to be exact. It's not give or take. It's been seventeen times exactly. And if I survive this trip, it will be eighteen once we get back.

Mitchell pulls his eyebrows together as though my words have a slight sting to them. As though he almost feels pity for me. But I do not need or want his pity.

I can wait. I will wait, anxiously anticipating the day when I can call her mine in every manner possible. Because she is worth an eternity of longing for.

Mitchell's pity is wasted on me.

I smile at him softly. "It's okay, though. I think I'm starting to wear him down."

I chuckle to myself but Mitchell only mumbles under his breath, lost in thought, "Yeah, maybe you are."

Chapter 8

I *can still remember* my old home in Stevensville. The one I had shared with Marcella. I remember heading to the kitchen one morning to make Julia breakfast before I settled into bed for the day. As I rounded the corner, Marcella sat stoically at the table, patiently waiting for me. The chess-board in front of her was arranged in a manner that gave Marcella the black pieces, which left the first move up to me. That was strategic too.

It was a game she had played with me many times before. Sometimes for pleasure but most often, it was a way to force me to spend time with her after we fought. It was her way of easing back into our normal routines.

"Staring doesn't move the pieces," I teased.

"Neither does sarcasm," she said coolly.

She wanted me to sit down and start the game so she could tell me whatever she was wanting to say. I knew that if I didn't hear her that morning, she would be ready again the next.

"Losing only makes you restless," I reminded her with a smirk.

She looked at me from the tops of her eyes in a sharp and even stare. "Well, it's a good thing I won't lose."

I smiled at her challenge and slid into the seat across from her.

As I looked over my pieces, contemplating my strategy, Marcella watched me patiently. "I've missed this."

Moving my pawn, I looked up at her. "Chess?"

A sly smile spread on her face. "A worthy opponent."

I chuckled to myself, thinking of all the ways Luther could never be a skilled chess player. He was too ignorant to formulate his own plan of attack and far too lacking to possess the adaptive nature needed to overtake the calculating tactics of another.

"So, Marcella. I was thinking about inviting Krista over for dinner to meet you formally."

"Oh," she said simply, considering her response. "How quaint. Is she going to be the guest or the meal?"

Not entertained by her tactless joke, I raised my eyebrows as a warning.

Rolling her eyes, she huffed. "Fine. Bring your stray over but don't expect us to braid each other's hair and gossip about boys."

Her words were tight and cold as I assumed they would be, but she added, "I suppose, however, that I could manage to put forth enough effort to pretend to have a soul for one evening if it appeases you."

"I wouldn't expect anything more from you, Marcella."

"Good."

We played silently for a while. And for a moment, it felt like old times. Marcella and I, alone in the world. Nostalgia lapped at me, reminding me of the comfort in belonging to a family.

All vampires have parts of themselves they must hide. However, Marcella did not need me to speak my dark sins, she knew them as her own. Not because she was a vampire, but because she was my mother. Sitting across from me was the only person in the whole of my existence who truly understood all of me. Marcella could see even the darkest parts of me without the dimmest light.

"I hope you know what you're doing this time, Nicolas."

Looking up at her, I watched as she moved her piece before continuing, "I successfully hid you for centuries from the Genesis. Kept them guessing. We were invisible. Until Claire. I knew I shouldn't turn her. I knew better but I did it anyway thought because you wanted her."

Claire was different. Claire was a mistake; I will agree to that. She was beautiful and young. Her life was full of family but she was alone. There was a part of me that honestly felt I could save her. That I could offer a family where she truly belonged. And perhaps, together, I could have helped her find herself and she could have healed me of my lingering memories of Ann. But that was naïve and foolish.

Without verbally acknowledging Marcella's words, I moved my piece, letting the light tapping sound of my bishop pad against the board be the only sound of rebuttal from me.

"Your feelings for Claire exposed us all. By choosing your desires over my own logic, I failed you. I was hopeful that you might do better than me. However, whether you admit it or not, this romance of yours is going to bring you to your knees. Instead of being sensible, you want to play house with a mutt and pretend that every other romance you've ever had hasn't ended severely." Her pitch deepened to emphasize her words. "And always for the girl."

She did not need me to answer. She knew she was right. Ann, Claire, Kate, all devastating endings. Even Hannah nearly died and she was only loosely connected to me.

With a smirk, she added, "Checkmate."

As my eyes scrolled over the board to find that I had, in fact, lost, Marcella's cold words continued, "And for heaven's sake, Nicolas, let us all pretend that the most damaging vampire in this room isn't you."

Marcella stood up and leaned close to my ear. "Love is a dangerous game. You will need to better at it than you are at chess."

With a cool, low chuckle, Marcella walked away, content that her point was made. And as fate would have it, everything she said turned out to be true...

*   *   *

The vibrating of my phone rumbles through the stillness of the dark car. It's enough to make Mitchell flinch in his sleep and enough to make me glad I did not turn the ringer on and risk waking him completely.

Seeing the name on my phone, I cannot help but smile a warm, lopsided grin. "Hey, I was hoping you'd call. I didn't want to have to wake you up."

Krista's voice is soft as she replies, "I can't sleep anyway. The bed's too empty."

"It's just one more night," I reassure her. "I should be back tomorrow sometime, but it'll be late. It's better if we wait until daylight to attack Salem and then it's a twelve-hour drive home." And doesn't include the seven times Mitchell is going to ask to stop for snacks.

I understand a werewolf's metabolism excessively burns through calories and that he cannot help his need to eat more frequently. After all, I am used to stopping for Krista constantly. However, stopping for *him* is unjustifiably maddening in a way that I cannot convince myself otherwise.

She lets out a heavy sigh. "It's going to be a long morning for me. Just waiting. You'll call me as soon as it's over, right?"

"I promise." I will call and I will drive home immediately. I will drive all night if I must. The sooner I am home to her, the quicker I can rid myself of Mitchell altogether.

"I talked to Tara," she tells me with a hint of humor in her voice. "She said you're avoiding her calls."

It's for the best. Right now, I cannot afford to have any distractions that might flare my anger. Not while I'm sitting so close to someone that I would love to take anger out on.

"I'll call her when I get back," I begin, "How is she?"

"Well, she's still pretty mad that we attacked her pack. But I think you might have smoothed that over a bit when you ditched Roddy. She's at least pleased that you didn't drag him into the mess you're headed to now. Besides, she's too busy to stay mad. She married Finn this morning so now she is *dating* her husband, which is such a weird thing to say out loud. I think Tara has enough on her plate right now that you probably don't need to dodge her calls anymore."

I smile to myself. Even if Tara is no longer angry, I will still wait to talk to her. There's no need to risk her wrath just yet.

"But, maybe, you should still avoid Roddy's because I'm sure he is still pretty peeved about it," she adds with a light giggle.

"Yeah, well, it was necessary."

"Oh, I'm sure it was. What about my brother? You haven't ditched him yet, right?"

As much as I would like to, I still need someone as a backup in case I do fail.

I click my tongue. "Oh, man. I knew I forgot something."

Despite her giggle, she tells me mockingly, "Ha, ha, you're so funny. Maybe that's why it has taken you five hundred years to find a girlfriend who will actually put up with you."

I chuckle to myself. "Ouch. That hurt."

She laughs lightly. "Liar." With a smile in her voice, she shifts directions. "So where is my brother? I don't hear his big mouth."

"He's bound and gagged in the backseat," I jest.

"Mm hm," she says disbelievingly.

This trip has been going much smoother than I expected. I mean, it would have been smoother with him bound and gagged in the backseat. And I'll still be glad to be rid of Mitchell tomorrow, once we get back. However, he has been much more obedient than I expected, very much like the well-trained pup I know he isn't.

"It's not been too bad. He surprisingly has slept a lot of the trip so that has been helpful," I tell her honestly.

Krista giggles lightly on the other end of the phone. "You think he's asleep, do you?"

Well, I certainly did but the sound of her giggle has me doubting myself.

"I guarantee he's been faking most of the time. Mitchell doesn't require any more sleep than I do. He's pretending to sleep so he can avoid talking to you. He used to do it to me all the time when I was little and obnoxious."

Faking being asleep. That cheeky bastard. Still, I suppose it is better than speaking to him for the entire car ride. Besides, I refuse to believe there was ever a time in which Krista could be annoying. I decide not to fixate on it.

Instead, I let the humor in her voice force a grin onto my face. "Well, I suppose I'm grateful for the silence either way."

Grateful for the quiet that has comforted me for the past few hours. And grateful that Mitchell understood as much as I do that his silence has increased his very chance at surviving our trip together.

That thought, however, is not necessary and certainly not prudent to say to the woman I sleep next to. So, I keep it to myself.

I do not wish to discuss Mitchell over the phone for the entire time

I have with Krista anyway, so I change the subject into something much more pleasant.

"Do you remember that time we stayed on a boat in the Mediterranean?"

Three weeks on a yacht and I just so happened to forget our phone chargers. She didn't believe that was accident then and she still doesn't. Although, I have never admitted to it, it wasn't. No calls. No interruptions. No wolves checking in… Bliss.

She giggles lightly as she remembers. "And you got your foot tangled and fell overboard. Then you tried to tell me it was on purpose because the water was so perfect."

"That water was perfect," I tell her.

"Yeah, it was," she says quietly, her mind fading away into a thought.

She is quiet for a moment, lost in the sweetness of her memories. Then with a quiet sigh, she adds softly, "I miss you."

"I miss you, too. One more day," I tell her as the city limit sign reflects in my headlights. "Hey, I just made it to Laramie, so I really do have to go. But I will call you when I'm on my way home."

"Okay. Talk to you soon."

"Very soon."

As I hang up the phone, I look at Mitchell pretending to be asleep. He looks somewhat peaceful—so much so, that his sleep may even be genuine. But whether he is truly asleep or simply faking, my actions will remain the same.

I slam on the brakes. Mitchell flings forward, nearly smacking his face on the dash.

He looks at me startled and unsure if he should be angry, and I cannot stop my impish smirk. "There was a deer," I lie.

Without believing me, Mitchell shifts himself in his seat irritably.

I park along the sidewalk near the bar that I need for my plans. "You remember what you're supposed to do?"

He nods. "Deception opens doors. Blah, blah, blah."

He tosses my own words at me like they are an exaggeration, but deception grants permission. And I need permission to enter the house that will give me Salem.

"Exactly." I stop the car, parking along the sidewalk, and turn toward him in my seat. "Remember, I only need three minutes. Stick to the script because if you tip them off and you blow this for me, I will feed you to them," I tell him flatly.

"Got it," he says dismissively as though he either does not believe I would leave him to die or as though he will not fail enough to find out.

Getting out of the car, I pull my coat up around myself and start toward the bar down the street. As I approach, I watch the humans spill out of the door of the two-story building. With brick on the second floor, the green paint of the lower level stands out in the night. The yellow lettering, reminiscent of days past, holds onto the historic charm the Buckhorn bar began with.

Pushing past the crowd near the door, I walk up to the bar. Leaning against the counter, I glance around at the walls that are heavily adorned, practically littered with taxidermy. A duck of some type forever frozen in flight. An elk staring back at me, forever keeping its secrets in a silent gaze.

As the bartender scans the room, I wave at him to get his attention. He walks toward me but as he approaches, a second, more captivating bartender cuts him off.

"I got this one, Heath," she says as she slides a glass in front of me. Smiling at me flirtatiously, she pours my drink as she confirms what she already knows. "Bacardi Black, no ice."

The male bartender shakes his head to himself, undoubtedly believing I am under the misguided notion that less ice equates to more alcohol but I am not that foolish. Nor do I care about the amount of alcohol in my glass. I cannot drink it. I can only smell it, inhale the scents of my past. Ice only serves to dilute the memories.

He may not realize this, but she does.

The pale brunette leans against the bar, knowing full well that it accentuates every curve she intends to flaunt as I stare at her familiar face.

"Miranda." Smiling wide, I let out a huff of air as though I am wonderfully surprised by her presence. "I was not expecting you to be here but I am so very pleased that you are."

That's lie. I did expect her. And she is exactly where I expected her to be and doing exactly what I expected she would do.

Playfully jeering, she raises her eyebrows. "Oh, how sweet, you remember my name."

I ignore Mitchell as he slinks in close, keeping himself along the wall near the door. Keeping my voice deep and even, I raise my eyebrows as tell her in a provocative tone, "Well, you were very memorable."

I lift the glass toward my mouth, lingering near my lips so that I can absorb the boldness of the rum. Closing my eyes, I inhale the rich oak from the barrel it was aged in. The savory, sweet molasses with hints of vanilla dancing within the intricacies of the aroma.

Her cool fingers graze over mine on the glass and I open my eyes to see her face near mine with only the glass in my hand between us. "I still am," she whispers.

I watch her for a moment from the tops of my eyes. She believes that I am dreaming of what I might do to her. And I am. It just so happens to be far from what she is thinking about doing. Still, I need her to buy what I am selling.

So, in a silky-smooth voice, I reply, "I bet you are."

My unwavering stare coaxes her to bite her lip. "A man with smile like yours could slay a thousand hearts."

"I'm not here for your heart, Miranda."

Like a cat playing with a mouse, she asks me suggestively, "What are you doing in Laramie?"

"Treaty negotiations with the wolves. Laramie is just neutral ground." I trail my fingers along her elbow as I add, "But I'm not opposed to a little reminiscing, if you're feeling nostalgic."

I let my gaze roll over her body, making it obvious that I aim to go home with her. Why I want inside her home is a nothing more than a lie; however, it is one lie that I need her to believe without question.

"You know me, I'm a sucker for making the same mistakes twice," she says with a mischievous grin.

I chuckle to myself lightly. "It was more than twice."

Leaning over the counter closer to me, she lays her hand on my chest, asking me with steam in her tone, "So once you get done walking the dogs, what exactly do you want?" Her hand slides along my neck, pulling herself further across the bar toward me. "My bed?" Leaning her mouth close to my ear, she asks, "My body?"

She glides her tongue along my jaw to my ear and drags her teeth, pulling at my earlobe.

Years ago, my heart would be racing in anticipation of an evening promising to be filled with blood and sex but that was before Krista. And despite how wrong this feels, I must play my part until I get what I need from her.

I move my hand to cradle her face, letting my thumb glide over her cheek as I whisper, "Covered in blood."

She lets out a hungry laugh. "Just like old times?"

I tilt my head to the side with a smirk. "Not exactly. I've learned a few things since then."

Her eyebrow arches with interest at my indirect challenge. "So, have I. Do you want the address?"

I side-eye Mitchell so she will take notice of him. Then looking back at her, I shake my head dismissively as though I don't want the werewolves to have her address. "I'll find you."

Resting her hands on my chest, she looks at me temptingly. "I always did like being hunted."

"I remember." I let the playfulness of my smile fade, leaving only determined hunger. "Someone better let me in when I get there."

"Just come on inside. But Vincent,"—she smiles with greedy expectancy, pulling her face toward me until her lips are nearly touching mine—"don't keep me waiting too long."

Leaning back, she taps her finger on the tip of my nose as she adds, "Oh, and um, happy hunting."

Smirking anticipatingly, she watches me as she walks toward another customer.

I leave my drink on the bar and walk toward Mitchell, smiling to myself. I got it. The invitation that I needed to enter her house, which happens to be a pivotal element to my loosely detailed plan.

As I pass him, I nod for him to follow me into the cool night outside. He pushes off the wall with a heavy sigh but, at least, he does follow.

He crosses his arms over his chest but it is not the crisp air that is biting at him so badly. "Subtle," Mitchell snaps cynically under his breath as we walk toward the car.

"It wasn't meant to be. I am in Laramie for one day and one night exactly. I do not have time to play coy," I tell him, being cautious not to say anything that would give away our real intentions to any patron who might overhear us.

"Is this your car?" I ask condescendingly as we approach the sedan, still pretending to not know Mitchell as well as I do.

"It's subtle," he says snidely, as he walks around the back of the car.

"It's sad," I tease.

Stopping by the driver's door, he replies irritably to me, "Just being around you makes me want to stab my own eyes out."

"You should then. Don't let me get in your way," I say, putting my hands up like a surrender.

Huffing loudly, he opens his door. "Just get in the car."

*   *   *

The car ride had been quiet, and I was glad for it. I spent most of my time looking out of the window, trying to forget the way Miranda caressed me. The lingering filth her touch left on my skin was different than I am used to.

I have flirted with humans to gain my meal but this felt too real. Perhaps it was because I already knew her once before or perhaps it was because Mitchell was watching, keeping me grounded in one world while I was tiptoeing in another.

Either way, I know what will make me feel better. Once I have bathed in Miranda's blood, the necessity of my actions will become undeniable. Washing away the grime, her blood will cleanse my skin until I no longer feel soiled.

Parked along a road with the engine off, the silence grows as I wait for the right time to enter her home to arrive.

"I know you have to be invited in that house," Mitchell starts softly. "I just don't think I could do what you did. The way you flirted with that girl. You're a better liar that than I am. I couldn't do that to Renee."

I look at him gently. He could. If it meant saving Renee, he would be surprised what he is capable of.

"It isn't a skill you should aim to perfect," I tell him passively. "There are only a couple of reasons a vampire will ask to enter another vampire's house. Sex just happens to be the easiest reason to sell."

It gives me a believable reason to be knocking on her door tonight and removes her reservations about letting me in. Given our history, this was a particularly easy lie to weave.

"I get that. But what if she wanted to take you right then? Like in the bathroom or something? How far would have been willing to go to get permission to enter this house?"

"Not that far." I look at him exasperatedly. That's the only reason I had Mitchell come inside at all. He was my excuse to bail without being suspicious if things escalated. The fact that he cannot see how obviously engineered my entire conversation with Miranda had been simply proves how short-sighted Mitchell truly is.

However, knowing that he is ignorant and brash does not make his accusatory comments any less irritating and I let my frustration show in my tone, "I wouldn't have let Miranda so much as kiss me without slitting her throat. The one thing you never have to question is my loyalty to your sister." Murder is forgivable, affairs are not.

One of my more important jobs is to prevent Krista from getting hurt, especially by me. I love her more than words can ever express, and I will never stop trying to prove that to her. But I have absolutely nothing to prove to Mitchell.

"Besides, it wasn't a concern because I happen to be smart enough to know exactly who I am manipulating. Miranda would never have sex in a dirty bathroom."

"Is she too classy for that?" Mitchell says sarcastically.

"Too discreet." My frustration makes the car seem suddenly tight as I shift in my seat. "Miranda brings food to bed, always. And she happens to be quite messy. A public restroom is just that, public. She would wait for me to come to her house, which is exactly where I need to be, which is exactly why I chose to play *her* the way I did. Do you understand, or is that too complex for you?"

Mitchell raises his eyebrows, nodding to himself as though my words stung as much as I meant for them to.

"I was just checking," Mitchell says irritably defensive. Only a blind fool would need to check. "She is still my sister, you know?"

"I haven't forgotten." It is the sole reason Mitchell still breathes, but there is no need to point that out right now. "No matter how little you think of my kind, we are capable of knowing how to love someone more than ourselves."

But that isn't entirely true. Vampires tend to be very selfish partners.

Mitchell stares back at me, silently, for a moment. Whatever trivial nonsense rattles through his head, he keeps to himself. And that's all for the better.

I grow tired of his childish games and questions. There is real work to be done and his drivel is nothing more than distraction for the task at hand.

Looking at the clock on the radio, I tell him quietly, "It's time."

Nodding, he gets out of the car as I grab a small dagger from the glovebox.

"Are you sure all of the vamps will be in the house?" Mitchell asks as I walk toward him.

Of course, I am. Otherwise, I would not have suggested this moment, no matter how badly I wanted out of that car.

As he pulls off his shoes and tosses them in the backseat next to his shirt, I indulge him. "This close to sunrise all the vampires will be home or staying where they are. There will be no unexpected guests, and if anybody happens to escape, the sun will force them to hunker down and hide. They will be no threat to us until night falls again. But by then, we will be gone."

Mitchell's eyes drift to the side as he nods to himself. He isn't nervous, simply processing his role in what we are about to do.

"Where do you want the claw marks?" he asks me quietly.

"Across the face," I tell him, touching my cheek with the dagger. "It has to look real."

Slipping off his pants, he tosses them in the backseat and shuts the car door. "Let's not tell Krista that it was me who scratched your pretty face," he jokes.

"You think I'm pretty, that's sweet," I tease. With a light laugh, I add with a smirk, "Besides, I tell Krista everything, except… I might leave out that the scratches were my idea."

Mitchell rolls his eyes. "Just get ready to run, little leech," he jabs indifferently, but hidden behind the flatness of his tone there is a hint of playfulness.

I smile to myself as he rolls his neck as though he needs to loosen his muscles and shakes his shoulders out, preparing to shift from a vulgar, contemptible human into a formidable beast.

His eyes flash open and they are no longer soft or human. Bright yellow eyes stare back at me for a mere moment before a growl rips out of him, forcing him to the ground onto all fours. He does not take long for him to shed his human form. Like a snake casting off its skin, his fur pushes the old version of himself free from the new.

His growl becomes animalistic and deep as his hands expand to compensate for his new paws. Controlling the transition between wolf and human forms equates to controlling the pain that can lie there. Willing shifts appear nearly painless, almost beautiful in the lack of violence. The wolf wants to be free. It encourages it with an effortless shift. It is the attempt to hold a wolf back that can break a man.

His hot breath fogs the night air as he exhales, gathering himself and his thoughts as they settle into his wolf state. He shakes his rust-colored fur as though to scatter the very remnants of his human from his mind.

Orange and brown like an autumn sky, his fur echoes the abundance of a harvest. But not simply the healthy fullness of a harvest but also the decay of things past their prime. The contrasting sentiments that his rust color evokes is almost pleasant.

The last time I saw his fur, we were surrounded by flames. It was the night I watched my mother die in my arms. But I cannot dwell on that now. There is simply too much that requires my complete attention tonight.

I attempt to force the consuming memory of losing Marcella back into the refuge of my mind as quickly as it appeared. But even the brief flicker of that moment forces a hard lump in my throat and a heaviness to begin to settle in my chest.

I attempt to clear my throat of the dry, uncomfortable tightening sensation but it is to no avail. I will simply have to deal with it until I can successfully distract myself with the events that are about to unfold.

Refusing to let Mitchell see the emotion his wolf stirs in me, I look at him callously. "Get on with it, whelp."

In an instant, he lunges at me, swinging his claws in one wide stroke. They cut into me, slicing deep grooves along my cheek. The air burns against my open flesh but still, I do not move. This wound was my idea. It must be convincing.

The attack, regardless of intention, forces my own brutish monster to the surface. My eyes glaze over into a black abyss, reflections as hollow as the space where my soul once resided.

My fangs extend, pressing against my lip with a hungry vengeance. My fingernails grow into claws, sharp as obsidian, longing for the chance to cover themselves in crimson.

I flip the dagger over my fingers, feeling the coolness of the blade roll over my skin as I kneel down in front of Mitchell's wolf.

With my face level with his, I catch the handle of the dagger in my palm. "That will do, doggie. Now, let's have some real fun."

I let a cold smile spread across my face and dig my shoes into the soft dirt as I turn to make a sprint toward the house several miles away.

I can feel the sun rising, urging me to hide despite its lack of control over me. Centuries of potential destruction bred into my blood still seeks out the threat of day. I can feel the shift from dark to light within me like the ticking of clock.

But I do not hide from the sun. Today, the sun is my friend; my ally to imprison the vampires in their home where an inescapable end is coming for them as quickly as this sunrise.

My feet push through the lush grass as I cross the field toward their house with Mitchell following close behind.

"Open the door," I call loudly, knowing that any vampire inside will be able to hear me.

Miranda would have told them to let me in, so no matter who opens that door, nobody will question why I am here or whether I am to be trusted enough to help. After all, they are expecting me.

Unsuspecting of my true intentions, a man opens the door and waves me toward him. "Hurry!"

Without slowing my pace, I rush past him, and slide across the floor on my side. I shove the dagger into the wooden planks of the floor to stop myself and use it to pull myself up in one seamless motion.

Lunging toward the vampire who had let me in, I bury the blade in his back. He screams in pain and disbelief. He knew I was coming here but he did not expect my betrayal. I pull the dagger from his back and kick him outside just as Mitchell closes in.

Mitchell jumps at the vampire, sinking his teeth into his face and pulls him to the ground. The vampire's punctured lung will hinder him but he will still be able to put up enough fight to stall Mitchell outside. The less vampires Mitchell fights, the better chance he has of surviving.

And even though I would not miss him, I am still obligated to return him to Bryant, alive.

I close the door as a blonde vampire rushes me, swinging wildly at me. Blocking her, I move one of her arms aside as she throws a second punch with her other hand. She is young and has not been trained, which I use to my advantage and easily block her again.

Grabbing her arm, I slam her back against the wall and sink the dagger into her throat until the blade taps into the wall behind her. Her eyes widen as blood chokes from her lips, spilling over my wrist.

Hearing another vampire moving upstairs, so I know I must end my attack with this blonde quickly. I pull the dagger from her throat and plunge it into her ribs, twisting it before I pull it back out. With four more rapid jabs, I leave her panting for air as blood curdles in her lungs.

Before I can finish her, the second vampire emerges on the stairs. He is a beast of a man with black eyes and even darker hair. Throwing the knife, I lodge it deep in his chest. The force knocks him back onto the steps. He rips the dagger from his muscles with an angry roar.

I scan the room for something that might be of use and my eyes land on the broom tucked just inside the doorway to the kitchen. After tossing the female vampire to the ground, I grab the wooden broom leaning against the refrigerator and snap the brush end off. A pointed, sharp end is much more useful than dirty bristles.

He rushes toward us as I stake the tapered end of the broom through the blonde vampire's stomach as she lies on the floor. Holding the handle, I use the broom as leverage to support my body as I kick him in the chest with both feet, sending him flying across the room.

I land on my feet, pulling the handle from her stomach and spinning it around to strike a human in the face as he rushes in, desperate to save the vermin he calls master. The cracking sound of the wood is little compared to the shattering of the bones in his face collapsing with the impact.

His body trembles on the floor. Although the human is not quite dead, there is no worry that he will get back up again. He will lie in his pain until he slips into the comfort of his death. He may not realize it as he lies on the floor unconsciously quivering, but my actions are a kindness for him. In death, he will no longer be plagued by monsters that creep in the night. In death, he can find his freedom.

The male vampire jumps at me with the dagger that I had thrown at him moments ago. Swinging the broom handle around like a staff, I strike the vampire across his knuckles. He cries out but does not drop the dagger. With another swing of the handle, I crack the wooden rod into his stomach, knocking him to the ground.

He finds his footing quickly, and charges at me once more. Sweeping the handle around, I take his legs out from under him and he crashes to the ground once more. I use the opportunity to shove the spiked end of the handle into his chest. This time, I do not miss his heart. Blood pools around the handle for mere seconds before his body fades to ash.

My fingers sift through the dusty rubble that used to be a man until they touch on the cold metal of a blade. Picking up my old dagger, I can hear more vampires stirring awake. The blonde vampire's chest heaves with gurgled, drowning breaths. I kneel close to her. Stabbing the dagger into her chest, I watch her melt away just as her partner had.

The creaking of wood above me urges me to look up at the large landing at the top of the stairs. Miranda glares down at me. Her black eyes lock to mine as a large man rushes past her and jumps from the second-floor landing onto his feet in the living room with me. His bald head shines briefly in the light from a floor lamp before he grabs it, jerking the plug from the wall.

I throw the dagger at the male vampire, striking him in the arm as I start up the stairs. Miranda rushes toward me but I do not plan on staying in this staircase for long. As the man pulls the dagger from his arm, crying out to release the pain, I leap onto the chandelier. Using it to propel myself over his head. I drop to the floor behind him.

I kick him in the spine, and he lurches forward, loosening his grip on the lamp. I rip it from his hands as he steadies himself. He springs toward me and I hit him in the chest with the broad base, knocking him back a step. Then, flipping the rod over my hands, I slam the base upward into his chin. Blood spatters into the air as his face is thrown back.

I swing the lamp around to strike him in the ribs, like one would strike a ball with a bat when I feel the sudden, cold plastic of the cord around my throat.

Miranda's feet press into my back as she uses her body to add pressure to the cord. I drop the lamp but only to claw at the cord as it slices into my skin. The smell of my own blood penetrates the air as warm fluid rolls over the collar of my shirt.

The bald vampire lunges at me with my dagger in his hand. I grab his arm to keep him from stabbing my heart but the dagger still buries into my abdomen. The pain is instant and burns through me as my blood reaches like fingers, stretching areas it isn't meant to be. If I had any air to let out, it would have come as a scream, but as it is, my breath is trapped.

Mitchell bursts through window and I'm sure he believes I am at a disadvantage. However, I have been in worst situations, and I'm not worried about failing just yet. Still, the surprise of the crashing glass does distract the large male enough for me to kick him in the groin. Hard, extremely hard, in fact.

The vampire doubles over in pain, clutching his groin with both hands. With his face lowered, I kick him in the nose, driving his nasal bones up into his frontal sinus. He snorts as though it might help him to dislodge the fragments of bone from his nostrils. But that is futile at best.

Mitchell pads toward us but I do not need or want his help. Backing up hard, I slam Miranda into the wall behind us. The jolt of our bodies loosens her grip on the cord slightly but it's enough for me to slide my fingers in between the hard cord and my raw, bleeding skin.

I slam my head into her face then pull the cord as I flip her over my shoulder, nearly hitting Mitchell as he sinks his teeth into the bald vampire. Twisting the cord around Miranda's throat like a noose, I swing her body over my head and slam her to the floor, shattering several ribs and dislocating her shoulder.

She moans in anguish, crying out with each breath. Her groans are lost in the shrieking scream of the bald vampire as Mitchell's teeth burns into the flesh, saliva scorching its way into every crevice of his wounds.

The male vampire claws at Mitchell. Grabbing his ear, the bald man pulls Mitchell back enough to wrap his arms around his throat. I know what the bald man is going to do because I have done it before. Crush the larynx and watch the wolf suffocate. It's easy and highly effective against werewolves because unlike vampires, wolves need to breathe.

Despite Mitchell's improvement since our last fight, he still isn't good enough for this fight.

Snatching it quickly from the floor, I swing the lamp into the male, knocking him back a few steps. With a swift kick in the ribs, I knock Mitchell back through the window. I pull the dagger from my abdomen and bury it into the vampire's chest. His body melts away, spilling ash over my hand.

Miranda struggles to lift her broken body from the floor as I walk back to her, wiping bloody ash from my hand on my pants. Without slowing my pace, I grab her by the hair and lift her up against the wall. Clutching her throat, I hold her firmly, pinning her.

Blood rains down in large droplets onto my arm as she coughs with each pained gasp. I plunge my hand deep into her abdomen, extending my hand upward until I wrap my fingers around her heart. With the added pressure of my hand, her breaths reduce to strained wheezing.

Leaning close to her, I whisper quietly, "Such a shame. You really were quite memorable."

Then I close my hand into a fist, crushing her heart. She fades into a pile of dirty ash sliding along the wall to the floor and one clump of ash still in my fist. Opening my blood-streaked hand, I watch as the ash streams from my hand to rejoin the rest of the pile on the floor.

Coming through the front door, Mitchell walks back inside rubbing his badly bruised ribs.

"That hurt," he says in a severe tone.

"Not as much as being killed," I offer back tersely.

The thick coating of Miranda's blood mixes with the ash on my skin and drags down my arm like sludge. Dripping from my fingers, it makes a light plopping sound as it drops to the floor.

Looking over my shoulder, I see Mitchell standing in his human form, staring at me cautiously. He does not appear as though he expects me to attack him. It is likely the simple sight of my black eyes peering out from beyond the ash of former bodies and the crisp crimson painting the room that rattles him.

I keep my voice cold as I ask him, "Are you just going to stand there with your mouth agape or are you going to find some pants to put on?"

His face relaxes into a look of annoyance before he looks at the stairs briefly. "Are you sure there's nobody else here?"

"There are no more vampires," I tell him honestly.

As he starts up the stairs in search of clothes that aren't coated in blood or ash, I add, "But there is a human in the basement."

Mitchell stops on the bottom step. "A sheep?"

A beating heart whose pain creeps through this house like a lowlying fog, covering and touching everything in its wake. Not a sheep.

Not enthralled. Her fear is real, like a rabbit full of constant panic, and it calls to me like a siren.

Not yet. But she will be. "She's a hare. I've never kept one, but I know what they are. She is a human, left alive and aware to endure the pain of bite after bite simply because their fear makes the feedings more fun."

Seriousness scrolls across his brow in a way that is all too easy to read. Surely, he knows my next words but still, they must be said aloud.

"We don't release hares back into the wild. There are two options for her: become a sheep or death." Hares have seen too much and their scars run far too deep to return to the life they once held.

"And since I am in need of a sheep, I'm going to make her mine." Waste not, want not, after all. "It is the closest thing to mercy I can offer her."

He steps down from the stair, his eyes trailing across the room as he considers my words. He can hear the truth in them despite the way his nature wishes to dispute them.

When his eyes meet mine, they are full of sadness yet understanding. "I want to watch," he mumbles in a hushed manner.

But he doesn't want to. He needs to. He needs to see the world his sister lives in, this mercy I speak of, instead of simply the death I so willingly show him.

Letting my eyes shift back into their bright green, I pick up a shirt from the floor. I shake the ash that used to be its owner from the fibers and toss it to him gently. "Get dressed."

Chapter 9

As *Mitchell slips the shirt* on quietly, I go to the sink to wash my hands. There is no reason to frighten the girl in the basement any more than she already is. And that is exactly what the blood dripping from my skin would do: frighten her further.

The blood coats the sink red as it swirls into the drain. I do not need to be perfectly clean. Just clean enough to convince her that I did not just slaughter a room of vicious vampires and their subservient human.

I hear his bare feet pad into the kitchen slowly as he attempts to find the clean spaces to step. I turn to see him standing in dusty pants staring toward the corner of the room. With a sober expression, he rubs his thumb over his lip, mulling over what he might see and how that might change him.

I walk over to him. While still stressing the importance of his compliance in my tone, I attempt to be as gentle as possible. "You will wait and watch from the hallway. Say nothing. Not to me and especially not to her. The more people she thinks are in the room, the more scared she will become. I want this to go quickly and calmly."

His eyes only meet mine long enough for him to nod and then drift away once more.

Patting his shoulder, I walk past him and follow the sound of her heartbeat to the basement door. With Mitchell behind me, we start down the stairs into the bitter darkness and toward the hopelessness that inches through the stale air.

Mitchell's feet smack against the stone floor quietly as he follows me through the hallway. With his hand on my shoulder, I guide him through the inky void. His eyes attempt to adjust to the scant light, but there is not enough light for even his werewolf eyes to make out much more than shapes.

Vampires are much more adapted to the black spaces we flourish in. Regardless though, I would not need them to find my way to her. I can feel her gloom. It steers me. Like a moth to a flame, I am drawn to her despair.

As I stop in front of a heavy, wooden door, Mitchell inhales sharply. He can feel the shift in the air around us, the unsettled dread that gathers here and plucks at the hairs on his arms.

The rich burnt color of the iron knob helps to hide the bloody prints, but I can smell them there still. I can hear her soft sobs from inside. Her breathy gasps are faint as she cries.

When I push open the door, I see her much as I expected. Lying in the center of the room on the cold stone floor is a frail woman. Young enough that I am not even sure she qualifies as a woman instead of a child. The life in her is depleted almost as much as her blood has been. She is not dead, but she longs to be.

There is not much furniture in the room to speak of, only one faded dresser along the wall with a small lamp struggling to cast a dim light for her. Even still, that single piece is out of her reach. Heavy chains weigh down her weakened body as the cuffs rub against old cuts they have worn into her wrists.

The only kindness they have offered her are a few dirty blankets that she is far too exhausted to even reach for. Her fiery hair is dull with dirt and oil. Caked in blood, it covers her face from view so much that even if her eyes were open and the lighting better, she would not be able to see us standing there.

Quietly, I step into the room. Mitchell stays in the shadows of the doorway as I had instructed him but I do not believe my words are what keeps him there. He stares at her, the grief in his eyes almost palpable.

This woman, cradled on the floor, is not what he was expecting, and the horrors of this situation imprint into his mind. Coming any closer to her would only make this moment more real, more immovable in his memories.

The salty scent of sweat clouds the already stifled air as I make my way quietly toward her. This is not sweat that is produced from exertion, however. This is different. It is the smell of fever. Sweat produced from a body fighting and losing. Sweat freezing to her stained skin in the cold air.

Letting my voice quiver with a false vulnerability, I sound nervous as I stammer out, "Hello?"

Her head raises quickly, fear pushing new raw energy into her body. As she scrambles into a seated position, her breath quickens, and I raise my hands to show her I mean no harm.

Letting my voice replicate the fear I feel radiating from her, I lie to her in a shaky voice, "It's okay. I won't hurt you."

Her eyes snap up to the ceiling like a rabbit listening for a predator, wildly anxious and alert.

I keep my eyes wide as though I am terrified by what I see. However, torment is not foreign to me the way it would be to a human and the horror in my face is a fraud.

Lowering my hands slowly, I ask in a calming tone, "Is there a key?"

I already know there will be a key. It is most likely stored in the dresser, somewhere in sight but not within reach. It is kept close to taunt her, to let her see that her freedom is close but that it is never within reach.

I do not need the key to remove the cuffs, but a human would. And currently, I prefer her to believe that I am human so that I may get close to her without causing any additional panic. Even though the added fear would improve the taste of her blood, this particular human has suffered enough.

The bright red of the busted vessels in her green eyes does very little to mask the fear as she lifts her puny arms and nods toward the dresser.

As I walk toward the dresser, she allows the weight of the cuffs to pull her wrists to the floor once more. The chains clang against the stone tiles. Her body is as tattered and thin as the gown that loosely hangs from her. Dirty and torn, the gown is much larger than she needs. However, it is likely the size she wore when she was placed here to starve and die a slow, tragic death.

I take the key from the drawer and watch as she musters the strength to lift her cuffs toward me. From some deep place inside of her that still longs to survive this, still wants to continue her existence despite all that she has been though, she mutters in a low, hushed voice, "Help me."

Her voice is feeble, like a stag teetering on the edge of complete collapse. Her words pull at a cut on her lip uncomfortably, opening slightly in the middle once more. The smell of the infection from her lip wafts into the air as I kneel down in front of her.

Her only words to me, pleading for pity, but I can only offer the peace that being a sheep can bring her.

Gently, I take her forearm in my hand as though I am planning to unlock the cuff. With the key in my fingers, I hesitate. I look at her battered face, letting the atmosphere quiet around us. She looks up at me, trembling. However, I am unsure of whether it is trepidation or the damp, chilling air that has her shaking so.

Her eyes meet mine and I have her. Locked in a calm enthrallment, she is mine and her body begins to relax even before I speak. So long as her eyes are locked on mine and I keep contact with her skin, I can hold this temporary entrancement. I can sway her thoughts with my very words, hearing them as if they were her very own. Like her brain is being paused and permitting me to play out a daydream of my design.

As long as she is under my control, she will not panic. Even if I explain what was about to happen, she would only be accepting. I do not always enthrall my sheep before changing them. I must admit, I enjoy when they struggle against me. However, there is only limited pleasure in crushing something that is already so broken.

Leaning my face close to her, I whisper slowly, keeping my tone soft and even, "You can trust me. I am going to make you forget any of this ever happened. Do not fight me. Just let me help you."

I keep my eyes green and my fingernails short as they must be for this type of thing, but my fangs extend out. Still locked on my eyes, she is unmoved. Her brain does not process the creature sitting in front of her. Her only thought is how this fanged beast will save her from this terrible place.

I move my lips to the base of her neck, and for a brief moment when my eyes no longer meet hers, she is set free of my enthrallment. My words still swirl in her mind, however, reassuring her that she wants my help no matter how frightful it may be.

Her skin snaps against my fangs as they sink into her skin and a rush of blood fills my mouth. Her breaths become quick and irregular, but she does not push away from me. She trusts that I can take her from this pain—and I will.

Drinking, I allow her blood to ease the burning in my throat long enough to mark her as mine. Long enough to tie her energy and life to my own. But not so long that I might risk her death.

Her body grows limp in my arms and she slumps against me as she fades into unconsciousness. Stopping myself there, I gently lay her limp body on the cold floor. Resting like this, she is much more peaceful, her soul has grown quiet, and her eyes flutter as though the sweetest dreams comfort her once more.

I remove the cuffs from her arms and pick her up. I will still need to call her to me to complete the process of making a sheep. I could leave her here for that but I won't. This dank basement is no place for any creature of mine.

As I walk past Mitchell, I hear him ask in a small voice, "Is she dead?"

If she were, I wouldn't be bringing her upstairs. What would be the point? "No. Only resting."

He follows after me with his brow furrowed, still disturbed by what he has seen. "So, she'll be a sheep when she wakes up?"

"Yes and no. There's a little more I need to do, but now that it's started, she won't wake up again until the process is complete."

In fact, if I were unable to complete the next steps, she would never wake and she would remain consoled by her dreams until she effectively starved to death.

I can hear his lips smack as he purses them. Gathering his thoughts, he lets out a forceful exhale.

"Are you all right back there?" I half-jest as we climb the dimly lit stairs.

"Yeah," he starts unconvincingly. "Has Krista ever seen you *make* a sheep?"

I could point out how foolish this question is since Julia was my sheep when we met and I have not made another until today. But Mitchell's voice still sounds rattled and uneasy.

Going against my natural reaction to call out his stupidity, I simply tell him, "No. I've explained it though."

The light from the living room illuminates my new sheep's skin in an eerie way. Malnutrition has grayed her skin into a deathlike wanness making this limp and lifeless body appear to be nothing more than a literal ghost of her former self.

Curiosity lightens up Mitchell's tone a bit as he asks, "You've told her everything about it?"

No, not everything. Only the relevant parts.

Nodding toward the couch that had somehow been pushed over, I instruct him, "Flip the couch up."

He hurries to it almost eager to have something useful to do as I add lightheartedly, "I have found that it is best to be honest with your sister. When I lie, she always finds out and she gets very angry."

Mitchell chuckles without meeting my eyes as though he is somewhere in his mind remembering his own encounter with her anger.

I lay the woman on the couch carefully. She cannot feel any pain in this state but it seems natural to be delicate with such a fragile looking thing.

Mitchell shifts uncomfortably as though what he is about to say offers him some difficultly. "Roddy told us about Krista killing Tara's alpha. That her eyes changed like a wolf, but that she was still human. Is that right?"

"Yeah." I push her hair, clumped and matted with dirt and blood, to the side.

"That's not something she should have been able to do."

My eyebrows come together. Shouldn't have been *able* to do? Even without understanding what his words mean, the statement alone sparks both curiosity and my defensiveness. Krista may be a wolf but she can do anything she damn well pleases. Small-minded dogs like Mitchell should be leery of supposing anything different.

Knowing that my defensive anger is premature doesn't hinder it from growing inside me. I keep my eyes on the girl in front of me, willfully stifling my instinct to voice my opinions.

Thankfully, Mitchell continues before I can, "Our eyes turn and our bodies don't only if we tap into our partner's strength. It's not like siphoning power, it's more like sharing in it; but it's only something that bonded or married wolves are able to do."

His words cool the heat that was eager to flare but I do not meet his eyes. I am lost somewhere in my thoughts. Krista is neither of those. Wolves cannot bond to vampires, and we certainly aren't married. I would have noticed if we were.

"So, what exactly are you trying to tell me?" I ask Mitchell flatly. I may not be as angry as I was just a moment ago but I am also not in the mood for stringing out a full conversation with Mitchell.

"My father has said for years that the two of you are bonded and he believes the change in her eyes proves it. I think it's why I'm here, so I could see for myself."

See what? Whether we've bonded. Thinking that her wolf would choose and bond, irreversibly to a vampire, is an impossible scenario.

With an exasperated sigh, I ask in a tone that only barely covers my annoyance, "Okay, well, if your father thinks we've bonded, why he hasn't given me his blessing?"

Withholding a blessing, while believing that his daughter is stuck in a relationship for life, is one of the most petty and ridiculous things I have ever heard of. How can Bryant pretend to love Krista while perpetrating such selfishness?

"You're not waiting on his blessing; you're waiting on mine." His words stop the air around me, like suddenly entering a tunnel. No breath leaves my body, no sounds echo in this house filled with death.

As he continues, I'm glad to have my eyes on the girl so he cannot see my face as his words twist around me, choking the air from my chest and leaving disdain in its place.

"For big decisions, my dad will ask his most trusted council to vote. It has to be unanimous and I'm the only one still voting no."

There is a part of me, albeit a small part, that appreciates his candor.

But a much larger part is fixated on the image of removing Mitchell's spine for all of the wasted years he has caused me. Mitchell has effectively been a roadblock on my path to everything I could ever want. A roadblock that would not be very difficult to remove.

"I think he sent me with you to change my mind."

I stand up to face him but am careful not to stand too close. The heat swelling in me makes it difficult to resist the urge to end his babbling. It would be easy from this distance. Mitchell is utterly useless to me anyway.

As much as I would like to close the distance and stand intimidatingly close, I stay here, a few steps back, where I can at least pretend that I tried to avoid the temptation.

"And? Has your mind been changed? Have you deemed me worthy yet?" My words come out icy and flat, lacking the condescending tone I intended so much that even an idiot like Mitchell can hear the anger stifled in them.

Mitchell puffs his chest slightly, annoyed that I am provoked. "No, you're not worthy. You're not half as good as my sister deserves."

I let out a frustrated chuckle, rubbing my hand over my mouth and trying desperately to hold back the words that fill my mind. Such a pious little pup.

"But…" he trails off bitterly. With a reluctant sigh, he shakes his head in defeat. "I do think it's possible that just because I don't want to believe it or even understand it, for whatever reason her wolf chose you and there's no reversing that. It's done. I don't get a choice. So, for me to continue to hold out, hoping she will choose another, is pointless."

His words halt the anger that was brewing inside me in an instant. My throat suddenly feels very dry, not like the burning of thirst I am used to; but dry, like a desert at high noon. Chills form along my arms, pricking at the hairs and urging them to stand as my skin becomes alive with nervous energy.

I am nervous.

His next words are imperative to how the rest of this trip is going to go. I am hesitant that he will offer the chance to marry Krista. I have been waiting to hear those words for so long that my parched mouth might just kiss him if he were to say them now. Well, I wouldn't actually kiss him but I would be overwhelmed, to say the least.

However, if he fails to say something of any use for me, it might just push me over the edge. The sudden rush of anger will undoubtedly flood back into me and make it very easy to remove him as an obstacle. Besides, who would know that it was me and not one of these of vampires lying in ash that killed Mitchell? It would literally be my word versus the dead.

And that is a very tempting position to be in.

He continues cautiously as though he recognizes the precariousness of the situation though I am sure he doesn't. Not fully anyway. I doubt he understands how very close he stands to a crossroad. More likely though, the wary sound in his voice is simply a reluctance to saying his next words at all.

"I think a wolf's bond would explain some things, like why she would want to be with you at all, or how she shared your strength the other day. But I also think it explains something else. Why people think you're not as bad as other vampires when we both know you are."

I have no argument. I am not a *good* person—vampires never are. I stand silent, waiting for him to finish his thought which does not take him long.

"I believe she shares her kindness with you. When people see glimpses of humanity, or compassion in you, it's hers. I think she literally makes you a better person."

My eyes drop, but not because I am ashamed. I'm not. I've always known Krista makes me a better person. I just never realized that there might be some other explanation for the tenderness I can feel that has been out of my reach for centuries.

The thought that the light in me belongs to her, as though I am carrying a literal piece of her inside me, is intoxicating.

There is another thought lingering there, however, a less wanting thought. If I share her light, that would mean I might share my darkness with her as well? My own hollow depravity might also be tainting and staining the edges of her.

"When we get back, I'm going to talk to my father and change my vote officially." His words stop my thoughts from going any further down a rabbit hole.

My eyes snap to his. He is serious. He's plans on changing his vote. Despite my best efforts, my face gives me away as a silly, lopsided grin spreads with the tangible hope in the air.

"You have the blessing of our pack, Nick."

I don't even correct him on my calling me Nick. I can't hear it anyway. My body screams for me to hug Mitchell but that goes against every fiber of my being. Plus, I could never live it down.

Instead, I let my smile widen with excitement. Ten years. It's been ten years. Asking, pleading, waiting, resisting killing Mitchell. And now it's here. This is the moment I have waited for.

I purse my lips but I cannot pull the corners of my smile down. There's nothing I can do about it, it is just a big, silly grin sprawled across my face.

"Well, I guess that means I have no choice but to make sure you survive," I half-jest.

Nodding, he replies dryly. "I guess so."

A thought sparks in my mind and my smile twists into a smirk. "You know, legally this means that we're going to be brothers."

Mitchell scoffs lightly to himself, rolling his eyes. "Yeah, well, vampires don't legally exist, so…" he shrugs off the end of his sentence as I chuckle to myself at his obvious discomfort in the idea.

Mitchell shakes his head and asks half-jokingly, "Don't you have something else to do other than stand here and gloat?"

He is right, of course. I do have things that need to be done, but instead of admitting that out loud, I simply nod.

I need to get my sheep ready to take home, and there are still a few hours before I plan to sneak into Salem's house. I want daylight to be completely settled in so that, hopefully, I can catch Salem off guard or even better, asleep. So, in the meantime, the hours should be used prepping my new sheep.

Not only do I need to finish binding her life to mine, my sheep also needs general care. She will need to eat and rest to build up her strength.

She is no good to me in this weakened state. One meal that lasts just a little too long and I would be out searching for a replacement and dumping another body. Neither of which is high on my list of things I want to explain to my future wife.

My future wife. No longer just a wishful statement but now a factual one. I smile to myself once more. I am going to marry her. And soon.

Stopping in the doorway, I look back at Mitchell. He didn't ask for my appreciation, but I know I should offer it to him anyway.

Softening my voice, I start, "Mitchell." He looks at me benignly as though there has never been reason for the hate we currently share. "Thank you," I tell him genuinely.

Mitchell shifts, uneasy by the unfamiliar cordiality between us. "Don't let it go to your head, I didn't do for you."

Nodding to myself, I continue on my way before the moment can turn sour, because with Mitchell, every moment inevitably goes south. Besides, I have plenty of things I need to finish here before I take on Salem, and we are running out of time. The sun is already peeking over the tree line.

As I leave the room, I focus my mind on the tasks at hand. My new sheep will need a name, probably Corrine. She looks something like a Corrine, but I won't know for sure until she's properly bathed. There is too much blood caked in her hair and dirt on her skin to see much of her appearance to say for sure if the name suits her.

I find a quiet bedroom upstairs and close my eyes.

Calling to my sheep is necessary. It is the final step that seals us together and ties any loose ends of our connection, ensuring that she will be my sheep and not just a hollow carcass that never wakes.

Mitchell did not follow me upstairs which is a relief. Without him, I can relax easier.

Calling a sheep can be dangerous. Not because of the act itself. It is the vulnerability of it. In order to bring her to me, I must first go to her. Not physically, that would be too easy.

Sitting quietly, I feel the air around me. Feel for the pulsating ripple of energy that spans from her to me. Like vibrations on a guitar string, her energy shivers against me. Cold and tingling along my skin, her aura plucks at me like a fly caught in a spider's web.

I have done this many times. Navigating through the netting of lingering energies to find my sheep is not difficult anymore. Her mind is open and pulls me like a black hole. I let myself drift along the trail her vitality and essence leads me until I feel myself glide into her mind like passing through water. There is no resistance given by her consciousness because it isn't hers any longer.

Every memory she made with family, every dream for her future, every piece of what made her is gone. She is not her own being any longer. Her mind belongs to me.

Her eyes open wide, but she is under my compulsion and my control. The vision from her human eyes is duller than I am used to, but I can still see Mitchell push himself back, startled. He was not expecting her to awaken quite so suddenly. I suppose I could have warned him—but where is the fun in that?

I flood her mind with images, like a map to where I am. Then, I sever the connection, knowing that she is coming to me. I open my own eyes, my consciousness back inside my own body.

The process always seems strange to people who have never created a sheep. They usually envision some sort of transitional period where my consciousness floats through the house like a ghost that slips into her and possesses her body. But it isn't.

Corrine does not have a consciousness of her own. When I began the process, every fiber of her being was rewired. Her mind, her body, her will, all belong to me. She is not her own being. She is an extension of me.

The walk from the couch to the bedroom upstairs is not far. Knowing that she will be here shortly, I start running her bath. She'll need cleaned to assess her injuries properly. Any that might need stitches or bandages will have to be addressed.

I hear her on the steps as I gather clean clothes from the closet for her. The clothes upstairs are simple, sweaters and jeans. Most likely for their own sheep. Upstairs bedrooms are usually reserved for the food.

I lay a soft pink sweater and a pair of black athletic pants on the bed as she enters. Nothing that will hold her bruised body too tightly for our long drive home.

She smiles at me, a pleasant smile that masks the emptiness which is typical in sheep, and the greed of flames rolls inside my throat. I am not hungry, but that does not simmer the fire. My monster anticipates me feeding. It knows that it's necessary. The final step in creating a sheep. The process begins and ends with a bite.

Now that I can see her better, I can tell that she is barely eighteen. She was just starting to live. Much too young to have her future stripped away in the night. But here we are, alone in this dim bedroom as the sun peeks into the windows at us.

The metallic scent of the old blood that has dried and flaked away clings to her skin as she tilts her head, exposing her neck. Submissive, her mind is willing and eager to please me. Her vein pulses against the skin near the nape of her neck. Drumming both visually and audibly, the throbbing vessels lull me toward her.

Gently, I place my hand along the back of her neck, allowing her head to naturally curve back into my palm and I sink my teeth into her neck. The rush of blood makes it hard to cut my meal off early, but I must. She does not have as much blood to spare as I would prefer. And anemia does nothing positive for the taste.

Corrine is younger than I prefer but beggars can't be choosers. I really did need a sheep and she really did need to forget.

I help her undress and clean herself, careful not to let the soap burn into her cuts. She is capable of adequately cleaning herself, but I want to assess her mottled body thoroughly. Delicately, I rub the sponge over her wounds as I expose them. Only a few cuts will need stitches and I will keep her enthralled while I sew them up. That way, she will not feel the pain of the needle as I stitch her.

Curiosity getting the best of him, Mitchell joins us upstairs after several minutes. He finds himself a spot on the end of the bed to sit and watch us in the adjacent bathroom. He keeps his eyes on the floor as though being near her while she is naked makes him uneasy. However, he refuses to go downstairs, the guard dog in him protesting.

Eventually, I do manage to coax him into fetching her a sandwich as I finish up with her. And once she is sufficiently fed and dressed, I tell her to rest again.

She cannot follow me toward my real goal of finding Salem and her tattered body could use all the rest it can get. Leaving Corrine asleep, I start downstairs and into the sullen basement once more. The time for me to kill Salem has finally come.

The sun is high by now. I can feel the heaviness of day, urging me to bunker down into some bleak crevice of the world despite my ability to walk in it. It is not uncomfortable, simply instinctual. A natural compulsion to bury oneself until the freedom of night lifts at you lightly, whispering for you to feel the chill of the air prick at your skin.

The farther we walk into the basement, the more Mitchell's solemn expression weighs down the corners of his mouth. The scent of rot and death in the stuffy air rubs against him unpleasantly. Like pushing through brambles, each scent scrapes against him harshly. For me, the familiarity of it is soothing, or it would be if I were here for any other purpose.

I used to dream of this. Hunting Salem. Seeing his eyes meet mine from under his dark, curly hair. Seeing the flash of realization when he recognizes his destruction has come at last. To feel his blood dripping from my fangs. To see his ashy remains blow away, disappearing from existence once and for all.

However, it was a dream I no longer believed would come. For years, Salem has been protected by the Genesis. Just out of reach for me to kill. But now, like this, there is something less satisfying about hunting Salem this way. Something almost disappointing.

There was no searching, no uncovering secrets, no months of planning the perfect ambush. It's just 'go to this location and kill this man'; it's too simple, like killing a mouse after it's already stuck in a trap. A lack-luster murder is almost a little sad. Yet, that will not cause me to hesitate to slice his throat from ear to ear.

Kneeling down near the end of the hall, I graze my fingers over the metal lid that is the entrance to the underground tunnel. This connecting tunnel is the main reason I choose this house as my starting point. Salem will not expect an assassin to raise up from the floor beneath his feet.

The lid is round and heavy like a manhole cover. My fingers find the lever lying flat, resting in its locked position, in the space cutout especially for it. Lifting the lever up, I raise it until the metal clicks into place and it stands upright like a handle mounted to the lid.

Not all of the underground tunnels have this type of access. Some are more like doorways and others are closer to storm drains. Escape tunnels like these are meant to be a means of egress during the day-light hours, not be aesthetically useful.

Using the lever as a handle, I slowly turn the lid, unscrewing it from the floor until the lid comes to a stop. The lid would be much too heavy for a human to lift. Even Mitchell would strain before he would undoubtedly manage to remove the cover.

The lid is heavy for me. However, I will not have any significant trouble with it. Besides, I have no desire for Mitchell to see me strain even the slightest under its weight. I lift the lid up and place it on the floor as though it is nothing more than a dinner plate.

There is an earthy scent from the water that escapes as I peer down the dark shaft that awaits me. The metal ladder is beginning to rust but not so much that it will impact the integrity of it.

A knot forms in my stomach as I stare down at the inky water. This is not a weak, mild human I am going to find. It is Salem. This is my moment. One of us will die today.

As Mitchell steps closer to glimpse into the tunnel, I hear him let out an exhale that sounds as if he had been holding his breath.

Surely, he is not nervous for me.

I clap my hand on his shoulder and wait for him to meet my eyes. "Two hours. If I don't make it back by then, burn everything."

He nods but he seems unsure, so I reiterate, "Everything."

This time, he only stares at me. Two hours is more than enough time to reach Salem's house, confront him, and return. Hell, I could probably kill Salem twice in that amount of time. But still, with all the hours of daylight to protect us, why not give myself some wiggle room. Too much time is definitely better than burning to death prematurely.

Climbing into the tunnel, I cannot help but notice that the water is not as deep as I anticipated for this time of year. It will likely get deeper as I go along so I am glad to be wrong in this.

Forgotten in a world without warmth or light, the water is cold as it laps against my skin. As it raises and touches the bottom of my ribs, my breath catches.

Chills form on my arms and I let my eyes glaze onto black. My vision with my green eyes is better than Mitchell's but still, the eyesight from my black vampire eyes is better.

As he drags the heavy cover back over the entrance, Mitchell's grunts echo through the narrow tunnel and disappear in the void that waits for me. He leaves a small open space for a moment longer and looks at me as though he is sealing me inside my own tomb.

Mitchell keeps his voice low, saying grimly, "Good luck." And just like that, he finishes closing the cover over me and my only source of light is extinguished.

Alone in the midnight darkness, the tunnel feels like a catacomb. The walls, neatly stacked bricks of old stones, are coarse to touch. Only the moss and slimy algae dare to soften them. Straight and strong, the walls reach up to a low, arched ceiling, not much taller than me at its highest in the middle.

Trudging through the frigid water, even my vampire eyes have a difficult time making out the walls. I run my fingers along the gritty stone simply to keep my bearings.

By the time the water reaches higher onto my chest, the tunnels begin to branch in three directions. I keep to the far right knowing that Salem's safehouse will not be much further.

The water deepens as I progress toward Salem's. Eventually, it becomes easier to swim than it is to walk, so I submerge myself and start down the correct tunnel.

Vampires do not need to breathe, though we do prefer to. Breathing is more comfortable than not. Swimming underwater allows me to get closer to Salem's home without any added sounds bouncing throughout these narrow tunnels. And right now, I will take all the advantages I can get.

The water floods my ears and clouds my hearing as I glide along. Nearly blinded in the stygian deluge, I feel my way along the bottom, careful not cause more than a ripple on the water's surface.

Knowing I will soon approach Salem's entrance, I drag my hand along the wall, feeling for the ladder. The metal is somehow colder than the water against my already numbed fingers as I grab hold of the bars.

Climbing, I rise out of the water slowly, being sure that not even the slightest splashing echoes as an alarm. My shirt drips but that sound is lost in the other ambient tapping of water that is constant here.

This lid is just as heavy but fortunately not as rusted as the previous one. This cover twists open without creaking or grinding against itself in protest. Laying the lid gently on the floor, I climb the rest of the way into the basement hallway.

There is no need for invitation into this house. As a safehouse, all vampires are welcome here. That open invitation is likely what led Salem here in the first place. No vampire who wishes to remain alive would let him hide out with them, not with the Genesis hunting him. He probably hoped that staying here alone, he could go undetected for longer than he had.

While the open invitation may have been convenient for Salem, it is also a liability since it indiscriminately lets killers like me inside as well.

On the walls, I see his attempt to keep the others out. Haphazardly painted in a barrage of different colors are crosses. Big and little, painful strokes of paint dashed on the wall by a vampire who could not stand to look at them. My eyes follow the crosses down both walls of the hallway. Like mopping oneself into a corner, these crosses effectively trap Salem upstairs as much as they stop vampires from entering here.

Except, these crosses cannot stop me.

Like the sun, crosses do not hold the same distress they once did for me. No more painful knot forming in both my stomach and throat simultaneously, choking my every fiber. No more pushing against my mind until I am forced to comply and evacuate the premises. All of that disappeared mysteriously along with my inability to walk in the sun.

Touching a cross, however, that is a different story altogether. I still need to be wary of keeping my hands to myself down here.

Walking silently through the hallway, I listen intently for any sounds that Salem may have overheard me sneaking in. As my eyes roam over the walls and doors in this tight hallway, my mind cannot help but to be curious as to what the rooms behind the closed doors might be like.

The hallway itself is much too narrow to bring any large pieces of furniture into the bedrooms here. Perhaps the rooms are large and spacious with inviting warm colors stretching out like a blanket in the grass on a cool summer evening.

More likely though, these rooms match the claustrophobic feeling the hallway invokes and were meant to maximize the number of rooms instead of the comfort of them. After all, this was always meant to be a safehouse and being safe does not require leg room.

I make my way up the stairs, careful that the old wood does not creak under my weight. The closer I get to the door at the top, the more the air shifts around me. Impending doom settles on my skin like the dew of a dreary dawn. Odious and dank, it clings to me uncomfortably and presses an overwhelming dread against my chest.

A vampire is here.

My eyes, still black from the tunnels, adjust to the limited light of the house as I step into a small kitchen. With the lights off and the windows painted black, it would be difficult for a human to see the bistro table along the far wall or the crosses that hang forebodingly, littering the floral wallpaper.

The room is fairly clean with very little dust resting on the light fixture above me. Someone must have been taking care of this home until very recently when Salem moved in. Now, they are probably distancing themselves from the house and, more so, from Salem, in fear of catching the attention of the Genesis.

Walking through the archway leading into a quint dining room, I can hear whispering leaching through the walls from the next room. Low and mostly incoherent, I can only make out fractions of words.

I lean near the wall, careful not to touch the painted crosses, and listen closely. The sounds I can make out are mere fragments of sharp sentences, certainly nothing that would indicate what the person is talking about. There is no need to worry about who they are speaking to, however, because there is only one voice coming from that room.

The smell of death swirls from beneath the door. Not the sweet, comforting aroma of a fresh kill, this death is old and smells of rot.

If I were to guess, humans were dragged in here with him when he holed himself into this house. They would have been made to hang these crosses since Salem's hands could not withstand the burning of even simply grazing his fingers over them. And he probably killed the humans as soon as their task was complete. But why he left their bodies decaying on the floor I cannot begin to understand.

Opening the door slowly, I glance into the room, hoping to have a quick survey of what I am entering before he notices me. The room is not huge, but it is uncommonly large for a house of this size. Along the wall, parallel to the front door, is a grand fireplace straddled by tall bookcases. A fire burns casting the only light in the room. The embers pop, throwing flakes of flame up the chimney as I scan my eyes over the bookcases.

The shelves are brimming with books of all sizes, some stacked across the tops of others just to make them all fit. There are a scattered items wedged between the books on the shelves: a globe, a couple of potted plants desperate for water, a taxidermied owl, and a few other oddities. Otherwise, it is a wall of dusty covers, many of which no longer have the title on the spine.

Facing the fireplace are two dark blue armchairs with a small table between them. The table is littered with leather-bound books nearly pushing the stained-glass lamp onto the floor. Perhaps my mother's journal is there among the loosely tossed books.

The crosses in this room are larger. They press into the air, making it thick to breathe.

"Failed," Salem mumbles in a whisper to himself, directing my attention to him. "Not her… Tried… Tried…"

Sitting on the floor under a particularly large cross, Salem seems too preoccupied to notice me enter. The human lying near his knees is swollen with decay. Salem dips his fingers into the thickened, rancid blood of the body.

Although he only dips his fingers, the sour blood coats Salem's arms passed his wrists as it courses over his skin. He smears the blackened sludge on the wall, writing letters from an alphabet that only exists in his mind.

To stare at him, I can nearly feel pity. These crosses have driven him to the brink of madness. To die like this, wallowing in filth, is not honorable. The lack of honor in his death will certainly detract from the glory of the moment for me.

His curls, once dark and loose, now lie wild and unbrushed. He shakes his head, dismissing whatever his scribbled writings are telling him. As pretentious as it may be, he used to dress like a rock star and his medium build used to stand tall and proud. Now, his frame slumps forward, the weight of his chaotic mind dragging him toward the floor.

"I hoped you'd come," Salem says so quietly that at first, I'm not quite sure if he is talking to me or himself. "I tried to kill her, you know? I tried, I tried, tried, tried, tried," he repeats absentmindedly.

Salem is hiding here because he killed Amelia. It is reasonable to assume that his mind is grasping at thoughts and memories too blurred to make any sense of them. It is just as reasonable, however, to wonder if his murder spree had not been complete. Perhaps, there was another person he wanted to kill before escaping. If that is the case, the name of such a person could be important information to gain.

Either way, I still have just over an hour before Mitchell sets fire to this house so I have plenty of time to find out more. Cautiously, I step closer. "Who did you try to kill?"

He snaps around, half shrieking, "Lilith!" His face twists like an injured animal. Then just as sudden, his face softens and his eyes grow into a wide stare. Whispering, he leans toward me as though he is telling me a great secret, "She lives. I tried... Tried and failed... Failed and tried..."

His words drift anyway into silence as he turns again toward the wall.

I should just kill him. Make it quick. But something inside me hesitates. Every time I have thought of this moment, I have been fueled by hate which only made his death that much more glorious.

But *this* is not Salem. This is a shell of him. I cannot feel the same anger for this husk of a man. Killing him like this will not be nearly as rewarding.

"Lilith isn't real, Salem," I tell him gently.

His eyes look at me sharply. "Can you really not see? It is so obvious. Isn't it?"

Keeping my distance, I lower myself to seem less threatening. "Lilith isn't coming for you. It's only me."

Suddenly tired, Salem looks back at the wall wearily. "You don't understand. She plots the demise of the species she loathes most. Time started with her. I was a fool to think I could stop her."

Though I do not understand what he is talking about, his words seem coherent enough that I begin to wonder. Maybe I can attempt to guide his wandering mind back to reality so that his murder will not be wasted. Or at least, I might decipher where the journal is in this mess before he dies.

Salem looks at me soberly. "Lilith will come for us. Both of us." His eyes drift aside as though he is remembering. "There is a way to stop her but Mother wouldn't like it."

Hearing him refer to Marcella as Mother grates against me in a way that makes me want to knock his teeth into the back of his throat. My mother's memory does not deserve to be tarnished by his voice.

However, reacting the way I would like to will not get me closer to the journal so instead, I look at him softly. "Salem, I'm looking for a journal. One that belonged to my mother. Do you know where it is?

His eyes snap to mine and speaks with a clear mind. "*My* mother! Never yours!" he shouts it at me. But at least, his anger had brought him back to reality, if only briefly.

When I do not readily respond, Salem turns wordlessly back to the wall.

"Do you have Marcella's journal?" I try to coddle his madness a bit by using my mother's name instead of calling her *my mother*.

Salem pinches his eyes shut and shakes his head as though my words clutter his thoughts. "It's not a journal. Just letters. Letters Mother wanted *me* to have. They stole them from *me*."

His breath catches as he recalls the letters that Marcella wrote to him and I find myself curious. This is not how I expected to confront Salem. His madness and the lack of heat in my hate is not something I would have considered.

Yet, I find myself wanting conversation with him more than his destruction. A feeling I am certain is nothing more than a fleeting moment due to the despicable condition. So, I am also certain that my declining anger will not save his life from my hands today.

"Why would the Genesis keep your letters? What did Marcella write about that was worth stealing?"

And for that matter, why not destroy them instead of hiding them and risking this very situation?

Salem looks at me blankly at first. "The letters are about you." Then in a flash, a spark lights in his eyes. "I can stop Lilith. I must. It's so simple. Mother will have to forgive me."

Something about the wild look in his eyes pricks the hairs on my arms. For the first time since I entered, Salem plans to do more than scribble on a wall. He doesn't want to write in blood; he wants to spill mine.

He smiles wickedly and lunges at me. I scramble to my feet quickly. However, his arms wrap around my waist and slam my body down onto the floor. The wooden planks protest loudly with the impact as my head smacks the floor, likely fracturing my skull. Pain radiates throughout my brain, blurring my vision briefly. For a human, this injury would be enough to end this fight. But neither of us are human and neither of us can afford to lose.

His claws swipe at me eagerly, cutting into my ribs with the strength and rage of a madman. Swinging my arm around, I strike his nose with my elbow and feel his bones shift under my arm. Blood ruptures from his nose, pouring onto my face and making it difficult to see; but Salem's eyes are wild and he seems unfazed.

Grabbing his shirt, I twist the fabric in my hand and use it to pull him toward me as I slam my forehead into his face. He shakes his head to clear his vision and loosens his grip ever so slightly. I use the opportunity to shove his body away from me and wipe his blood from my eyes.

With blood still smeared across my eye-lids, I jump to my feet. Salem's eyes meet mine, crazed but determined. He stares angrily at me for a mere second and starts to rise. Before he can get his footing, however, I kick him in the ribs and send him flying into the wall. His body rolls down the recent writing on the wall, smearing the thick, dark, human blood.

The force of Salem hitting the wall sends a wave of trembling across to the bookcase. Several books topple over and crash to the ground. Salem lurches at me nearly as soon as his feet touch the floor.

I kick at his throat, hoping to use his momentum to add to the force of my foot. Instead, Salem is ready and grabs my ankle. His fist bursts into my inner thigh, rupturing blood vessels as the fibers of my muscle rip from the strike.

My opposite knee wavers, wanting to buckle, but somehow, I manage to keep from falling. If Salem were clear-headed, he might have applied the strike properly and broken my femur but luckily, he did not. There will be massive bruising and I will likely have a limp for several hours after my adrenaline wears down. For now, this will not be enough to stop me.

Sucking in a breath from the pain, I grab the largest thing I can reach, the taxidermied owl from the shelf of the bookcase. Standing on a tree limb with fake shrublike plants concealing a solid base, the owl is perched with its wings tucked neatly by its side. This only makes it easier to manage in my hands as a weapon.

The tree limb and base are bulky, and I use every bit of their weight to crash into his cheek. He stumbles back a step and releases my ankle. The corner of the base cuts into his skin, puncturing a hole in his cheek. The amount of blood and the look on his face as he touches his face tells me that the puncture goes completely through to his mouth.

Tossing the owl aside, I close the distance between us and punch at him. He blocks my fist and responses with his own, but we were trained similarly. His counterstrike is predictable, and I grab his wrist easily. Striking low, my flat palm cracks against his ribs. The snap of his rib echoes upward toward the ceiling as though it can flee from this fight any more than either of us can.

Salem stumbles back a step, his foot slipping slightly in the mucky blood on the floor and I seize my chance. Shoving him back against the wall, I pin him so that he cannot escape my punching. One fist follows the other into his ribs, an onslaught of pain and cracking of narrow bones. Dust falls around us from the ceiling as the vibrations of my strikes shake the wall. Like glitter dotting the air, the dust swirls around us.

Screeching through his pain and frustration, Salem pushes me hard enough to send me back several steps until my calf hits the armchair. Knocking the chair backward, I topple over it, resurging sharp pain in my bruised thigh.

The chair crashes to the floor and smacks loudly against the hardwood. As soon as my feet land, I kick the chair despite the protest of my leg and launch it toward Salem. He moves quickly aside and the chair crashes into the wall near to him. It fractures into pieces strung together by bits of torn fabric.

Salem rolls the broken chair leg under his foot and uses the momentum to kick the splintered wood up into the air and catch in his hand. He shifts the wood in his hand, preparing to use it as a stake. But I do not plan for it to be lodged into my chest today.

Picking the small table between the chairs, I dump the stained-glass lamp and the books onto the hardwood. The glass litters the floor like fragments of a rainbow skirting across the ground. Papers scatter beneath the second chair and hide behind leather-bound books.

My purpose for the small table is to create my own stake but Salem's reaction causes me to stop mid-air. His eyes grow wide as he looks at the strewn books dispersed among the shards of colored glass. "My letters!" he shrieks in a shrill cry.

His impulsive cry gives away more than he realizes. At least now, I won't have to search through all of the books in this room. Once he's dead, I can narrow my search to these books on the floor for the journal or letters or whatever has caused us both so much trouble.

Fury drives his steps. Charging quickly, he grabs me and slams me into the wall. The drywall caves around my body as though it is soft clay. The depression of my body holds me like a mother cradles a child. Salem lifts the stake up to finish me but his anger blinds him. His moves are sloppy and easy to deflect.

He keeps me against the wall as he lowers the stake toward my chest. Taking hold of his wrist, I twist his arm. His skin rolls under my hands, like wringing out a wet rag. His flesh rips and blood oozes from between my fingers. Only when I feel the bones snap under my grip does the stake drop to the floor.

Salem looks down desperately for his lost weapon and I use his minor distraction to attempt an escape from his clutches. Pushing myself further up the wall, my back sweeps over the crosses that he painted there. I let out a scream as my flesh melts against the cross, pulling away the skin that sticks to the paint.

The smell of charred skin wafts into the air around us, which I am sure gives Salem great pleasure. Necessary as it may be, the pain of crawling over the crosses weakens me. Instead of landing on my feet, my already waning leg buckles and I collapse onto my knees.

Salem jumps onto my back, his claws digging into my flesh once again. His fingernails coat in bits of flesh and stain red with my blood. A warm trail of my blood slithers down my back between my shoulder blades as I grab him. Pulling him forward, I heave him over my shoulder and drop him onto the floor.

He grabs at my leg, his claws ripping deep into my calf. Blood paints my pants, making the fabric cling to my skin. I punch into the drywall, grabbing a fistful of gypsum dust and bits of paper from the wall. Then, I toss the drywall powder and particles into his face. Salem cries out, scratching at his eyes in a desperate attempt to dislodge some of the grime.

My fist flies toward his skull, hoping to collapse it against the wooden planks. However, Salem is fast and he kicks me in the stomach hard enough to launch me across the room. He flips up, landing on both feet and charges after me. But I am done with this fight. This ends now.

I run toward him and jump toward his chest. Wrapping my legs around his neck, I use my momentum to flip him over me and fling his body into the floor. The house shakes with the force of him slamming into the ground.

Stunned by the impact, Salem chokes out a breath. In that split second, with his back on the floor, I flip toward him and land over him on all fours. More quickly than he could have anticipated, my hand pierces the soft space beneath his sternum. Blood pools around my wrist as my fingers reach up inside chest, making their way through the squelching soft tissues.

Squirming, Salem cannot break from my hold and with each movement, the waves of pain ripple across his brow. My hand wraps around his heart and his face freezes in panic.

His end is here. The fleeting moments he has left dangle in my fingers. I smile at him coldly, letting him absorb that it is me who is taking this from him. Me, the boy from the alley. The boy he stole everything from. The boy he cursed with an immortality ruled by a hunger that can never truly be satiated. Me, Nicolas Rider, is delivering his death.

With my hand inside his chest, his breaths are uneven and raspy. Still, he manages to choke out a hoarse voice, "Thank you."

No. His death cannot feel like a gift. He cannot thank me. He cannot be grateful for it. He deserves pain. He deserves a lifetime of it.

This is too quick of an end for someone like Salem. This cannot be how he dies. I cannot give him a lifetime of pain, but I will give him a death that is filled with it.

Grabbing his hair with one hand, I let my other hand slide out of his chest. The pain and weakness left from my hand's wake is enough that Salem is able to do little to resist me. As I drag him across the living room, his feet kick with the little fight still left in him, but his flailing doesn't even slow my stride.

Opening the door, I toss Salem into the dirt, into the sun, and into his fiery finale. His skin sears in the light, blistering and bursting like boiling water. Screaming, he claws at himself desperate to remove the flesh that scorches, melting into him.

Pain begs him to move but keeps him from getting far. Unable to do much, Salem rolls on the ground, collecting dirt in his blistered skin. His painfilled shrieking draws a smile on my face as I watch him writhing in the filth where he belongs.

His skin peels away in patches until his crying quiets and the air grows still. I lift my eyes from the ash that used to be Salem and see Mitchell standing near a tree. His face is one of both disgusted and disturbed. I cannot imagine how he feels about watching Salem burn or how I must appear now. My black eyes peer out from a face coated in blood, and not all of it mine.

"It's done," I tell him flatly, nodding toward the house. I let my fangs and nails recede as Mitchell follows me quietly.

He lets out a heavy sigh as though he is releasing his concerns that he might have to burn this house down. If I didn't know any better, I might even think that Mitchell hoped I would survive.

As Mitchell comes inside, he surveys the room before coming the rest of the way to where I kneel. Beside the toppled table, I sift through the books on floor.

Slowly, Mitchell approaches me. "Are you okay?"

I look up at him but I cannot determine whether he is asking about my injuries or my feelings after murdering my maker.

I shrug away his concern and return to my task of finding the journal so we can get out of here. The more distance we can put between us and this mess, the better. What I want more than anything is to be home with Krista.

Not home to our little house; but home. With Krista. She is my safe place. The one person I don't have to put on a performance for. I can exhale and just fall into her.

Twelve hours. That's how long it takes to get back to Stevensville from here. The Lock is, without a doubt, my own personal hell, and the last place I would choose to be. That place and that pack are a thorn in my side. But right now, there is nothing I wouldn't give to be there.

"What exactly are we looking for?" Mitchell asks. His question is useless, however. There is no way for me to guess what the journal looks like.

"I'll know when I see it," I mumble to him. Just then, my hand grazes over a book of pressed papers bound together by string. Wrapped in leather and tied tightly, the bundle is not large. Much of the book fits in my palm with the papers neatly folded inside.

"This is the one," I say in a whisper.

My thumb rubs over the burned initials on the reddish leather: *MV*. "Marcella Varro," I tell him. "It's her maiden name."

No longer able to stomach her husband, Marcella had chosen to go by her former name instead of the keeping the name she despised so much. Beyond that, she never spoke much of her husband. At least, not to me.

Emotions I had not expected wash over me now. My mother touched this book. These letters are her words. And when I read them, I will hear her voice in them. My eyes grow heavy with tears that want to fall. I clench my jaw, holding them at bay.

Mitchell must see the moisture set in my eyes but he says nothing as I cross my legs and sit on the floor. I unwind the string from around the book, unsure of what I will find inside.

After having been pressed in so tightly for so long, the letters do not fall from the book when I open it. I stare down at them for a moment before I take the first letter from the top.

I contemplate whether I should even read just this one. We need to leave. But the letter calls to me. My mother's words are in my hand.

I open the first letter slowly but it isn't a letter at all. Names and dates are scrolled across the parchment and it takes me longer than it should to determine that it is family tree. Marcella's family tree.

Mitchell peers over my shoulder as my finger traces Marcella's writing.

"That's her," I say, tapping her name on the ledger. I trace the line to Noah. "This is her son. She said I looked like him. It was why she had Salem turn me," I add, shaking my head.

Confusion sweeps over me when I see the line continue. Noah died; that's what she told us. But not only is there no death date listed by his name but Marcella tracked his family. He had a full life. He had a wife and children. Everything she made Salem take from me, Noah had.

Noah. My finger trails further along the fading lines. His son, Ezra, and daughter, Valerie, both listed on this old fragment of a paper in worn handwriting.

Both of his children had children of their own. Noah got to be a grandpa. The thought of it leaves a bitter taste in my mouth. I was robbed of my life while Noah didn't lose any of his. True or not, that is the thought that echoes in my mind.

That is, until my finger touches the next name and my breath catches.

Noticing my change, Mitchell leans toward the paper to see better. "What is it?"

But it's not what. It's who. Me. That's my name. Vincent Thatcher, born June 19, 1387.

Mitchell tugs at the corner of the paper slightly so he can see better still. "You and Marcella are blood relatives?"

"No," I say but then almost just as quickly, I reconsider. "Maybe." I shake my head as it swarms with too many thoughts to hear any one specifically.

"I'm not sure," I finally admit. Was I related to Marcella? Could she be my great grandmother? If we did share the same blood, it would explain why I look so much like Noah but nothing else.

This doesn't make sense.

I was her favorite. Marcella had no problem admitting that to the rest of our family, so why would she keep our relation from me? There is no clear gain from hiding this. Marcella could have used this information to further cement my loyalty to her. And the Marcella I loved would have.

Mitchell taps the bottom corner of the paper near my thumb, pointing to a circle with a vertical line through it. "I know this symbol. It's the mark for the Aros. They're one of the oldest werewolf packs that I know of. What do they have to do with any of this?"

Unable to focus on any one of my scrambling thoughts, I rustle through the letters, all neatly pressed and folded, desperate to learn more of the puzzle that lay before me now.

"As little as they can, I imagine," a smooth and icy voice chimes from the doorway.

I turn to see Mila standing near the door, apparently able to withstand the sun like me. She smiles at me with a haughty sense of superiority.

Handing the book of letters to Mitchell, I stand up to face her. "Hello, Mila."

Behind me, I hear Mitchell rise from the floor, wrapping the string tightly around the letters. He does not follow me as I walk toward her but instead takes a few steps backward.

I cannot tell if he is nervous or simply subconsciously putting more distance between Mila and the book. If he knew her at all, however, he would be nervous.

She does not need permission to enter this house and yet, she lingers just outside. It's the crosses. Mila isn't waiting for my invitation; she *can't* come in. She may be able to walk in the sun, but she is not as free from the burdens of being a vampire as I am.

Her piercing pale blue eyes look nearly white as she smiles coldly at me. Her fingers clasp the weighty medallion charm on her necklace as though holding it is a habit. I have seen her with it before and it obviously means more to her than she tries to let on.

Stopping a few feet from her, I cross my arms over my chest. "I wish I could say it was nice to see you again, but it rarely is."

Her eyes narrow, but I only smirk. "I would invite you in, but something tells me you can't." I wave my hand at the crosses on the walls. "I'm sure that must be very annoying for you."

These crosses are meant to keep vampires out. They are hard to look at directly even from across the room, and being in the same room as this many crosses would burn into a vampire's brain like a branding iron being stuck to flesh.

Impossible to think of anything, the pain is so piecing that either the vampire will certainly leave or his mind will. Salem had forced himself to live under them and they had driven him mad.

With a huff, she shifts her weight. "Don't be smug. It's unbecoming. Especially after I came all this way to see you, puppet."

Her voice dances over her last word. The Genesis knows how to get me to bend to their will. They have never been shy about using me. And Mila has never played coy about admitting it.

My smile drops. "What do you want, Mila?"

"Oh, come now. I thought we might be friends in this." She rolls her hands over themselves like a wheel. "What is that saying, enemy of an enemy is a friend?"

I click my tongue. "I've hated Salem for as long as I can remember but he was never enough of an enemy for me to consider you a friend."

Mila shifts uncomfortably. "But you do have friends. Someone told you where to find Salem and the book. If you tell me who it was and give me the book, I might let them live."

Any name I give her would be a death sentence. I shrug. "Lucky guess."

She huffs lightly. "Let's just get to the point, shall we? While I do thank you for removing Salem and retrieving the letters, make no mistake: those are *my* letters. And I am here to collect them. So, go ahead, be a good boy. Hand them over."

Not a chance. I need these letters more than Mila does. The first paper gave me a small hint of what I might find and I cannot afford to lose them now. That family lineage presents a puzzle that needs answered. Not just for me, this needs to be solved for Krista.

Whatever answers I might find could be the key to shaking loose from the Genesis once and for all. Krista deserves a future without the Genesis. Marcella would not have sent these letters to Salem if they weren't significant.

"Those letters are addressed to Salem. You stole them so you should be able to recognize that I am stealing them now."

She pushes her blonde hair behind an ear. "You might be able to hide in this hovel of a house until I leave but I will come for the book. And if I were you, I wouldn't bother hiding it from me. I know how to make you to talk."

Her mouth twitches as she adds, "Krista. That's her name, isn't it?"

I am certain she notices the anger rip through me despite the way I try to conceal it. Mila and her band of merry psychos have threatened Krista before.

They hurt Krista to make me cave into promising them something in the future. I still don't know what they will eventually want from me or whether I will be able to protect Krista when they inevitably come for it.

Mila came here for this. She came to watch me squirm and fold to her. She knows that I couldn't save Ann from Salem. And I couldn't save Marcella from Mitchell. She wants me to believe that I can't save Krista from the Genesis.

Stirring up my old wounds is a strategy that seems to be working. My mind works over the possibilities: either hand the book over or Mila will certainly follow me home to Krista. She may even beat me there.

As much as I do not like either option, Mila knows which one I will ultimately choose. The Genesis won't kill Krista. They need her to manipulate me. But they do not need to make someone bleed to hurt them and the Genesis are good at finding inventive ways to make someone suffer. They have proven themselves quite capable of most anything.

Before I can answer, I hear the thud of something in the fireplace. With the heat of the quick flame warming my back, I did not even need to see the book to know what has happened. But still, I look.

Mitchell stands empty-handed as the book burns brightly. The old, fragile paper ignited easily. Despite it only being in the fire for a moment, the book is already far too charred to be saved.

I turn my eyes back to Mitchell, who looks at me nervously. "I'm sorry, Nick, I—"

Raising my hand, I cut him off. "Stop talking."

Mila lets out a hard chuckle but it does little to cover her irritation. "Not the most obedient pup, is it?"

Although I am not overly pleased that because of Mitchell I get to watch my mother's letters disappear into the flames, Mila's words grate me more. I insult Mitchell, not her.

"Most strays aren't," I tell her flatly. Then with a false sense of innocence, I point to the fire and add sarcastically, "I hope that wasn't your only copy."

Her eyes narrow on Mitchell but it is me she speaks to. "Strays tend to have short lives. His will likely be shorter than most."

I step in front of Mitchell, blocking Mila's view of him, unsure why I should feel territorial about him at all. "His death belongs to me, just like Salem's did."

That isn't why I don't want her to kill him, though. If someone else were to murder him, I would be just as pleased as if Mitchell dies by my hands.

Looking sharply at Mitchell, Mila huffs. "You can have your stay of execution, for now. But remember that any time I wish it, Casiana can and will enthrall Nicolas to kill you," she says, pointing at Mitchell.

And Casiana can do that. I am already inclined to want to kill Mitchell, so convincing me through enthrallment would be easy for her. I wouldn't need much persuasion to push me past any hesitation to follow through.

Then with a wicked smile, she adds playfully, "Can you imagine the fallout of such a thing?"

Yes, I can.

Chapter 10

With Corrine taking up the entire backseat, stretching out far beyond what her restraints in the basement would have allowed, the drive was mostly quiet. Both, Mitchell and I remain trapped in our own minds.

My thoughts keep circling back to when Tara and I had planned to start traveling around and digging up answers wherever we could. We never put our plans into action and a part of me wonders if that was a mistake. If anything would be different if we had continued our quest for answers.

Once I realized that drugs can and do affect me, I was eager to know why. However, before we even started, there was a quarrel between my mother and me that forced me into a sort of hiding. Looking back, it seems silly for a vampire as old as myself to hide like a spoiled child but I did.

Tara and I decided to suspend our search. Snooping about would have only drawn attention to us. It would be easier to avoid Marcella if Marcella could not find me.

That suspension was only meant to be a pause. However, once I met Krista, everything changed. I no longer cared about where I came from, only about where I was going. I could only see my future. And that was something I hadn't given much thought to before. I couldn't just walk away from her to search for answers. Especially when I thought those answers would have ultimately changed nothing.

However, that was before I knew much about the Genesis. Looking back, perhaps it was a mistake to abandon my search. Perhaps with the appropriate answers, I could have spared Krista from ever knowing Mila or Casiana at all.

Perhaps I waited too long. Perhaps, any answer I may have used to free us now has just been reduced to ash.

As we pass the sign for the state line, I am grateful that Mitchell breaks the silence and my thoughts. "Who's Casiana?"

"Amelia's second in command," I mutter toward the window.

"Amelia?"

Oh, right. Of course. Mitchell doesn't know the Genesis. I have never liked or trusted him enough to bother explaining them. "Amelia was the leader of the Genesis until Salem killed her."

"So, now Casiana is the leader?"

"Maybe she always was." Salem had mumbled something at the house about killing the wrong one. Maybe Amelia wasn't the target he thought. Maybe her position as leader was simply a decoy to protect the real person in charge.

"What do you mean?" Mitchell asks curiously.

"I'm not sure," I tell him honestly. My assumption that Amelia was not the actual leader of the Genesis is just that, an assumption. It isn't based on any facts, only a feeling.

"Is Mila third in command?"

"No, I don't think so." As far as I know, Mila is Casiana's personal assassin, even though Casiana is more than capable of killing any person she wants to on her own.

"I think Mila's loyalty is exclusive to Casiana and vice versa. You'll see them both wear the same necklace, and if one knows something, the other seems to know it too."

"Like a hive mind?"

I laugh to myself. "They're bad guys, Mitchell, not pod people. Mila and Casiana are like their own little cult within a bigger, more dangerous cult."

Mitchell nods but it is clear that there is far more needed for him to truly understand.

After a few moments of blessed quiet, Mitchell again breaks the silence. "Can all of the vampires in the Genesis do that sun trick like you and Mila can?"

Despite the difficulty we've had over the past few hours, I smile at his simplicity. Walking in the sun is no trick. But the truth is, I don't really know how many other vampires were changed in the same ways the Genesis have changed me.

Raising my eyebrows, I look at him. "Mila and I are not the same. She is way meaner than me," I say it like a jest but it is no joke. Mila is vicious.

Mitchell chuckles to himself but almost instantly, his face becomes serious. "You're bleeding."

Yes, I am aware. The blood from my calf had matted to my pants before we even left the house but that was not enough to clot it quickly.

My leg hurt. My thigh has been badly bruised; my calf shredded. I had hidden my limp from Mitchell. However, the blood had pooled in my shoe and leaked onto the floorboard of this car and that was something I apparently couldn't hide from him.

When I don't respond, he continues, "You're bleeding a lot." He says it with much more concern that I would expect from him.

This time, I look at my leg to acknowledge that I know how much I have lost. "Hm." I nod. "Don't worry about it. I'll get more later."

Mitchell's face snaps from concern to shock and I cannot help but to laugh. "I'm joking, relax."

Well, sort of joking. Hunting would help me heal but I have resolved to wait until Mitchell is not around to drink from Corrine.

Mitchell half-smiles as we pass a weigh station. "Hey, Nicolas, I want you to know why I threw that book in the fire."

Waving his words away, I stop him. "You did the right thing. Krista is more important than anything in that book. I was going to end up giving it to Mila anyway."

"I know you were," Mitchell blurts out. "I couldn't let you."

Leaning forward, Mitchell reaches behind him to the small of his back. The car swerves a bit as he manages to pull something out that had been tucked in his waistband under his shirt.

My breath catches as my eyes roll over the leather. There, in his hands is my mother's letters bound by string in a neat little book. Her initials burned into the dark cover.

He switched it.

"I didn't want to tell you until I was sure we weren't followed." He holds the book toward to me but I only stare at it as though it might be a trick in a dream.

I am not sure if Mitchell says anything else. If he does, I do not believe I would hear him anyway. I can barely hear my thoughts over my heavy breathing.

Forcing my hand to reach for the book of letters, I swallow hard. My mother's letters are here. And they are mine.

I lay the book in my lap for a moment. The smooth leather is much newer than any of the parchment paper inside. My thumb traces over the burnt initials carefully.

I thought this was gone, taken up in flames. My last bit of my mother ripped from my grasp no sooner than I touched it. I steady myself with a long exhale and untie the string holding the book together.

The letters are still neatly folded; though the haste in which some were pushed back into the stack when Mila had interrupted is evident.

The family lineage is still on top and needing to be examined further but I want to go deeper into the pile. I want to see my mother's handwriting and read the words that were once in her mind. I want to remember the way she spoke, the pauses in her sentences. I want to feel her here with me in these letters.

I open the very next letter in the pile, not knowing if these are stacked in any specific order…

August 20, 1409

To my dearest Salem,

When you read this, you already undoubtedly realize that you have been deceived. I have tricked you. This is true, but not because you are a fool. Yet, it was I who was the fool all along. You see, I believed the Genesis when they said they were my friend. I trusted them and I loved them dearly. But that love was one-sided. They only wanted to use me as a means to get to him.

I am not proud of the things I've had to do. Nor am I pleased that I must leave you behind. I will miss you dearly but I will continue on knowing that your ignorance of my true intentions will protect you from my treason.

The man you turned last night, Vincent, is a very special man. He is a descendant of one of the purest werewolf lines and the key to harnessing a very destructive power. My Noah was a part of this plan as well. However, I was naïve to it. Noah had been hidden from me, and subsequently from the Genesis, until the innocence of youth had long dusted away and he was no longer of any use to them. However, his grandson was left exposed and vulnerable. And when I learned what the Genesis intended for Vincent, to steal a child born to him, one both pure and innocent, I knew I must stop this once and for all.

I hope one day you will see that there really was only two options: turn Vincent or kill him. And killing Vincent will never be something I could bear, and therefore is not truly an option at all. He is my blood, and I owe him my protection. My love I will offer him freely for I could never turn from the face that looks so much like my own sweet boy. You must understand, it is blood that binds us beyond reason.

Heed these words: there can be no children born to Vincent. The entire bloodline must come to stop, for any child born from his line is destined to become a harbinger of our world's demise. The only way to change this future was to prevent him from becoming the wolf he was meant to be and to stop the child that was growing in his fiancée's womb. Stopping the family line is the only way to stop her. And she must be stopped. Lilith cannot win.

Please know that while it grieves me to write this, I sincerely wish you the best of life and please know that I will always long to have been a part of it.

Your forever mother, Marcella

With tears rolling down my cheeks, I fold the letter again and place it top of the stack. Getting through these letters will be more difficult than I anticipated. Even in this first one, there is too much for me to process.

One, the Genesis want me for something so destructive and dangerous that it frightened Marcella. Frightened her enough to destroy my life and abandon Salem, whom she dearly loved.

Two, when we were attacked in the alley by Salem, Ann was pregnant. She wasn't given even a hint of mercy and perhaps didn't even know that she was carrying my child. But regardless, Ann died in the mud with my child in her womb. And Marcella, my mother, knew that when she ordered their deaths.

Lastly, I was born to be a werewolf. The very thought of it makes me feel dirty inside. I am in love with a werewolf and can recognize the hypocrisy of what I am feeling. But Krista is not me. She is meant to be a wolf. I am not. Being a vampire is far too natural for me to have ever been anything else.

Feeling unsettled, I cringe inside. Wolves hide behind the guise of protecting humans. In reality, they are rude, temperamental, mouth-breathing cretins. I refuse to believe I could have ever been one.

Me? A descendant of wolves. A bunch of mutts huddled together and clamoring around each full moon. Afraid to embrace the animal that lives in them and truly hunt.

I am a vampire. I was meant to be one. And there isn't a single part of me that denies how much I would crave being a monster if I weren't.

But I am different. I have known that for some time.

I wouldn't have thought it was possible but I can only come up with one reliable explanation. The Genesis must have awakened my wolf somehow. I don't know why the Genesis would have ever wanted to change me into this thing? This Nexus. But it would explain why I can walk in the sun and how I bonded to Krista in the way only a wolf can.

I am not simply an altered vampire like I had been led to think. A Nexus, a link between both worlds. Call it what you like, I am a hybrid.

A vampire stuck in a wolf's world. Hybrid or not, I want nothing to do with their ridiculous rules. I absolutely will not have an alpha. I take orders from no man and, certainly, not from any beast. Nicolas Rider does not bow.

* * *

The rest of the drive remained quiet. Mitchell attempted to start conversation only once but quickly give up when it was obvious that I was not responding. The few words I did speak to him were flat and indifferent, and centered around switching drivers each time we stopped for food or gas.

The letters had remained on my lap, untouched any further, until our last stop before we reached Stevensville. At which point, I put them in my bag in the trunk. Hours before, I had accepted to myself that I would not be able to read any more while in this car. I did not want to learn anything else with Mitchell sitting so close. I needed to be alone for this.

The drive seemed to last much longer than the twelve hours that had lapsed in reality; but finally, the buildings become familiar and Mitchell pulls up in front of the hospital to drop me off.

A small smile lights his face as he nods his good-bye to me. It is the same dopey grin he had a couple of hours ago when I first told him that Simone had the baby.

When I heard the news, my first reaction had been to groan, knowing that Warren's unavoidable 'I told you so' speech would be waiting for me. But Mitchell, this standoffish oaf, genuinely beamed for a baby that isn't his. Mitchell was so obviously excited about the addition to their pack that I couldn't hold back my lopsided smile then or now.

Shaking my head at him, I watch him drive away before I head into the hospital. The anger I felt when I first discovered Marcella had been lying all along has begun to cool and I am grateful for that, even though I am still not happy about being a werewolf in even the slightest of ways.

The past ten hours calmed the sting of learning that I am, in the smallest part, a werewolf. And being a hybrid did allow me to bond with Krista so I suppose it isn't all tragic news.

I did not dare tell Mitchell what I had uncovered. I need to understand it better before I can let any of the pack know. Krista is the only exception to that. And still, I have no idea what words I will use when I start that conversation or how she might respond to it. I'm not even sure how I should be responding it.

Hybrid. Nexus. Whatever anybody wants to call me. I feel like a foreigner in my own body. Tainted and stained.

I wish Marcella had told me. I have so many questions. I wish even more that she were still here to answer them now. She would be mad that I killed Salem, but not surprised. And she would forgive me for it, like she always did anytime I disappointed her. Now, I understand why.

The elevator doors open to the third floor breaking my thoughts. Even before I leave the elevator car, I see Krista standing near the infant viewing window.

Smiling softly, she watches a sweet baby sleeping. I assume it is Simone's but it doesn't really matter whose child it. It isn't hers. And it never will be.

Marcella's letter said that any child of mine would bring destruction, and for once, I am grateful to be sterile. The last thing I want to bring into Krista's life is more destruction.

Stopping near her, I nudge her arm gently with my hand. The smile that spills across her face fills me with warmth. She wraps her arms around me as tears flood her eyes.

Holding her tight, I nuzzle my face into her neck, inhaling her scent along with the mixed smells of the hospital. I do not care to decipher the various aromas. I simply let her scent comfort me, cradling me in her embrace as her soft, brown curls tumble over my cheek.

Her hand rubs my hair. "I've been counting the hours. I dreamt of this moment."

She means of the moment I returned home to her, but this is a moment I have dreamt of too. More times than she realizes.

"If you want to tell me about it, we can go home," she offers. And I do. I want to tell her everything.

Leaning back enough to see her face, I place my hands on both sides of her neck. "I will, but first there is something more important I need to tell you."

Her eyebrows furrow, a bit unsure of whether my seriousness indicates my next statement will be welcoming or not.

My thumb glides along her jawline as I tell her, "Krista, I have been alive for a long time. And I don't have a lot of firsts to give you. I can't go back in time to make you my first kiss or even my first love. But you are the only person I have ever watched the sun rise with. You bring so much light into my dark world that I don't ever want the sun to come up without you next to me."

Her cheeks push up into a soft smile, her skin warming against my hands.

"Krista, you're my first sunrise but I want you to be my only one." Lowering myself to one knee, I continue, "Will you marry me, Krista?"

Her breath catches even before I have the ring box open. Her hand covers her mouth but only for a second as tears fill the edges of her eyes. "I thought you wanted my dad's blessing."

"I have it."

She blinks hard a few times, letting out a forced exhale. Clearly, she did not expect me to have his blessing and perhaps a part of her thought that without it, I may not be completely serious about this.

But I am. This is the one thing in my life I know is completely real.

Standing up, I add, "I only your permission now." As I cradle her cheek in my hand, a tear rolls over my fingers. "And I hope I have it because I desperately want to marry you."

Brushing my hair with her fingers, she playfully shrugs. "Well, if you're desperate."

I chuckle lightly at her jest as she grabs the collar of my shirt and uses it to pull her lips close to mine. "Nicolas Rider, I would marry you a thousand times and in a thousand ways, if it meant I could keep you for even one more day, so yes, I would be devastatingly happy to marry you."

She kisses me, softly at first. Her lips are smooth and inviting as her fingers twist through my hair. The tears that had dampen her cheeks still linger on her mouth, leaving a salty taste on my lips.

Her grip on me tightens, pushing a heat to roll through me. I have longed for this moment. The moment when there is nothing standing in my way. She is mine. And the way her mouth moves with mine tells me she has wanted this day to come as badly as I have.

Moving her arm to pull me closer, her elbow catches the ring box in my hand, and it tumbles to the floor. The ring pops from the cushion holding it but it does not go far, landing near her shoe.

I smile widely at her. "There's probably some old wives' tale about dropping the ring during a proposal," I tease.

She bats her eyes pretending to be innocent.

Kneeling once more, I take the ring in my fingers and look at it. This is the last time I will hold this ring without knowing where to place it. It has an owner now. It belongs to my wife.

My wife. I smile at the thought.

Looking up at her, I take her hand gently. Biting her lip bashfully, she attempts to hold back some of the smile that is pouring from her.

I slip the ring on her finger and press my lips to the back of her hand.

So close to her, something stops me from moving. It a scent that mixes with Krista's own. It had been weak before so I hadn't given it much thought. My smiles fades as I recognize the scent that has evaded me for weeks. I was so stupid to not have seen it before. It was so obvious.

Suddenly weary, I close my eyes, resting my forehead against Krista's stomach. Unaware of what stirs in my mind, she rubs her hands through my hair, affectionately.

I turn my head so that I can place my ear against her abdomen. Her hands stroke my hair delicately as I listen to her stomach acids grumble. The thumping of her heartbeat deep in the vessels that run along her spine is plain and clear. Even the sound of her diaphragm stretching with each inhale is unmistakable. Those are expected sounds; but they are not the only sounds coming from inside her.

Beneath her warm skin, I hear something faint. Something that forces me to stop my breathing merely to hear it more clearly. Something that causes my fingers to brush over her shirt. Deep inside, there is a very fast beating of a very tiny heart.

The sound of Krista's voice is dim at first, dulled by my own distraction. Her fingers rest on my head as she lightly taps my shoulder. "Are you okay?"

I stand up once again, more frazzled than I would like to appear. This is not the time or the place to say anything about the child growing inside her. Someone could be watching, listening. The Genesis could be.

Besides, what would I say? Marcella ruined my life once to prevent this very thing. Pulling myself together quickly, I nod, convincing Krista that whatever was on my mind must surely be due to the past week of fighting I have faced.

Delicately trailing the fingers of my free hand along her cheek, I look into her eyes and lie flawlessly, "Everything's perfect."

She accepts my lie and smiles back at me without any worries to crease her brow. But everything is not perfect. Everything is far from perfect.